PROOF

The Novel

PROOF

The Novel

Ted D. Berner

Dawn,
The Proof is
everywhere!
Rodger gflm
AKA: T.D. Berner

GRIGORI
Publishing

First edition from Grigori Publishing, August 2015

Published in the United States by Grigori Publishing LLC
Box 966, Lincoln, MT 59639

Cover design by: Ebook Launch and Jeanine Henning, jeaninehenning.com
Cover illustration by: Mike Brown and Benjamin Wood
Editing by: Mindy Wilke
Book design by: Maureen Cutajar, www.gopublished.com

Library of Congress Control Number: 2015942423

ISBN: 978-0-9964156-0-6 (hardcover)
ISBN: 978-0-9964156-1-3 (paperback)

www.proofthenovel.com

Printed in the United States of America

I would like to dedicate this book to all the loved ones I've lost during the writing process, including: my friend and father-in-law Leonard, my brother-in-law Butch, my loving mother Evelyn, our beautiful dog Marion, and my friend and brother Rick.

There were giants in the earth in those days; and also after that, when the sons of God came in unto the daughters of men, and they bare children to them, the same became mighty men which were of old, men of renown.

GENESIS 6:4

PREFACE

SHORTLY AFTER THE turn of the twenty-first century, a friend and co-worker pointed out a verse in the Bible to me that I've been fascinated about ever since. Genesis 6:4 briefly references an ancient civilization that is so amazing, but for some reason, has been brushed aside and forgotten by mankind. I was so fascinated by this lone verse in the Bible, that several years later, I began the long drawn out process of researching everything I could find regarding that long lost civilization that was glossed over in the Bible. I eventually wrote this novel, which is hinged around that one verse.

Did giants really once roam the planet earth eons ago at the dawn of the human race? According to the Bible and many other ancient texts and legends, they did just that. I was and still am amazed at all the legends and folklore from around the world that seem to back up these fantastic stories. Is it possible that the unexplainable megaliths scattered around the globe are a telltale sign as well? Over and over again, stories surface from the locals that live close to the ruins that do in fact support the connection.

If anyone ever said that writing a book is easy, it wasn't me. Although I can honestly say it was exciting not to mention surprising doing the countless hours of research required and the countless hours were just that, countless. If I had it to do over again, would I still embark on such a task? Without thinking twice, the answer is "yes." Only because the topic was and still is such a fascination to me.

ACKNOWLEDGEMENTS

FIRST AND FOREMOST, I want to thank my wife, Christine, for putting up with me throughout this entire process. Living with me is hard enough despite the fact that I'm obsessed by the unknown.

I would also like to thank everyone else who was involved starting with Tony Greenan, for had it not been for him I may never have paid any attention to Genesis 6:4 to begin with.

My good friends, Jim Heisler for reading my unedited drivel as I spit it out and Bill Gable, for taking the time to read his first novel ever.

Mindy Wilke for taking on the task of editing a manuscript written by a first time novelist.

Hope Quay, who with her eloquent way with words, helped smooth out several of the lumps along the way.

Robbie Gehring, who spent a whole day of his young life reading my novel to see if his old uncle made any sense.

Lloyd Brown, who while suffering in pain with a broken back, took the time to see just how zany his new neighbor was.

Nicole Miller, who took some of her precious time, confirming what she already knew, that her uncle is a little peculiar.

Tessa Gehring, who spent several hours making sure this novel would end up on the best sellers list.

Author Elizabeth Cain, her husband Jerry, and my brother Steve for helping with the last minute cleanup.

Maureen Cutajar for fitting me into her busy schedule and formatting *Proof the Novel* for publication.

The Universe itself, for throwing me a bone when it came time to figure out what to put on the cover.

The ever so talented Mike Brown, for taking that bone and starting the process of bringing it to life on paper.

Benjamin Wood, for transforming the creature to match that with the imagination of the author.

Andrew Winkler, for bringing the cover to life with 3D animation.

Brian Parsons, for dramatic effect through audio.

Paul Gieselman, for the awesome website that proved to be indestructible, even though the author personally tried to destroy it.

Of course, the All Mighty himself, for creating all that is and for allowing us to have this wonderful experience we call life. And last, but most definitely NOT least... Thank you.

FACT OR FICTION?

THE LEGENDS, FOLKLORE, non-character related individuals (other than Zelma Shultz), and books discussed in this novel, are NOT the creation of the author, but do or did exist, or if fabricated, were done so by someone else in the distant past. The only things made up by the author, are the characters and the things they do. Everything else? You be the judge.

DOCUMENTED:

IN NOVEMBER 1946, Bedouin shepherds discovered ancient scrolls in caves just northwest of the Dead Sea some thirteen miles east of Jerusalem. They are now known as the Dead Sea Scrolls. Among the parchments, several of them are books from the Old Testament in the Bible with several other religious texts that were never included... the Book of Enoch is one of them.

PROOF

The Novel

CHAPTER 1

"IN THE BEGINNING *God created the heaven and the earth.*" This was probably the most famous opening sentence in any book ever written, Ty Larson thought. He read on, most of the next few verses echoed familiarity from the first time he'd read the Bible back in high school. Then, all of a sudden, there it was… a few short sentences in Genesis chapter six that were going to change his life forever:

And it came to pass, when men began to multiply on the face of the earth, and daughters were born unto them, That the sons of God saw the daughters of men that they were fair; and they took them wives of all which they chose. And the lord said, My spirit shall not always strive with man, for that he also is flesh: yet his days shall be an hundred and twenty years. There were giants in the earth in those days; and also after that, when the sons of God came in unto the daughters of men, and they bare children to them, the same became mighty men which were of old, men of renown.

Ty could hardly believe his eyes. Why had this not jumped out at him before? What did it mean? *"The sons of God came in unto the daughters of men and, they bare children to them?"* This sounded like something straight out of Greek mythology, but Ty had been raised to believe the Bible was fact, not myth.

It was hard to believe it took an assignment in the final class of his college career—an archaeology class—to make him notice these intriguing verses. It was only a fluke that he'd ended up taking this class in the first place. He was graduating a semester early with a degree in criminal justice, and he only had three final credits to take. There were several other electives that would've fulfilled the requirement, and had the school's computer system not been down during enrollment, he never would have seen the alluring blonde in line for this class swaying his decision. He knew all too well that he probably would've taken an easier way out with an Art Appreciation class. Now, however, archaeology had his full attention.

The assignment was an end-of-the-semester paper regarding any Biblical links to the ancient megalithic structures scattered across the globe, which was what led Ty down the road to where he now sat. If these passages had anything to do with his assignment, he didn't know, but it definitely was going to require some investigation, and after all, investigation was his passion.

Deciding on a major had been easy. Ty had always been interested in criminal justice, to no one's surprise. Several of his family members on his father's side were in the CIA, FBI, or some type of law enforcement. Although his father had never pushed him to follow in his footsteps, Ty found himself heading down the same path, hoping to get a career with the Central Intelligence Agency. Investigation of any kind had always intrigued him, so applying to the criminal justice program at Alexandria University had been an easy decision and had done nothing but fuel his passion even more.

Ty reread the verses over and over again, his imagination running wild. Who were the Sons of God and who, or *what*, were the giants in the earth? His thoughts kept slipping back to what little he knew about the characters in Greek Mythology. Zeus, Apollo, and Poseidon were some of the gods, but what about the progeny of the gods and humans like Hercules and Achilles? Achilles was involved in the once-considered mythical Trojan War with the city of Troy, the ruins of which had been discovered by Heinrich Schliemann in 1868. Could the rest of these stories possibly have any truth to them as well? And if they were true, what kind of world would this have been?

It took several taps on Ty's shoulder by the librarian—reminding him that the library was closing for the night—to break the trancelike state that had overcome him. He'd been in such deep thought that he'd totally lost track of time. Looking at his watch, Ty was surprised to see it was nearly 11:00 p.m. He knew where he needed to go next, but his visit to the church would have to wait until morning.

TY AWOKE WITH the sun shining through his bedroom window and realized he must've finally fallen asleep sometime after 3:00 a.m. His mind had been racing most of the night with the possibility of the Sons of God taking daughters of men and what their offspring could've possibly been. *"Giants in the earth"*… what did that mean? With something that sounded so spectacular, he couldn't fathom how there were only a few short verses dedicated to a story of such magnificence.

He didn't waste any time getting out of bed; before he knew it he was dressed, out the door, and in his car on his way to the church. Even with only a couple of hours of sleep, he felt the same adrenaline rush he used to feel in the starting blocks right before the gun sounded during an important race. Ty's exceptional athleticism had earned him a full-ride scholarship for the university's track team. If he'd pushed himself a little harder, he probably could've even qualified for the 2012 summer Olympics in London. But wanting to focus on a career instead, he made the difficult decision of giving up the sport. He missed it immensely, but his future—hopefully with the CIA—mostly kept his track shoes in his running bag these days. Now, he just ran occasionally to stay in shape and relive the glory days.

The parking lot for the church was empty of course, it being a Thursday, and as he parked the car he tried to remember the last time he'd seen Father Mac. They'd met long ago, way back when Ty was just starting the first grade. Although both of Ty's parents had grown up in a small town in Montana where his father and grandfather had worked for the border patrol (Ty was even born out west), the family moved to Alexandria, VA—and to Father Mac's parish—when Ty's father started working for the CIA. Ty and his brother, Eric, had been raised as Christians and going to church was normal for Sundays except on rare occasions. Since he'd moved out on his own though, he hadn't even thought about going… until now.

Ty wondered if the priest would remember him or even still be at this parish. Maybe he should've called first. He shrugged his shoulders and hoped for the best. *It was too late for that now*, he thought as he got out of the car.

The smell of fall was in the air as he started up the worn granite steps. This was one of the oldest churches in the city, maybe one of the oldest in the entire Northeast. As a child he never really noticed the grandeur of the building, only remembering the long climb up the crowded steps that led through the oversized double doors. Then, followed by what seemed like an eternity of shuffling through the large congregation to eventually find an empty spot on one of the rock-hard pews big enough for a family of four.

Fueled by excitement of the answers that could be waiting for him, he topped the stairs two at a time as he approached the beautiful ornate, hand-carved mahogany doors. Ty half expected to hear an eerie creak as he pulled the doors open, but surprisingly they opened without a sound and with ease as though they had just been oiled. It took a couple of seconds for his eyes to adjust to the dimly-lit entryway. Instead of continuing on through the next set of double doors into the main cathedral where the church services were held, he almost instinctively proceeded down the stairs where he'd always assumed their priest had lived.

The stairway made a ninety-degree turn halfway down and ended at the start of a long, wide hallway that stretched the length of the building. There were four doors off the hallway, two on either side. He'd always imagined it looked like a dungeon down here, but instead it was almost like walking into a museum of religious relics from the 1800s.

Before he had a chance to admire the artwork, he noticed that the first door he came to was ajar. He knocked and pushed it open. "Hello?"

As the door swung open, Ty saw an elderly man dressed in a brown robe, sitting at a desk, look up over his glasses.

"May I help you?" the man asked.

Ty didn't think he looked like Father Mac, but it had been over ten years since his last visit to the church, so he inquired, "Father Mac?"

"No, I'm Deacon Jones. Father Mac should be in his study across the hall."

Thanking the deacon and closing the door behind him, Ty proceeded across the hall and knocked on the door. At least now he knew Father Mac was still alive and well.

Through the door he heard what sounded like the rustling of papers and a chair scrape across the floor followed by footsteps getting closer. The knob turned and the door slowly opened and sure enough, there he was, Father Mac, just as Ty remembered him: a noble-looking man with kind eyes. The years had wrinkled his face and his hair was not the dark salt and pepper it once was, but rather, entirely grey. Nonetheless, Ty recognized him without a doubt.

"Father Mac!" Ty said with confidence.

"Yes?" the elderly man replied.

It was obvious he was trying to put a name to the face, but Ty didn't really expect the priest to remember him... not after all these years.

"I'm Grant and Marion Larson's boy... Ty." He said with a sudden pang of guilt at the thought of how long it'd been since he'd been to church.

"Ah yes... Tyler! It's been a while. I'd assumed you were on a mission spreading the Lord's word in some far-off land," the priest said with a sly smile.

Ty recalled the priest had a sense of humor and responded with a smile. "Well, actually, I've been working on my degree at the university and, God willing, I hope to finish this semester."

Father Mac returned the smile and asked, "Didn't I read about you in the sports section of the Alexandria Herald a few months back? It sounded like you'd be training for the Olympics about now."

Ty shook his head. "No. I decided to try to graduate a little early. I need to get five years' experience in the field before I can apply at the CIA. I'm hoping to start a career there, but to do that I had to forget about the Olympics."

"Well I'm sure your parents are very proud of you and all you've accomplished, Tyler, no matter what. Tell me, what brings you down to my little corner of the world?"

"Well, Father, I must admit that I haven't read the Bible for some time now, but I began to read it again the other day and I came across something that was rather puzzling." Ty decided to skip over exactly how he had found all this. Somehow, he just couldn't bring himself to say he was only reading the Bible for an assignment.

"Oh, yes," Father Mac replied. "There are numerous passages that might make one scratch one's head. Believe me, scholars and translators have been fighting this battle long before either of us were even thought of. Which is the one you found?"

Ty opened the Bible he'd brought with him. "I was only a few pages into it, and here in Genesis, chapter six, where it says—"

Before he could finish, Father Mac interrupted, "And you were wondering about the Sons of God?"

"Actually, yes. How did you know?"

"You're not the first to inquire about that. The way it's worded can make it very confusing," the priest explained. "There've been some who've confused the Sons of God with fallen angels who procreated with human women. Although this is an exciting thought, nothing could be further from the truth. We've studied these verses very carefully and the Sons of God are merely the sons of Seth, or the Sethites, and the daughters of men are the daughters of Cain, or the Cainites."

The priest went on. "The Sethites were good people who lived according to God's word, while the descendants of Cain were evil and turned their back to the Lord. The Lord didn't approve of the unions between the Cainites and the Sethites, because the moral character of the Cainites became like a cancer that spread throughout humanity. This was the reason that the Lord brought on the Great Flood... to rid the earth of these sinful people and their sinful ways."

Father Mac continued for quite a while, with various references throughout the Bible to corroborate his response.

Ty's adrenaline rush had faded almost as fast as it had come. "That's it? It's no more than that?"

The priest saw the look of disappointment on Ty's face and instinctively tried to soften the letdown with some humor. "Maybe if you came by to visit a little more often, like, say, oh every Sunday, these kinds of things wouldn't come as such a surprise."

Ty gave the priest a grin and said sheepishly, "I'm sorry for my absence. Things have just been so hectic with school and track these past few years that it seems like I've hardly had any free time for much else." Ty glanced at his watch and realized he was going to have to leave if he didn't want to be late for his only class.

The priest could see his intent. "Oh, I'm just kidding, Tyler. You can stop by and visit whenever you want, and as often or as little as you'd like. The doors are always open."

Ty thanked Father Mac for his time and promised his visits would be more frequent. They said their goodbyes, and with the wind taken out of his sails, Ty turned to leave.

As he exited into the hallway, he noticed that the deacon's door was slightly ajar. In the back of his mind, he wondered if the deacon had been eavesdropping on their conversation, remembering that he'd shut the door behind him when he left.

Who cares? Ty thought. He was still in a state of shocked disappointment over the priest's explanation of the verses that had gotten him all fired up to begin with. It had seemed so obvious that something incredible must've happened so long ago, but if something was too good to be true, it probably was, and the priest would know.

Ty was still internally grieving at his unfortunate dead end as he walked up the dimly lit stairs and was just about to the main floor when he felt a slight tug on his jacket. Thinking he must've snagged himself on the handrail, he turned around and was startled to see the deacon right behind him.

"Oh! Deacon, it's you," Ty exclaimed in surprise. "I'm sorry, did I forget something?"

The look on the deacon's face was stern. "The book of Enoch!"

Ty was at a loss for words and utterly puzzled. The deacon kept a firm grasp on Ty's jacket as he repeated himself, "The book of Enoch! In there you will find the names of the ones you seek."

"Names? Of the Sethites and Cainites?" Ty was more than a little confused now.

"No!" the deacon demanded, almost seeming upset. "This is one thing Father Mac and I disagree on. Read the book of Enoch!" The deacon let go of the jacket and disappeared down the stairs, as silently as he had come.

Ty stood there frozen, wondering what the hell had just happened. The Book of Enoch? He remembered just reading about Enoch in Genesis, but there were only a few sentences at most, and he didn't remember any such book in the Bible.

He turned and continued out the double doors in a slight daze. Strangely, the doors made that eerie creak that had been absent upon his arrival. Looking up, he noticed the sun had disappeared and a dark overcast had settled down upon the city.

CHAPTER 2

TY WOKE TO the sound of other students getting up from their seats indicating the end of the period. He realized that he must've nodded off somewhere in the latter half of class from his lack of sleep the previous night. As he started to gather his things, he noticed his professor, Dr. Eisenberg, looking at him; Ty was sure his little nap hadn't gone unnoticed.

"I hope with this being the last class of your college career, you don't take it too lightly, Mr. Larson," the professor said to Ty as he was walking out.

The professor spoke with a slight accent that sounded somewhat European. Ty knew he'd been all over the world on archeological digs since his twenties and appeared now to be in his sixties. His features were very distinguished with lines etched in his face resembling a road map of his travels. The professor was a very personable, yet stern man, with a way about him that made his students want to please him. Ty enjoyed his class and always found the professor's stories exciting, which made it all the more embarrassing to get caught sleeping.

"Sorry, Professor," he apologized. "I was up late last night, but I can honestly say I was working on your assignment."

"Oh? Was it the prize for the best research offered that spurred you into action, or was it your love for archaeology?"

Ty smiled. He hadn't forgotten the professor had told the class that the National Archaeology Association was sponsoring an archeological trip to the Middle East. Dr. Eisenberg had offered to take with him the student who came up with the most innovative research in the final semester assignment. Although the thought was enticing, Ty was convinced surely one of the archaeology majors would be able to top him, but that wasn't holding him back from getting caught up in the excitement of his budding theory.

"Well, that's sure quite a carrot to dangle in front of us. I'm not sure I can beat a class of archeology majors, but I hope to at least give them a run for their money." Ty told the professor, not wanting to elaborate on his progress just yet.

"Well, in that case, I guess I don't mind quite as much if you use my classroom to catch a few winks. After all, it is for the greater good of archaeology. Now enjoy your weekend and I'll see you next week all rested. And remember, Ty, 'leave no stone unturned,'" he said, probably to help keep him motivated. The professor always had a way of making his students feel like they might actually discover something new.

Ty nodded and exited the classroom. Waiting in the hall, he saw his classmate, Tom Bruiner, leaning against the wall. Tom sat next to Ty, so he obviously saw him taking his little snooze as well.

"Hey, dude, late night at the pub and you didn't give me a call to join you?" Tom was one of the archaeology majors, but still had a few years left before graduating.

"Nah," Ty laughed. "Just got caught up in a bad movie and had to finish it." He still didn't want to tell anyone his wild theory just yet.

"Yeah, I know the feeling," Tom said. "Sometimes you get so far into a movie and no matter how bad it is you still have to finish it. Hey, I gotta run, but just wanted to let you know a few of us are going down to O'Reilly's Saturday night around 9:00 for some drinks and maybe a game of pool, so hopefully you can join us."

"Well, maybe… I have a few things I need to get caught up on, but if I get a chance, I'll stop by." Ty was doubtful, knowing that he was probably going to be researching Enoch.

"Okay, hope you can make it. See you later. Oh, and by the way… I think *you know who* might be there," Tom said jokingly and punched his arm before he turned to leave.

Ty grinned as he waved goodbye. He'd been so caught up with his research that he hadn't even thought about breaking the ice with the beautiful blonde who was the reason he ended up taking this class to begin with, but if Celeste was going to be there, maybe he'd make it after all.

THE UNIVERSITY HAD an adequate library and he used it every once in a while, but Ty preferred the local one that was only a half block from his apartment. It'd been built long ago, like so many other buildings in the area, which gave it even more appeal. The book selection was far superior to most others, too, having a pretty impressive selection of hard-to-find books.

Ty quickly forgot about Celeste as soon as he got to the library and found a quiet spot where he could start his research into Enoch. He took out his King James Version of the Bible and looked through all the Books in both the Old and New Testament. Just as he thought, there was no Book of Enoch. He did remember reading a little about Enoch before, however, so he opened his Bible up to the index to see where he was mentioned:

Genesis 5:18-24, Hebrews 11:5, and Jude 1:14 & 15. *Well, I might as well start at the beginning,* Ty thought, and flipped through the pages to Genesis 5:18:

And Jared lived an hundred sixty and two years and begot Enoch. [19] And Jared lived after he begot Enoch eight hundred years, and he begat sons and daughters. [20] And all the days of Jared were nine hundred sixty and two years: and he died. [21] And Enoch lived sixty and five years, and he begat Methuselah: [22] And Enoch walked with God after he begat Methuselah three hundred years, and begat sons and daughters. [23] And all the days of Enoch were three hundred sixty and five years: [24] And Enoch walked with God: and he was not: for God took him.

Ty had just read these same passages yesterday, but still didn't really know what to make of them. He didn't think it was pertinent to what he was looking for at the time, so he didn't give it much thought. *"He walked with God"...* what did that mean? Whatever it was, it sounded pretty amazing, but why was there so little about Enoch? Ty thumbed ahead to Hebrews 11:5:

By faith Enoch was translated that he did not see death; and was not found, because God had translated him: for before his translation he had this testimony, that he pleased God.

Ty thought how confusing the Bible could be and realized how people could spend so much time studying it, but the little he'd read so far made it sound like Enoch must've been very important. He flipped ahead to Jude 1:14:

And Enoch also, the seventh from Adam, prophesied of these, saying, Behold, the Lord cometh with ten thousand of his saints, [15]

To execute judgment upon all, and to convince all that are ungodly among them of all their ungodly deeds which they have ungodly committed, and of all their hard speeches which ungodly sinners have spoken against him.

He couldn't believe it. That was it? Someone who walked with God after all and possibly didn't even die, yet he was only referenced in a few short sentences in the Bible? But the deacon told him to read the Book of Enoch. If there isn't a Book of Enoch in the Bible, then where would it be? Ty remembered a program he'd seen on TV about different biblical characters' writings that, for some reason, were never included in the Bible; maybe this was one of them.

This seemed like a good time to get on a computer and check the internet. He plopped down at the vacant computer in the middle of a row of several stations and typed in, *"The Book of Enoch."*

"The Book of Enoch," "The Secrets of Enoch," "The forbidden Books," "The Banned Books from the Bible," and several more titles came up. It definitely looked like he wasn't the only one interested in Enoch. He scrolled down to the first one that looked like reliable information. The first few paragraphs talked about who Enoch was: the seventh from Adam and the great grandfather of Noah.

Ty realized with a sense of awe just how long ago the events he was contemplating had taken place. *If I only had a time machine*, he thought. It seemed the deeper he delved into this, the more muddled everything became. Ty had always preferred sitting down with a book to reading off a computer screen, but his curiosity was mounting. He wasn't going to search or wait for the book this time.

The first few chapters of Enoch seemed to be a vision that revealed, among other things, an impending destruction of life on earth: *"all shall be afraid, and the Watchers be terrified."* This was the first he'd heard of the Watchers. Who were they? Ty read on, then he came to something that sounded very familiar:

It happened after the sons of men had multiplied in those days, that daughters were born to them, elegant and beautiful. And when the angels, the sons of heaven, beheld them, they became enamoured of them, saying to each other, Come, let us select for ourselves wives from the progeny of men, and let us beget children.

He was stunned. This seemed to reiterate what he'd just read in Genesis the other day, almost verbatim. The Sons of God taking daughters of men, and having children? He read on:

Then their leader Samyaza said to them; I fear that you may perhaps be indisposed to the performance of this enterprise; And that I alone shall suffer for so grievous a crime. But they answered him and said; We all swear; And bind ourselves by mutual execrations, that we will not change our intention, but execute our projected undertaking.

Ty had a decent vocabulary, but execration was a word he'd have to look up. He opened up another tab on the computer and typed the word "execrations" into the search engine. After just a split second, there was the definition: "to invoke a curse on, to declare to be hateful, to denounce." Were these beings denouncing the Creator over nothing more than lust? It sure sounded like it.

He read on with his excitement gaining momentum, then there they were, just what the deacon had told him—names!

Then they swore all together, and all bound themselves by mutual execrations. Their whole number was two hundred, who descended upon Ardis, which is the top of mount Armon. That mountain therefore was called Armon, because they had sworn upon it, and bound themselves by mutual execrations. These are the names of their chiefs: Samyaza, who was their leader, Urakabaraneel,

Akibeel, Tamiel, Ramuel, Danel, Azkeel, Saraknyal, Asael, Armers, Batraal, Anane, Xavebe, Samsaveel, Ertael, Turel, Yomyael, Araxyal. These were the prefects of the two hundred angels, and the remainder were all with them. Then they took wives, each choosing for himself; whom they began to approach, and with whom they co-habited; teaching them sorcery, incantations, and the dividing of roots and trees. And the women conceiving brought forth giants, Whose stature was each three hundred cubits. These devoured all which the labour of men produced; until it became impossible to feed them; When they turned themselves against men, in order to de-vour them; And began to injure birds, beasts, reptiles, and fishes, to eat their flesh one after another, and to drink their blood. Then the earth reproved the unrighteous.

It took Ty a second to digest what he was reading. This sound-ed incredible! It was definitely not the view Father Mac held. This was, literally, angels procreating with human women and produc-ing children… giants, no less—just as the few short sentences in Genesis had so briefly mentioned. Why had this not been elabo-rated on in the Bible? He continued reading:

Moreover Azazyel taught men to make swords, knives, shields, breastplates, the fabrication of mirrors, and the workmanship of bracelets and ornaments, the use of paint, the beautifying of the eyebrows, the use of stones of every valuable and select kind, and of all sorts of dyes, so that the world became altered. Impiety increased; fornication multiplied; and they transgressed and corrupted all their ways. Amazarak taught all the sorcerers, and dividers of roots: Armers taught the solution of sorcery; Barkayal taught the observ-ers of the stars; Akibeel taught signs; Tamiel taught astronomy; And Asaradel taught the motion of the moon. And men, being destroyed, cried out; and their voice reached to heaven.

Ty paused for a second. This sure sounded a lot like Greek mythology all right. Could there be any merit to this at all? "They descended upon Mount Armon." Was Mount Armon a real mountain? Ty opened up another tab to look it up and to his surprise, there it was, only now the mountain was called Mount Hermon, located in Lebanon. *Lebanon?* Ty thought. Only a couple of weeks ago, his class had been studying some very perplexing ancient ruins in Lebanon.

In Baalbek, Lebanon, beneath the ruins of the Roman Temple of Jupiter lay some of the most mysterious stone work in the world. It wasn't the ruins of the Romans that were so mysterious or even the civilization before them, but those of some unknown culture long before... one that appeared to be much more advanced.

Although the Roman ruins were very impressive, they were built on top of the most mysterious ancient ruins on the planet, ruins that consisted of the largest carved stones on earth. These megaliths were so enormous that even with our modern-day cranes, they couldn't be moved. More massive than a railroad boxcar, at almost seventy feet long, fourteen feet wide, fourteen feet high, and weighing an estimated 1000 tons, they had been carved from nearby quarries, moved uphill and over rough terrain to the temple site, then somehow lifted up and stacked precisely into place. They fit together so perfectly that a sheet of paper couldn't fit between them. These massive stones were ten times the size of the huge blocks that were used in the construction of the pyramids in Egypt!

There were some people who tried to explain this ancient, advanced civilization with speculation about extraterrestrial astronauts thousands of years ago, but Ty had always been skeptical of this theory. He thought for a moment... *might these fallen angels, the Watchers, be responsible for these ruins?* If these Watchers existed and were some kind of being similar to the Creator, then they would certainly be aware of all the forces in nature that the world had to offer, which might include some physical way of levitating heavy objects. There was always a new phenomenon of the earth being discovered that made it obvious that man still didn't know everything about the world in which we lived. Or, perhaps the explanation was simple brute force used by the half breeds—the giants—to lift the enormous building blocks.

What about the fact that some of the stones that were finished were never put into place? It was as though whoever had started the megalithic construction had been interrupted for some reason. Interestingly enough, according to the Bible, it would have been around this time that God had caused the Great Flood of Noah. Obviously, a world-wide flood would put a stop to any construction.

He brought up a map of the area to see how close Mount Hermon was to Baalbek. Chills went down his spine when he saw the results… they were literally a stone's throw away from each other. Could this just be a coincidence? Ty's father had always told him to be wary of anything that appeared to be coincidental, and his uncle had always stressed that there were no coincidences.

The next question Ty asked himself was: *who else believed the Book of Enoch to be true?* Judging from Father Mac, it was apparent that mainstream Christians probably didn't, but the deacon did and surely he wasn't alone. Ty went to a different web page to see what else was said about Enoch. *Well I'll be damned*, he thought. The Book of Enoch was part of the Dead Sea Scrolls, found in 1947. Apparently the early Christians, along with the Jews, had viewed it as scripture. And yet, for some reason it wasn't included in the Bible and was all but forgotten, except by the Ethiopian Orthodox Tewahedo Church.

Although the internet could definitely save some time with most research, it was Ty's experience that sometimes it was better to get things straight from the source. Now it was time to find an Ethiopian Orthodox Tewahedo Church. With that, there was one more task for his search: where was the closest one? Just as Ty assumed, there weren't very many in the United States, but to his surprise, five of them were in Washington, D.C. That was odd. New York City, the most populated city in the country, only had two. Why would there be so many in the nation's capital? In any case, D.C. wasn't very far away, so it looked like Ty's parents— who had moved to D.C. some years ago—might get to see their youngest son this weekend after all.

CHAPTER 3

IT WAS A short train ride from Alexandria, Virginia to Washington, D.C., a trip that Ty had made many times over the last four years to visit his parents. Usually he caught up on some sleep from his late nights studying, but this time he was going to take the opportunity to look over the reading material he'd found at the library. The only book about Enoch they had was titled, *"Fallen Angels and the Origins of Evil,"* by Elizabeth Clare Prophet. It included the Book of Enoch, along with the author's view of the Watchers and other scriptures relating to Enoch.

Although he hadn't been able to find a book on ancient levitation, he was able to find a sizeable paper written about various myths and actual historical accounts on the subject, which he'd printed and brought with him. He thought that if the mysterious ancients in Baalbek were moving such enormous blocks of stone around, perhaps some sort of levitation had been used. According to the article from the library, there were a few different ways in which this was possible including: magnetic, electromagnetic, aerodynamic, optical, and the one that piqued his interest the most... acoustic.

At the beginning of the paper was a section titled, *"Myths and Megaliths,"* which turned out to be exactly what he was looking for. It seemed there were many legends around the world that spoke of this "transportation" of huge blocks of stone floating from the area they were quarried to the sites where they now reside, and almost all these legends involved the use of sound.

In the highlands of Bolivia at the ruins of Tiahuanaco and Puma Punku near Lake Titicaca, lay numerous carved blocks of stone weighing one hundred tons or more from quarries over ten miles away. The workmanship of the stones was impeccable and rivaled anything that could be done today with modern technology. Although nothing is really known for certain about the people who lived there, some of the surviving legends speak of the founder god, Viracoha, constructing the site at the beginning of time and causing the stones to float through the air to the sound of a trumpet. Another story tells of Viracoha creating giants to move the stones, then for some reason he became angry with the giants and caused a flood to destroy them.

Ty thought this sounded eerily familiar, so he read on. In Mexico, on the Yucatan Peninsula, were the remains of the Mayan city of Uxmal. According to legend, the city and its pyramids had been built by a race of dwarfs who, by whistling, were able to move the stone blocks for construction into place. Easter Island was another place with huge stone statues, called Moai. Some were over thirty feet tall and weighed as much as eighty-six tons. Local legends there spoke of priests making the Moai float from the quarries to various locations around the island.

Another such legend involved the walls of the ancient city of Thebes. According to early Greeks, Zeus' son, Amphion, moved large stones into place by playing his harp. There were even stories of the Egyptians striking huge blocks of stone used to build the pyramids with some sort of instrument, producing a sound that caused them to float through the air. And then there it was, Baalbek. According to legend, the first city had been built before the flood and then later rebuilt by a race of giants.

Ty had to stop and think about this. Everything else had indicated that the half-breeds or giants had been wiped out by the flood. Was it possible that some of them survived? According to the Bible, Noah and his family were the only people to survive. *Was it possible this account wasn't completely accurate?* It did appear that some things had been left out of the Bible. Maybe this was another one of them.

Ty was definitely not a Bible scholar, although his grandfather had been, but he figured he was going to know a lot more about it when this was all over. After he thought about it for a while, he remembered the Biblical story of David and Goliath. That definitely happened *after* the flood, but was it possible that Goliath was one of the half-breeds or just someone who was abnormally large like he'd always assumed?

Ty recalled reading something back in high school that referenced all the different civilizations throughout the world having stories of a great flood that wiped out mankind; the number was staggering. Interestingly, though, some of the stories included the inhabitants going to mountaintops to escape the water. Whether there was truth to any of this was debatable, but one thing was certain: many unbelievable stories had a grain of truth imbedded in them somewhere. Now, it was just a matter of figuring out how much truth was imbedded in *this* story.

Ty looked up as the train started to slow. Union Station was approaching, which was the end of the line and his stop. As the train rolled to a halt, he stood up to get closer to the door to try to get ahead of the wave of people who were about to exit. Even though crowds didn't bother him much, not being bogged down with the masses would definitely save some time. Tactfully picking his way through the crowd, he made his way out of the station to the street. Outside the air was crisp and a bit sharp on his face. Zipping up his coat, Ty ducked his head against the cold and turned up the street.

The Ethiopian Orthodox Tewahedo Church was about six blocks from the station and since he hadn't been training for track any more, he thought the walk would be good for him. He'd phoned his dad earlier to see if he could pick him up at the old Carnegie Library at Mount Vernon Square in a couple of hours, which would give him plenty of time to visit the church first.

Before Ty left the library last night, he read a little about the Orthodox Ethiopians to get an idea of their belief structure. They were definitely Christians, but concentrated more on the Old Testament than most sects and included more books in their Bible, such as the Book of Enoch. Amazingly enough, the Orthodox Ethiopians also claimed to have possession of the Ark of the Covenant from the days of Moses. Apparently it was in a church in Ethiopia, but the only person allowed inside was a priest who guarded it with his life. This, of course, made critics skeptical of its existence.

The closer Ty got to the church, the more nervous he became. Showing up to see Father Mac had been one thing, but this was even more unnerving. With no idea what to expect from his venture, the prospect was becoming more and more intimidating with every step. The only thing that took the edge off a little was the fact that he knew the Orthodox Ethiopians believed the Book of Enoch to be true.

The street was loud from the traffic this time of day, but Ty was so deep in thought that hardly any noise seemed to reach his ears. As he approached the block where the church was supposed to be, it became apparent which building it was: a small, two-story stone building resembling a typical Roman Catholic church from the late nineteenth century, tucked between the neighboring more modern-looking structures. Unlike Father Mac's church, the stairs leading to the front entrance of this building went down one flight below the street level. Ty descended the stairs, curious about what he'd find inside. He reminded himself that churches were supposed to be places of sanctuary, a thought that seemed to calm his nerves a bit as he walked in.

The inside was dimly lit with candles throughout, several rows of pews on each side and several pictures of Christ on the walls. Breathing in, he recognized the faint odor of incense in the air. At the far end of the room, two men in long white robes wearing brimless dark brown hats stood beneath a large wooden cross fastened to the wall. Both had rich, dark skin and one was obviously much older than the other. As he walked, he scanned the room once more. Other than the two robed men, he was the only other person inside. They stopped whatever they were talking about and focused their attention on Ty as he approached.

He introduced himself. "Hello. My name is Tyler Larson, and I'm a student at Alexandria University. I was wondering if either of you could tell me about the book of Enoch? I read that if I wanted expertise on it, this was the best place to go."

The younger priest took a step forward and smiled. "Ah, yes. Welcome. It is always a pleasure to meet newcomers who seek information on our books. We would be more than willing to help you find your answers." The man spoke with a heavy accent. Ty had no trouble understanding him and somehow, his speech made the whole experience seem all the more legitimate.

So Ty proceeded from the beginning. He told them everything, including the possible chance to go on the trip sponsored by the National Archaeology Association, his questions regarding the Watchers and the giants, and even his discoveries and theory on levitation of the huge stones throughout the world by some sort of sound.

After he finished his lengthy story, the two priests exchanged a curious glance and said something to each other in a language that Ty didn't recognize. They looked at him, then the older of the two took a deep breath and began to speak in a very thick accent.

"Your passion for this truth is quite obvious and very commendable," he said. "For many years, all Christians and Jews believed the texts you are researching to be true. The reasons behind these stories' exclusion from the Bible as you now know it are purely political, but we have kept true to the full version." He paused for a moment, glancing at the other priest, then continued. "The Watchers were not myth, they existed just as described in both the Book of Enoch and the Book of Jubilees. The giants of which you speak are a bit more complicated. The term 'giant' came from the Hebrew word *Nephilim*, which actually means 'fallen.' However, do not confuse the *Nephilim* with the fallen angels—the Watchers—all texts make a clear distinction between the two."

Ty found himself in a state of awe; it took a moment to absorb what the priest was saying. Theorizing had been one thing, but to actually hear this coming from a high religious figure who believed it to be true was putting a new perspective on everything.

The priest continued with his explanation. "'Giants' is the English translation, which probably came from the Greek word *gegantes*—meaning 'titans'—were the actual progeny of Gods and humans from Greek mythology. It is because of the *Nephilim* and their actions here that the Lord flooded the earth."

"But what about after the flood?" Ty asked. "What about Goliath, was he one of the *Nephilim*?"

"You are a very observant young man," the priest responded. "Noah and his family were not the only survivors of the Great Flood.

There are other *Nephilim* mentioned in your Bible who also survived. Moses killed the one named Og, who was said to have an enormous bed made of iron to support his great stature. It is told in the Book of Jubilees that the Lord allowed ten percent of the *Nephilim* to survive the Great Flood." He paused for a moment, glanced at his partner and then lowered his voice. "Even today there are those who believe they are still among us."

Ty couldn't believe what he was hearing... *still here?* Before he had a chance to respond, the younger priest whispered something to the older one who nodded then turned back to Ty. "We must attend to other matters now, my boy. My apologies."

In unison, they turned on heel and began to make their way further into the recesses of the church. They had only taken a few steps, however, when the elder turned back and looked into Ty's eyes, almost as if he was peering into the depths of his soul. "Be careful, my son," the priest warned dauntingly. "Sometimes, that which we seek is not what we truly wish to find."

The priest held his gaze a moment longer then turned to walk away. It took a couple of heartbeats before Ty could move. What was happening? Was this yet another piece of a fantastic puzzle that was unraveling before him? He was caught up in thought, but by now, the priests had almost reached the far end of the church and Ty realized he really should leave. Everything seemed a blur as he opened the door to go with thoughts of the *Nephilim* still racing through his mind. The light of the sun blinded him for just a moment as he stood in the threshold of the church, energizing his feeling as though he had just awoke from a dream.

THE ELDER OF the two priests stopped and watched the door close as the Larson boy left the building. As soon as the door clicked shut, he gave a gesture to the other, who nodded and withdrew into a back room. Once alone, he reached inside his robe and pulled out a small portable intercom and spoke into it. The language he spoke wasn't English, nor was it the one in which he'd spoken to the younger priest earlier. Indeed, this was a language that hadn't been heard in over five thousand years.

At the same moment, as the Larson boy walked out the front of the church, a camera lens slid through a closed curtain in a window across the street. As it captured the young man walking away from the house of worship, a figure emerged from the dark alleyway that led to the back entrance of the church. Ty Larson walked on, appearing to be lost deep in thought with no way of knowing or reason to suspect that his every move was now being watched.

CHAPTER 4

TY DIDN'T KNOW exactly who'd be there to pick him up after his visit to the church. He'd called his dad, Grant, and if he wasn't working late, he was usually the one waiting for him. Otherwise, his mom, Marion, would be the one to get him.

The sun had started to set as Ty walked up the street toward the library next to Mount Vernon Square. He was still in a state of disbelief at what had just transpired. Everything he believed about the history of civilization was now in question. Could things actually have happened this way? If so, what about the *Nephilim*... was it possible they might still exist? And if they did, where were they now and how could they possibly hide from the prying eyes of the human race?

With all this whirling around in his mind, he didn't even notice he had reached the base of the library stairs, or that his father was leaning against the railing, until he was almost on top of him.

"Hey, Dad! Glad to see you didn't have to work late tonight." Ty smiled, trying to cover his total distraction and gave his father a hug. "I'd ask you what's been going on at work, but I know you couldn't tell me anyway."

"Yeah, some things never change, but at least they let me out every once in a while," his father said with a grin. "Good to see you, son. You always make our day when you come to visit. Your mom's at home whipping up one of your favorites, so we'd better not drag our feet too much. That backpack all you brought?"

"You're the one who taught me to travel light, Dad. '*You never know when you might have to flee the scene in a hurry,*'" Ty said, then smiled after mimicking his father's familiar warning.

"I guess you must've been listening to me every once in a while, then," his father said and returned the smile as they started down the sidewalk toward the parking lot.

Approaching the numerous rows of cars, Ty asked, "So, Dad, are you still driving the same old jalopy, or did it finally go back to the earth?"

"Oh yeah, it hasn't made it into the long term recycling bit yet, but we might have to upgrade it to keep your mother happy. I think she's a little embarrassed to be associated with it anymore… at least she doesn't feel that way about me yet," his father added in jest.

FATHER AND SON continued to visit while they walked to where the fabled car was parked. The CIA vet had a lifetime worth of vigilance training, but as he chatted with his youngest son, his guard was down just enough that he never noticed the man step out of the shadows and write down their license plate number.

"SO, TY, YOU said on the phone that you were coming up here to do some research for a class. Anything you care to elaborate on?" his father asked him when they got in the car.

Although Ty had been reluctant to talk about any of his new ideas to anyone except for Father Mac and the Ethiopian priests so far, he always felt he could talk to his dad about anything. They'd always had a good relationship and being in the CIA, Ty's dad had been exposed to several bizarre-sounding events that were actually true, so Ty didn't hesitate to run his ideas by him.

"Well," Ty began, "I don't know where to start, Dad. The last couple of days I've been reading some things that seem so incredible that it doesn't seem possible there'd be any truth to them. Except there's always more. Every time I think one thing is too crazy to be true, something else backs it up, so maybe there's some merit to it after all. Have you studied the Bible in depth at all, Dad?"

His father thought for a moment. "Well, not like your grandfather, but I've read it a couple of times, although I can't say that I've really studied it. I thought this last class of yours was an archaeology class, not a religious one. What's up?"

"Well, let me wait until we get home, so I can tell both you and Mom at the same time. Maybe getting a couple of different perspectives on it will help."

"Sounds good to me," his father replied. "I know your mother will love to hear what you've been up to. It can be frustrating for her when I can't tell her what I've done all day, but that's the way it is in this business."

They continued to get caught up on the rest of the way home. Although Washington D.C. had only been Ty's home for his high school years, after which he'd moved back to Alexandria to go to college, it definitely felt like going home and always gave Ty a warm feeling. As they pulled into the driveway, Ty imagined he could see his mother through the kitchen window working over the stove, but unfortunately, because of what his mother referred to as his father's overwhelming paranoia, the curtains were always drawn any time the sun was down.

Ty and his dad were joking and laughing with each other as they walked into the kitchen where Ty's mother was standing over the sink rinsing off a head of lettuce. Upon seeing them, she put it down, grabbed a towel and half dried her hands as she rushed toward him.

"My baby!" She exclaimed, engulfing him in a hug that squeezed his ribs together. "Oh, it's so nice you're home! I hope you're hungry, I made one of your favorites."

Ty had smelled the mulligatawny as soon as he had walked in. It was an Indian curry chicken soup he had fallen in love with after watching the Soup Nazi episode on a Seinfeld rerun.

"Yours is always the best, Mom, and it's good to see you, too," he said after the air reentered his lungs as she let go of him.

They spent a few hours enjoying dinner and catching up on each other's lives. Ty had forgotten all about his recent endeavors for the first time since he'd gotten tangled in it all, until his father asked, "Well, son, I gotta know. Tell us about this mystery project you're working on. The suspense is killing me."

Ty nodded and leaned forward, his face serious as he proceeded to tell them what had transpired over the last few days. He didn't leave anything out, even his theory about the possibility that levitation moved the unexplainable megaliths scattered around the globe. Once he'd finished he looked at them and asked, "Well, am I crazy or do you both think I might be onto something?"

His mother spoke first. "Oh no, I don't think you're crazy, Ty, I think it's healthy to have an active imagination. By the way, how's Father Mac doing?"

Ty's heart soared at his mother's enthusiasm, but didn't let it show. "He's doing quite well. He's hardly aged at all."

While Ty and his mother were talking about Father Mac, he noticed his dad got up and went into the living room and came back with a Bible in his hands. Sitting down, his father opened it up and read for moment.

"Well I'll be," Grant said in amazement. "I can't believe I never heard of this before. You say the Book of Enoch elaborates on this?"

"You must've read Genesis six four, and I did bring a copy of the Book of Enoch with me. You can borrow it for a bit if you want to read more," Ty offered.

"Sure, I'd love to, son," his father replied.

Ty could tell his father had something on his mind. His face had the same look on it that he'd get when he was thinking about something from work that he couldn't talk about. After a few seconds of deep thought, his father excused himself from the table and stepped into the other room to make a phone call.

Ty looked at his mother. "Some things never change."

"Oh, I know. I'm so used to it that I hardly even notice anymore," she said, and turned the conversation back to whether or not Ty had a girlfriend, and was he eating well at school?

After a few minutes, his father returned to the kitchen and looked at Ty. "Son, I think we may have something down at the office that'll be of interest to you. I just had to double check to make sure it's not considered a national security issue, and it's not. So if you want, I can take you to the office tomorrow and show you something that I'm sure you'll want to see. You can come too, Marion."

Ty's curiosity was piqued. "Sure! Can you tell me what it is?"

"You'll have to wait and see. We still have some protocol to follow first."

His mother looked utterly shocked. "See, Ty, this is why I need you to visit more often. Home for three hours and we've already been invited to CIA headquarters."

The room was silent for a moment, then everyone broke into a laugh. Ty's mom didn't get invited to Grant's office very often.

They visited more after coffee and grasshopper pie until it was time to turn in for the night. Although Ty was enjoying visiting with his parents, he couldn't stop wondering what it was his dad had to show him.

MEANWHILE, AS THE lights were turned out at the Larson house, the amber glow of a cigarette lit up the dark void in a parked car in the shadows across the street, less than a hundred yards away.

CHAPTER 5

IT WAS GRANT'S habit to start his day with a five-mile run somewhere through the neighborhood, either to one of the nearby parks or down along the river. This morning was no different, except today, once he was out of the house, he noticed the parked car across the street a couple of houses down that was out of the ordinary. Although the windows were tinted, he thought he'd seen a stir of movement come from inside the vehicle. It was most likely nothing more than a visiting family of one of his neighbors, Grant thought, but he'd been trained not only to notice these kinds of things, but to be wary of them. There was a mantra he'd heard years ago that he now lived by—nothing could be anything. This morning, with his new awareness of the out-of-place car, he consciously turned up the street—running away from the car—so he could return from the rear to get a closer look.

During his run, his thoughts kept slipping back to what Ty had told them at dinner the previous night. He himself had always wondered how these ancient civilizations had moved huge

stones with such primitive technology. It did make some sense
that if there were God-like beings living here, they'd know the
physical properties this world had to offer. With the passing of
several thousands of years and the possibility of a great deluge,
who knows what might've been forgotten? And if there were giant half-breeds, their size and strength might be all that was
needed to move the enormous slabs of stone.

As his run was winding down with only a few blocks left,
Grant turned his thoughts back to the car parked near the house.
The possibility of anything suspicious seemed highly unlikely, but
it was something he had to consider as a result of his cautious nature. The car had not moved in his absence, still parked exactly
opposite of an overhanging Yellow Birch. He came up behind it
from the opposite side of the street to be as discreet as possible.
Grant had always had great vision. Both eyes were still better than
20/20, so as he approached the car, he was able to clearly make
out the license plate number while his gaze remained inconspicu-
ous. He kept jogging right up to the front door as always and
went inside not giving the car a second glance.

Ty and Marion were sitting at the kitchen table having coffee
upon his return, too immersed in their conversation to give
Grant's presence much attention. He took a quick shower then
joined them, knowing he'd have to wait until he was at the office
to have the license plate number checked out. He was still thinking there was probably nothing to be concerned about, but it was
in his nature to be suspicious.

They all had breakfast together, reminiscing about the good
old days of Ty and Eric's childhood, then Grant looked at his
watch and realized it was time to go. He usually didn't work on
Saturdays, but he didn't want to be late for the appointment he'd
set up with his co-worker and longtime friend, Will Grable, concerning Ty's project.

"Well, we'd better get a move on so Will doesn't have to wait on us," Grant said as he got up from his chair. Ty and his mom both agreed so she quickly cleaned off the breakfast table while Ty gathered up his things and headed out to the car.

As Grant was backing out of the garage, he eyed the car across the street curiously, which stayed stationary as they made their way to the end of the neighborhood. At first it appeared as though it wasn't going to move as they made their first turn onto Washington Avenue, but after two blocks and right as they were making their next turn onto Jefferson Boulevard, Grant noticed the sedan was now in trail. He knew it could all still be a coincidence, but he also knew that with every turn the sedan duplicated, the odds of that were dwindling. The Agency—what people who worked for the CIA called it—had spent millions of dollars every year training their agents on everything from how to tell when someone is lying to how to tell if you're being followed and how to deal with it. Grant had played this game before, in training sessions, but now, this was no exercise.

Once on the 495, it was about fifteen minutes to his exit. If he had been alone, he would've intentionally driven past the Agency and then doubled back at the 123/George Washington Memorial Parkway interchange, but with his family on board and his reluctance to scare them with what might be a false alarm, he decided to go the back way via the 193 to see if they would still have the uninvited company behind them.

Both Ty and his mother obviously noticed the late turn off, then Ty spoke up, "Hey Dad, did they move headquarters since my last visit, or is this the preferred way on the weekends?"

"Funny, son," Grant replied. "Actually, there's been a motorcycle for sale parked in front of this little deli that has been catching my eye for the last couple of weeks, so I thought we'd get a little closer look to see what it is and maybe stop by on our way back and ask some questions."

Grant made up stories from time to time over the span of his career, so he had some experience with these spur-of-the-moment untruths, although he still felt guilty about telling them to his family. Motorcycles really had always been an interest of his, to Marion's dismay, and he actually did want one someday when he had more free time.

"Now, Grant, don't you think you're a little old for that?" Marion asked in a comical tone.

"Well, if I wait much longer, I will be for sure," Grant responded as he winked at Ty.

"I think I'll stay out of this one," Ty said then looked out the window.

They turned on to the 193 and drove about a block, past where there actually was a deli and, to Grant's delight, absolutely no motorcycle out front.

"Well, it looks like I waited a little too long. Somebody finally must've bought it."

"Thank God!" Marion acted relieved, "I mean, I'm sorry, hon, that's a bummer," It was now her turn to wink at her son.

All this time Grant had been keeping an eye on his mirror, and after about two blocks, the same sedan was still behind them. This was definitely no coincidence anymore.

Just a few more minutes and they came to their turn. Grant drove toward the Agency, and it was no surprise that the sedan didn't follow. After all, who in their right mind would go up to the front door of the CIA headquarters if they didn't belong there? Grant had no idea who or why anyone would be following them, but only a few yards ahead were the resources to find out.

CHAPTER 6

THE CIA HEADQUARTERS at Langley, Virginia was a famous site worldwide; Ty had lost count of how many times he'd seen it featured in a film or a book. While the general public only got to see the impressive structure from brief snippets in the movies, Ty had been more fortunate. Even though he had the opportunity to visit the Agency on occasion with his father, he still felt overwhelmed every time they drove up the lane as the building still seemed larger than life to him. This time though, a new excitement was rising up inside of him as well, an anticipation that even trumped the excitement he had felt on his first visit.

Usually everything that went on at the Agency was done on a need-to-know basis, all very low key. Even secrets had secrets. Every once in a while there'd be some information they could release to the public, but that was pretty rare. Ty knew his dad took his job very seriously. He knew whatever his dad had to show him today wasn't classified, but whatever it was he was being taken to see, it had been brought here for a reason.

With it being a Saturday, Ty had expected the Agency to be a little slower, so he was amazed to see the amount of activity going on. Men and women with ironed shirts and polished shoes were rushing about just as if it were mid-week. Inside the main lobby, the first thing that always caught Ty's eye was the CIA seal in the center of the floor. With the help of Hollywood, this was probably the most famous part of the building. Every time he saw it, it reminded him of the picture taken of George Bush, Sr., standing in the middle of the seal when he was the head of the CIA.

Will's office was in the Science and Technology department, which was in the opposite end of the complex from his father's office. The Science and Technology department was a part of the building neither Ty nor his mother had ever been to before, although the hallways all had a similar look to them. While walking to Will's office, Ty started to feel like a mouse in a maze and knew there would be a piece of cheese behind one of the doors they were approaching. They finally came to Will's office, with the door open and the light on. Despite being with the CIA for several years now, his pleas for an office with a window had fallen on deaf ears. According to Ty's father, this was something Will could frequently be heard grumbling about, and knowing his dad's sense of humor, Ty was sure he had some fun with it at Will's expense.

"How's everything in the Bat Cave?" Grant said as he knocked on the door and pushed it open wider.

Will looked up from behind his computer and smiled. "Ty, Marion, good to see you again... and I see you brought the Joker with you."

Will stood with a chuckle and embraced Marion and then Ty. Almost immediately, a strangely shaped object with a cloth draped over it sitting on the desk caught Ty's eye. His excitement must have shown on his face, as Will seemed to catch on right away.

"Ah yes, the reason for your visit. I won't keep you waiting, Ty."
Will pulled the cloth off the object with a little flourish, like a
magician doing a trick. "Ta da!"

They all stared in amazement, which quickly turned to confusion. On the table before them was some kind of mechanical
contraption that looked like it came from the pages of a Dr. Seuss
book. There was a metal copper-colored sphere about the size of a
basketball attached to a silver metal frame at two points on opposite sides of the sphere. The frame had a round ring base and a
vertical ring about three inches wide encompassing the sphere—
but not touching it—with about an inch gap between the two.
Mounted inside the vertical ring (again not touching the sphere)
were eight sets of three tubes about a half-inch wide, spaced even-
ly apart. On the ring base were what looked like two sets of guitar
strings running perpendicular to each other, spanning the center
of the ring directly under the sphere.

As fascinating as this was, Ty had absolutely no idea what it was
supposed to be or what it had to do with what he was researching.
Glancing at his mother, he saw his own confusion reflected on her
face as she was apparently wondering the same thing. They just
stared in silence until Ty's father spoke up. "Well, Will, you've obviously stolen the show again, but I think everyone's a little lost."

Will smiled, then broke his silence. "I'm sorry, I just get a kick
out of seeing the expression on everyone's face when they see this
for the first time. Ty, I hear this is something that's probably of
some interest to you. What do you think it is?"

Ty thought for a moment then shook his head and shrugged
his shoulders. "Honestly? Well, it kind of looks like an engineer
somehow got a steel guitar to mate with a gyroscope and together
they had a bottle opener?"

His father laughed. "Good one, son. The first time I saw it, I told him it looked like something you'd surely find in the Bat Cave."

Will looked only slightly amused. "You guys are hilarious… and Grant, I think you can put that Milkman theory to rest."

Everyone laughed except for Marion, who furrowed her brow and gave Will and Grant a disapproving sneer, then jokingly muttered something about just how much more desirable the milkman might be.

Will cleared his throat and quickly changed the subject. "Ty, have you ever heard of John Keely?"

Ty thought about it for a second. "John Keely? No, I don't think so. Who is he?"

"Actually, the question is. Who *was* he," Will responded. "John Keely was an inventor who lived from 1827 to 1898 in Philadelphia and spent fifty years of his life working on various machines that used sound to power engines, levitate objects, and even disintegrate solid rock. This particular machine is called a sympathetic transmitter, and supposedly when the right chord is played on a zither, it can make steel balls float in the air."

"Wow! Does it actually work?" Ty looked at the machine, then back to Will.

"Well," Will replied, "That's the funny thing. Keely could make it work—and did—in front of several witnesses on several different occasions, but no one else has ever been able to duplicate the demonstrations after his death. He had a lot of critics who thought he was a fake, but he was always able to convince the stockholders that he'd discovered an unknown force capable of generating an enormous amount of energy. It was from a demonstration given to a group of scientists in 1872 that sparked enough interest from investors that the Keely Motor Company was formed with a capital of five million dollars. Eventually, the stockholders became impatient with Mr. Keely's secrecy and delays of a working motor, so even though they still believed in him, they filed suit against him and eventually quit funding his work. Mr. Keely did, however, still have one source of funding: the wealthy widow of a Philadelphia industrialist, Clara Jessup Moore. She was a strong believer in his work and continued to fund his research until his death in 1898. It was then that the Philadelphia Press did an investigation of his workshop and found hidden lines in the walls leading to a three-ton sphere in the basement that they thought must've contained compressed air to secretly run his demonstrations."

Ty was a bit puzzled. "So, he was a fraud?"

"Well," Will started again, "what I just told you is what's known to the general public. Personally, I think there's more to the story. You see, back in the 1800s, there were several secret societies that were very popular, such as the Freemasons, the Illuminati, the Sons of Liberty, the Knights of the Golden Circle, and possibly even the Skull and Bones, to name a few."

Ty interjected, "Did he join one of those?"

"I don't know," Will said shrugging his shoulders. "But it almost seemed that soon after the demonstration in 1872 that sparked all the interest in his work, Mr. Keely took on a different demeanor. I think all his demonstrations after that were a little questionable and, oddly enough, the device he'd demonstrated which had gained all the support was never seen again. Some think that shortly after the inventor let the cat out of the bag, so to speak, about the unknown energy force he'd discovered, if a secret society had recruited him—willingly or otherwise—they didn't want the world to know about this force."

"Oh!" Ty interrupted, "so that must be why he went to all the trouble of rigging his shop with hidden lines of compressed air, to make it look like he was still onto something without actually divulging what it was he'd discovered. In fact, I'll bet he knew he'd probably eventually be found a fake and maybe even hoped for it."

Will nodded. "Well, that's what I think, and it does make

sense. We do know that the funding he received still went into the company. If he was a fraud from the get-go, one might think at least some of the money he was receiving would've been abused, but that wasn't the case."

"Was the rich widow who financed his work involved in any secret society at the time, or was her husband?"

"Very good questions, Ty. I really don't know, but it wouldn't surprise me at all if they were."

"So how did the CIA end up with this gizmo?" Ty asked.

Before Will could answer, Ty's dad butted in, "Sorry guys, I've something I need to take care of in my office. Will, would you mind escorting these two over when you finish up?"

"Sure, we'll be over in a few. Want me to buzz you before we head over?" Will asked.

"If you don't mind. Thanks, Will. And, Ty, if he tries to talk you into buying some Iraqi Dinar, you may want to think twice about it." With a smirk on his face, Ty's father turned and started down the hall. Several years earlier, Will had talked Grant into buying the Iraqi Dinar, assuring him it was going to revalue any day and be worth millions… that was ten years ago.

Once Grant was gone, Will shook his head and turned back to Ty to answer his question. "What was I saying? Oh, right, how'd we end up with it. When the Philadelphia Press did their investigation, they weren't the only ones involved. In those days, the CIA didn't exist, but the State Department was around, and they somehow must've pilfered this before the press showed up. From there it was shuffled to the Signals Intelligence Service, which doesn't make any sense to me, because they were more into code breaking than anything else, although they were very good at keeping secrets. It then ended up with the Office of Strategic Services—OSS—who were the predecessors to the CIA. We obviously then inherited it by default. It was never considered a national security threat, but no one really knew what to do with it, so it's been packed away in storage ever since. I only came across it because the boys in charge of the storage department were going through everything and reorganizing things into an electronic file. I guess somebody thought it was time we got caught up with the times, since this is the Science and Technology Division, so here it is."

"So what'll happen to it now?" Ty asked.

"Unfortunately, once we're done looking it over, it goes back to storage. Who knows when it'll be looked at again, if ever. I have to admit though, this is the best part of my job," Will added. "You wouldn't believe some of the strange things that I've seen come through here over the years."

"You mean to tell me you guys really do have a warehouse full of stuff, just like in the Indiana Jones movie? Is the Ark of the Covenant in there, too?" Marion joked.

"Sure, along with Noah's Ark and the flying saucer from Roswell… it's a rather large warehouse."

Ty could see why his dad got along with Will so well, the similarities in their sense of humor were uncanny.

"So, just a couple more things to tell you before I'm done boring you," Will continued. "I've seen pictures taken of this device from back in 1872, and something is definitely missing from it. I don't know if it was intentionally removed, or if it was broken when it was being transported at some point." Will shrugged. "I guess we'll never know, but there's another thing that's rather strange. When I opened the crate this was in, I noticed a small, folded piece of paper wedged into a crack. It had oxidized so much over the years it looked like part of the crate, and I almost missed it."

"Really?" Ty finally took his eyes off the machine to look at Will. "Was there anything on it?"

"See for yourself," Will opened a drawer in his desk and pulled out a plastic baggy containing what almost looked like a fragment from the Dead Sea Scrolls and handed it to Ty. He held it a little closer to the light to get a better look. The wording had faded over the years, and it was just barely still legible. Two words were written on the piece of paper; *Yar-lha-sham-po* and *Belial.*

Ty looked up at Will. "What do they mean?"

"That's the same thing I asked, and after a little research, it appears that the first one is the name of a god in Tibetan mythology and the second sounds like a demon from the Bible, perhaps. What it has to do with Mr. Keely, if anything, is a mystery."

"Do you mind if I jot them down so I can look into it a little more?" Ty asked.

"Be my guest," Will replied. "Just let me know if you find anything interesting."

"You bet," Ty said as he wrote the words down on a piece of paper and tucked it into his wallet.

"Well, unless you want to look at this a little longer or have any more questions, I think I've told you about all I know about Mr. Keely and this contraption."

Ty and his mother took one long last look at the machine. He was amazed at the craftsmanship and wondered at the possibility of it ever having done what the inventor claimed.

"I sure do appreciate this, Will."

"No problem. I'll give your father a call to see if he's ready."

Ty nodded as he was digesting everything he'd just heard: a machine built in the 1800s that could levitate things and possibly disintegrate them as well? Not only that, but the name of a possible demon from the Bible and a god from Tibetan mythology along with it? How were they tied together? Here he'd never given mythology much thought, but in the matter of a couple days he was beginning to think there might be some merit to it after all.

Will interrupted Ty's thoughts. "Well, if you two are ready, I'll take you down to Grant's office."

"Thanks again, Will," Marion spoke up. Ty wasn't sure his mother was quite as enthralled in all of this as he was, but something about her being at his side through the visit had made the experience seem even more real.

MEANWHILE, BACK AT his office, Grant felt troubled as he hung up the phone. He'd run the license plate number of the sedan that had been following him through the system and had gotten no results. There was absolutely no record of such a number in all of New York State. He'd seen numerous phony New York plates over the years and if this one was a fake, it was a damn good one. However, the thing that troubled him the most wasn't the potentially bogus plate, but the fact that the computer system he'd used to trace it had been accessed the previous night to trace his own.

CHAPTER 7

TY'S TRAIN BACK to Alexandria was scheduled to depart at 4:35 that afternoon. Although Grant and Marion would always try to talk him into staying a little longer, he told them if he left now he'd have some time to work on his paper and still maybe get together with his friends later. He mentioned it probably would do him some good to take a break from his research and clear his head a little, but the honest truth was that the more he found out about this project, the more exciting it became. Grant had to agree with his son. Could there actually be some truth to any of this? Every clue seemed to lead to something so bizarre it was almost inconceivable. Grant could see how there seemed to be enough evidence to make his son want to dig a little deeper.

They had just enough time to stop for a late lunch. The majority of the conversation was about Mr. Keely's machine. It seemed so incredible that someone might've stumbled onto an ancient technology so powerful... and then for some unknown reason there was a chance it could've become lost again. Marion brought up the parallels between the disappearance of the inventor's machine and the stories about innovative gasoline engines capable of incredible fuel mileage suddenly vanishing, accompanied by rumors of involvement of the big oil companies. If there had indeed been a cover up in the Keely matter, might it simply have been over money?

Although this was all intriguing, Grant's thoughts were not focused on the mysterious case of Mr. Keely, however, but the idea that someone with access to the Agency's computer system had traced his license plate. There was no way of finding out who was responsible for the trace, but there was a time stamp whenever the computer was accessed, which was right about the time he'd been picking up his son at Mount Vernon Square. Because of this, he was suspicious the reason they'd been followed that morning had something to do with Ty. The reason was a mystery—did it have something to do with the Ethiopian Orthodox church he said he'd visited? Grant had the authority to have someone from the Agency keep an eye on his son, and hopefully find out who might be watching him and why. He decided not to say anything to Ty—about either of the tails. Grant couldn't chance tipping off whoever was following his son by having him know about it. The only thing that gave Grant any comfort at all about the situation, was that he knew he would have two of his best men watching over his youngest son.

On the way to the train, Grant kept one eye on his rearview mirror, but noticed that whoever had been following them earlier was now nowhere to be seen, but he vowed not to let his guard down again.

AS THEY PULLED up to Union Station, Marion tried one last time to convince Ty to stay a little while longer. Although Ty wished he could, he really needed to get back and get some work done on his paper. He had less than a week before it was due, and he was starting to feel a little of the pressure that all the excitement from his discoveries had been masking.

So they said their goodbyes, and Ty promised to let them know when he got home. He waved one last time before he passed through the center doorway leading to the lobby. He'd always admired the architecture style used for the station. Just looking at the magnificent building sparked Ty's imagination, nudging his thoughts back to what had started his quest. To think that thousands of years ago structures with huge blocks of stone were, in some cases, quarried many miles away from where the building site was erected and done with such precision and without the tools that modern technology had to offer. There was no shortage of theories on how these feats were achieved, and the simple truth was that nobody really knew for certain how the ancients did it. Could there really have been God-like beings, along with their half-breed offspring, somehow involved? A few days ago he would've scoffed at such an idea, but now he wasn't so sure.

The line at the ticket booth was unusually long for a Saturday, but Ty didn't seem to notice. He could hardly believe the events that had transpired lately. The Ethiopian priests made it sound like they believed some of the half-breeds might still be alive; that sure was a spooky thought. If it were true, why hadn't any of them been seen? Undoubtedly someone or something of that stature couldn't go unnoticed for very long.

The thought that Keely might've been part of a secret organization such as the Illuminati or the Freemasons put a whole new twist on what he was researching too. After all, the only thing he was trying to prove was some connection between Biblical times and huge stone structures, but this is where the path was leading him, and he simply couldn't just look the other way.

The train ride back was over before he knew it, and after he came out of his self-induced trance, he realized he hadn't turned his cell phone back on. He checked and had two messages: one was from his mother, and the other was from Tom. Ty still hadn't decided if he was going to meet them at O'Reilly's, so he thought he'd wait to call Tom until he knew for sure.

As the train rolled to a stop, he looked up and noticed an attractive blonde make eye contact with him as she stood up to depart. Ty smiled and remembered that Celeste was going to be with the group tonight. Maybe he should make time to go and try to get to know her a little better.

Ty got off the train and headed for the parking lot. He found his car in the row where he always parked and was a little peeved to see someone's advertisement pinned under his windshield wiper. He'd always thought this was a pretty futile attempt at marketing, not to mention that he viewed it as littering. Not once had this marketing ploy gotten any business from him; in actuality, he usually threw it away without even looking to see what they were trying to sell.

Then, as he was in the process of crumpling up the ad, he realized something wasn't quite right. He looked around the parking lot, and not one other car had a piece of paper on the windshield. Not one! He looked at the wrinkled piece of paper in his hand and opened it back up. The ad was for some organization called A.R.E., Association for Research and Enlightenment. Ty again looked around the parking lot, only this time he wasn't looking at windshields. This time, he realized as the hairs on his arms stood on end, he felt as though he was being watched.

CHAPTER 8

TY'S APARTMENT WAS only a few minutes from the train station, but during the drive he'd decided he would meet up with his friends after all. If nothing else, it would help get his mind off the craziness that seemed to be consuming him. Who knows why his car was the only one in the lot with an ad under the wiper? Maybe his car had been there longer than the rest, or maybe whoever put it there only had one left, or maybe someone was playing a joke on him. Anyway, whatever the reason, the more he thought about it the more he figured there was probably a good explanation for it. He'd at least have to find out what goes on at A.R.E. just to satisfy his curiosity, but that was all the effort he'd put into it, and for the time being, it could wait until morning. What he was going to do now was drop his car off at his apartment, quickly check his email, and walk down to O'Reilly's.

Ty lived in a nice neighborhood (considering what he paid for rent), with lots of mature maple trees and a few elms and oaks. It was that time of year when the leaves were just starting to change

color. Although the area was very pretty in the spring and throughout the summer, the autumn in the northeast had always been his
favorite time of year.

His apartment was on the corner of Fourth and Main in the
residential area, but there was no parking allowed on the street in
front of the building, so he'd always turn at Third Avenue then
turn again into the alley that led to the parking lot in back. The
lot was small, and there was only one covered parking spot for
each apartment.

As he pulled into his space, he noticed a small oil slick on the
right side. *Oh great,* he thought. His car had quite a few miles on
it, but it'd always been mechanically sound, and he was hoping it'd
last at least until he graduated. He made a mental note to check
the oil in the morning to see where the leak was coming from.
Hopefully it was nothing serious.

He shut off the engine and grabbed his overnight bag, then
looked one more time at the crumpled flier. It almost looked like
it was printed directly from a website's homepage. There was an
oval emblem in the upper left corner that had a dove in the middle, and just over the top of the dove it read, *"Edgar Cayce's
A.R.E."* Under the dove it said, *"Your Body, Mind, Spirit Resource
Since 1931."* Edgar Cayce... he'd heard that name before, but
where?

Ty folded up the flier and put it in his coat pocket. He got out
of the car and started the short walk toward the eight-story building that had been his home for the last four years. Both entrances
required a key to access the lobby. He let himself in through the
back door and went down the hallway that led to the elevator.
The rent was cheap, which was good, and he lived on the top
floor, which was by choice. Sometimes the elevator was out of
commission, and Ty never knew if it was going to be operational
or if he'd see the familiar "out of order" sign posted. To his delight,

it looked as though it was working, but he could see it was already on the eighth floor, so he'd have to wait for it to come back down. In his opinion, it was the world's slowest elevator, although it was still a little faster than taking the stairs (which was what he often did).

As he waited, he couldn't help but think of what great leaps in technology there'd been over the span of man's life here on earth, or so he had thought just a few days ago. If what he was in the process of uncovering was true, though, he now had to wonder— had there really been any advancement at all? If some sort of levitation was used to erect the ancient megaliths eons ago, then what other forces of nature had been forgotten? Is it possible that we are actually less advanced now than we were thousands of years ago? The thought seemed absurd, but to manipulate gravity to those extents would be an immense breakthrough that seemed almost impossible to achieve in this day and age.

The elevator finally arrived and the doors slowly squeaked opened. Ty got in and started the slow ride to the top, all the while thinking it probably would've been faster to take the stairs. The elevator finally made it to the top floor, coming to a halt, the doors opening sluggishly into the quiet, drafty hallway. His apartment was at the end of the hall, facing Main Street. He'd only formally met a couple of the other tenants on his floor, but had seen most of the others in passing, except for the last two at the other end of the hall.

Just as he reached his apartment, he glanced at his watch to see how late he was going to be and realized he'd forgotten to call Tom to tell him he would indeed be coming. Picking up the pace, he unlocked the door to find the same messy place he'd left behind yesterday. *I'm going to have to fire that maid,* he thought as he chuckled to himself while tossing his bag on the little coffee table in front of his 1980s model nineteen-inch screen TV. There were only three rooms in his place: a living room/kitchen combo, a small bathroom, and his bedroom. It always amazed him how big a mess he could make in such a small apartment, but that was just one of his many talents. Actually it really wasn't that bad, it was just that some of his things didn't really have a home.

He looked around to see if he needed to do anything before he left again. Then as he started to turn to leave, he noticed his computer was on. That was odd. In the last few years he tried to become "greener" by conserving energy and shutting things off before he left. It must've been the flow of adrenaline fueling his excitement that allowed him to leave it on. Shrugging it off, he realized that at least computers were smart enough to go into hibernation mode if they hadn't been used in a while. But still, it was odd.

The flashing power light on his computer reminded him that he wanted to check his email. Not much, just a little junk mail and a couple of messages from Tom reminding him about tonight. Ty closed his email and made the conscious effort of shutting down his computer for certain. Now it was time to relax.

He again took the lethargic elevator and reached the lobby after its descent. It was empty, which was usual for this time on a Saturday. Ty left the building out the front, and began his walk to the pub. The sun had already disappeared for the night as he started his trek down the partially-lit sidewalk. The temperature drop had become noticeable as well, with a light breeze accentuating the fact.

Although he was going out to try to unwind from the excitement his research was generating, he still couldn't help thinking about what the world might've been like so long ago if any of this was true. Levitation may have been just one of the physical properties that was known about. What if some of the other legends, such as Zeus throwing lightning bolts, also had some truth to them? After all, electricity is all around in nature, being able to manipulate it and control it in some way might not be so unlikely. And what about the enormous magnetic field that the inhabitants of the earth lived in? Ty knew that magnetic fields are the principles that make electric motors work, along with numerous other devices, and here the earth was engulfed in the largest magnetic field we could possibly ever have access to. If there was some way of harnessing any power from that and the ancients knew how, what other feats might they had been able to do?

According to the Bible, there were all kinds of feats accomplished that seem to be impossible today. Several of them were by Christ, and after Ty thought about it, if there was anyone who would know about all of the forces of nature, and of any possible way of manipulating these forces, it would've been him. Everything from walking on water, turning water into wine, even raising the dead—all had been done while Christ was flesh and blood. Most Christians refer to these acts as miracles, but what really is a miracle? Doing something with amazing results that's not understood? Would talking to someone on the other side of the globe with a cell phone have been considered a miracle in Christ's day? For years, Ty had thought that these events in the Bible probably did happen, but that they had to have been done somehow within the physical laws of the immediate world, not by magic. When the disciples saw Jesus walking on top of the water toward their boat, Peter had initially started out to meet him and had actually made it a little ways, before he started to sink— and Peter was no doubt an ordinary human.

A car horn sounded at the upcoming intersection bringing Ty's awareness back to his surroundings. He realized he was close to the pub, and he didn't really remember the past few blocks. The residual light from the sunset was now completely gone, and the glow of neon from the local small-business district was like an oasis of light in the otherwise poorly lit neighborhood.

As Ty waited for one last car before crossing the street, he looked around, noticing there was someone walking about a half a block behind him. He usually had a good sense of awareness. But the fact there had been someone behind him for who knows how long without his knowledge made him a little mad at himself for getting so caught up in his thoughts and not paying attention to much else. From the time he was a young boy, his dad had taught him a lot about self-preservation, covering everything from self-defense to handgun training. Although Ty had never been a fighter, he was more than capable of defending himself, if the need arose.

As the last car passed through the intersection, he hurried across the street, crossing into the local neon jungle. There were three delis, one pizza place, a couple of small grocery stores, a pharmacy, three little pubs, and a small clothing store, along with some other small shops, all in a one block area. It wasn't a touristy part of town, and it didn't have any major chain stores, both of which were appealing to him. Also, with the university close by, there were always a lot of students in the neighborhood, and they were a vast part of the clientele in the local businesses, especially the pubs. He hurried the last half a block past the grocery store and the small pizza place to the pub.

This neighborhood had several buildings dating back to the early 1800s, and O'Reilly's was one of them. It was initially built as a combination court house and police station, but was never completed when the funding was cut off, attributable to stories of an affair between the land owner and the county commissioner's wife. The building sat vacant for several years and wasn't converted into an Irish pub until the late 1800s when an immigrant from Ireland, Jack O'Reilly, traded two horses and a mule for the abandoned building.

Ty entered the pub through the narrow doorway as a small group of people were leaving. The place was rather quiet for a

Saturday night, but that was normal when the university football team was playing out of town. He looked to where he and his friends normally sat over by the pool tables, but didn't recognize anyone. Just as he was about to take his phone out to give Tom a call, he heard his name called from the other side of the bar. There was Tom sitting alone motioning him over with a beer in his hand. Ty smiled, waved back, and walked over.

Ty looked at his watch. "Am I that late, or did you scare everyone off already?"

Tom laughed and said, "Actually, when I told everyone that I'd invited you, they couldn't get out of here fast enough."

"Oh yeah? So, you're saying there might be some beer left for me after all?" Ty said as he shook Tom's outstretched hand. He'd only known Tom since the start of the archaeology class, but they hit it off right away. They had a lot in common, such as similar personalities, the same taste in music, and a lot of the same interests. Although Tom never talked about his parents, he was also originally from Montana and was here on an academic scholarship. Tom had just started his freshman year, but he was actually several years older than Ty. Unlike Ty, Tom didn't go to college straight out of high school. He'd been working for a concrete company in Houston for the last nine years before deciding to go back to school.

Tom gave a crooked smile and eyed the pitcher of amber liquid, which was about a third of the way full. "Sorry man, proclaimed by yours truly. Seriously though, what were you doing that was more important than me and beer? I almost gave up on you."

"Oh, I went up to D.C. to see the folks last night and just got back. Are we the only ones to show up?"

"By only ones, are you asking if Celeste is still gonna show?" Tom asked with a smirk, then poured a beer into an empty glass and slid it in front of Ty.

Ty tried to play dumb. "Now why would you say that? I think we've said like two words to each other."

"I know, and what's up with that? You can't tell me you're too busy." Tom was taking six classes this semester, which kept him incredibly busy, so he liked to give Ty a hard time about only having one class to worry about. Tom didn't give Ty a chance to reply before he said, "Actually, she did stop in and even asked about you."

Ty tried to read Tom's face to see if he was joking. "Sure she did."

"No, seriously, dude, she did, and when I told her that I hadn't heard back from you, she finished her drink and decided to go home."

Up until now, Ty didn't really know if she was interested in him, but now it looked like he may have a chance after all.

"Oh well, maybe that'll teach me not to be late anymore," Ty said, trying not to look as if it mattered much. They ordered another pitcher and continued to visit.

"Are you going to the game next weekend? Literally everyone is going, but I'll be holed up working on Eisenberg's paper. How's that going for you by the way?"

Ty thought about telling him about the wild path he was taking with his research but realized just how preposterous it sounded and decided against it. God-like beings mating with human women and creating giants with supposed super powers just seemed too far-fetched to talk about at this point, and that wasn't even starting on the levitation.

"No, dude. No game for me either. Not sure yet about my angle on that topic, but I've got to get moving on it for sure."

SEVERAL PATRONS HAD come and gone as they were talking, but there'd been two who arrived a couple of minutes apart, shortly after Ty arrived, who just quite didn't fit the mold of the local college students. If Ty had gotten a closer look at the man behind him on the street… he would've recognized the first of the two.

CHAPTER 9

As the evening progressed, Ty remembered the flier left under his wiper and thought he'd run it by Tom. "Hey Tom, have you ever heard of Edgar Cayce?"

Tom looked at him and replied, "Don't tell me you're into psychics now, Ty. Hell, I'm starting to worry about you a little."

Ty thought for a second. "What are you talking about?"

"Are you kidding me?" Tom asked. "I thought you lived in front of the History Channel, and you mean you've never heard of Edgar Cayce?"

"Well, I think I may have heard his name before, but anything to do with magic or voodoo usually goes in one ear and out the other."

Tom gave Ty a serious look then said, "Believe it or not, this guy was the real deal. I've seen a few documentaries about him, and I honestly think he was genuine."

Ty looked skeptically at his friend. "Don't tell me you actually believe in that sort of thing? Who should be worried about whom?!"

Tom shook his head. "No, man, I'm with you on most of these self-proclaimed psychics, but this guy was different. Literally everyone who had tried to disprove him came away a believer. Everyone!"

Obviously Tom was very passionate about the topic, so Ty became a little more serious. "Okay, tell me about this guy, then."

Tom took a swig from his beer, paused for either thought or dramatic effect, then began. "Well, Edgar Cayce was totally amazing. He was born in the late 1800s and I think he died somewhere in the mid-1940s, but from the time he was a kid, he displayed some kind of psychic ability. I guess he wasn't the best student in the world, but supposedly one time he fell asleep on one of his school books—which he hadn't read at all, by the way—and when he woke up, he knew the entire contents! But that wasn't what made him famous. What made him famous was his ability to diagnose and treat people's ailments. The weird thing was that he'd have to lie down and kind of put himself in a sleep-like trance, then someone would ask him questions about the person with the medical problem, and he'd tell them what was wrong and what needed to be done to cure them. The person wouldn't even have to be there... hell, all he needed was a name and an address and someone to ask him the questions while he was on a couch in a trance. And he wouldn't remember any of it after he woke up. These were what they referred to as 'readings.' A lot of his patients were people who'd been to real doctors who were unable to help them and almost always were misdiagnosed. Believe me, there were plenty of skeptics, but like I said, everyone who came and tried to disprove him always left a believer. Early on, some of his clients would ask him questions about things like stock picks or where to find oil, which he'd tell them and he was always right, but strangely enough after answering questions concerning monetary gain, he'd become physically ill. He finally had to have his wife be the one to run the readings, so people couldn't slip in those types of questions."

"So," Ty interjected, "how do they explain what he was able to do?"

"Who knows," Tom responded. "According to Cayce, he thought everyone was able to do what he did with a little practice, although I'm not sure who'd want to. Something about it was physically draining, in fact it sounds like that's what finally killed him. He knew—I think from one of his own readings—that he should only do two a day, but he was such a compassionate man he couldn't turn people down. He'd do several more than two each day until he finally dropped over dead."

Ty was silently mulling over how any of this could be physically possible when Tom asked, "So, why the interest in Cayce all of a sudden?"

"Oh, someone put a flier on my car at the train station while I was visiting my parents. The emblem said 'A.R.E.' with Edgar Cayce's name, and I thought it sounded like a day spa or something."

Tom thought for a second then said, "You know, Cayce built a hospital in Virginia Beach, which isn't too far from here, and I think it's open to the public now. Every reading that he ever did was written down and recorded and is still there."

Ty shook his head. "That's actually really interesting. I don't know though… I really don't approve of advertising that way. Honestly, I think it's a cheap ploy. And what exactly are they selling, anyway? Do they charge a fee to get into the place?"

Tom shrugged his shoulders. "Beats me, but I know he never charged anyone when he gave them a reading, although I guess he did accept donations. Maybe that's what they want?" Tom looked at his watch and must've noticed they'd been talking for almost three hours. "Well, buddy, I'd better call it a night. Some of us have more than one class to worry about."

Ty grinned. "Hey, I paid my dues. If you hadn't decided to wait until it was almost time to draw social security to go to school, you would've been done a long time ago. By the way, where did you park your walker?"

At thirty years old, Tom was considered a nontraditional student as far as undergraduates went, so he was surely used to the jokes by now. "Ha ha, very funny... are you sure you're old enough to be in here? Maybe I should have the bartender check your I.D. again."

Laughing, they both downed their beers and stood to leave. Tom offered to drop Ty off on his way home, which Ty considered, but decided that with his apartment being so close, he should walk instead.

The temperature had dropped even more in the last few hours, and Ty could now see his breath, which was a sure sign that winter was just around the corner. He zipped up his coat all the way and started the trek back to his apartment. The traffic on the streets had all but dried up, as most people were probably home in a nice warm bed, which was starting to sound like a good idea to Ty too. He was only a block from the bar and already regretting turning down Tom's offer. So with that thought, he decided to jog back to his apartment. After only about half a block, however, his pace quickened into more of a sprint. Although he hadn't been in training for a while now, he was still probably one of the fastest people in the country, and the remaining five block run was over just as his hands started to feel the cold. Once in the lobby of his building, he kept his momentum going and ascended the eight flights of stairs, the only thing slowing him down was his effort not to disturb any of the other tenants.

Ty's heart was pounding as he entered his apartment. Since leaving the pub, he'd been thinking of Edgar Cayce's ability to diagnose and cure people's ailments. How was that possible? Was this yet another force of nature that the fallen angels knew about? It may not have been as advanced as Christ's ability to heal the sick or raise the dead, but certainly it was along those lines somehow. Maybe it was possible that every action or reaction ever done by anyone or anything—whether it's a thought, a heartbeat, or something as small as cellular activity or even the movement inside an atom—somehow left an imprint on the fabric of space-time. If that was the case, then if someone could somehow sense and decipher these "messages," it would be possible to know everything from the past to the present. After all, the neurons in the brain not only receive, but also transmit electrochemical signals, and the enzymes in a cell cause numerous unique chemical reactions that might just leave such a "fingerprint." Maybe Edgar Cayce had this ability. That would explain how he was able to understand what was going on in someone's body. Maybe Christ not only did the same, but was also able to manipulate the actions inside the cells somehow in order to heal someone. This was way over Ty's head, but he was sure there was a physical explanation. Obviously, not one that mankind was aware of at the present time but something explainable nonetheless.

He took off his coat, threw it on the bed, and turned on his computer. The mindreading capability of Edger Cayce wasn't really what he should be focusing on right now, but it did spark enough interest to think about researching the man before he called it a night. Once his computer was warmed up and ready to go, the first website that came up was edgarcayce.org. The first page looked exactly the same as the flier. Just to make sure, he grabbed his coat and pulled out the folded piece of paper: exactly the same, someone had merely printed the homepage from the website, just as he'd thought. What a strange way to advertise. If they were looking for donations, wasn't there a more effective way? Then he started to get a strange feeling again. *What if he was specifically targeted by someone? But why?* He hadn't even known who Edgar Cayce was, and he wasn't into psychics anyway. Nothing about this seemed to make any sense at all. He continued to look at the website, and then something caught his eye. He clicked on it and the title read, "Edgar Cayce Readings on Ancient Mysteries." He began to read the first paragraph:

> *While in the trance state, Edgar Cayce's ability to peer into the past with uncanny psychic accuracy was demonstrated repeatedly. This type of information is called "retro-cognition" and the Cayce readings attest to the variety of material available in this manner: previous happenings in an individual's life, including accidents or forgotten traumas; as well as ancient history, including the geological evolution of the planet and details of tribes and civilizations that predate recorded history.*

Ty gave this some thought. With the way he rationalized how Cayce's ability might be physically possible, then all this might've been a reality. Tom emphasized that Cayce's skeptics all left as believers after trying to prove him a fraud. *Civilizations that predated recorded history?* Might Cayce have known something about the Biblical civilization on earth before the flood, the same civilization that Ty had been trying to research?

Once again, he started to get the feeling that the flier placed on his car was no accident, but who or why someone would do that didn't make any sense at all. After hearing the deacon's and Ethiopian priests' viewpoint on the fallen angels and the *Nephilim*, his thoughts and theories were obviously not new ideas. Was he being targeted? He tried to consider the possibility of this being some sort of elaborate prank, but simply couldn't figure out who would possibly have that much time or why they would want to leave the flier in the first place.

Ty glanced back to the computer screen. On the left side was a list of some of the Ancient Mysteries that Cayce must've talked about. From talking to Tom, he'd already started to become a believer in this Mr. Cayce, but when he got about halfway down the list, he came to a topic that made him freeze in his tracks. What he saw on the screen was incredible. Another story Ty had always regarded as a fairy tale was about to take on a whole new meaning: the fabled legend of Atlantis!

CHAPTER 10

ALTHOUGH TY HAD stayed up late working on the computer, his internal alarm clock still went off at 5:30 a.m. regardless. He normally jumped right out of bed and started the coffee, but this morning he lay there wondering about the strange road his quest was leading him down. Was it possible that the legend of Atlantis was true? If it was, might there be some connection between Atlantis and the civilization he was now chasing? And was it just a coincidence he'd been introduced to Edgar Cayce, or was he being pushed? The latter made no sense at all, for who'd have anything to gain? The bigger question now, though, was Atlantis? Really? He was becoming so unsure about everything. He had so many questions. In fact, the only thing he felt certain of was that what he'd found in the days that had just transpired were all somehow connected. Everything was just so cohesive, in a weird, seemingly unstructured way. Now, though, he had to try to find a way to fit this new piece into the puzzle. There had never been any doubt in his mind the Atlantis story was just that, a story, another myth just like Zeus and Hercules. Although Atlantis had always been fun to fantasize about, he'd always thought it was invented ages ago by someone with an overactive imagination, most likely Plato's. If such a great civilization really had existed, unquestionably there would've been some clues left behind that could prove it. Right? He couldn't believe he was actually starting to give it some serious thought.

The Edgar Cayce website confirmed what Tom had said, that the A.R.E. was located in Virginia Beach, which was only about a three-hour drive. He initially planned on spending the day working on his paper and maybe even going to church, but now he was thinking about taking a drive to see what this place really had to offer. After all, he still had a lot more research to do before he could connect the dots and make a strong case for his theory.

With the excitement beginning to build, Ty finally got out of bed and started some coffee before jumping in the shower. He made it a quick one, and by the time he got out and dressed, his coffee was done brewing. Filling his mug first, he then hastily grabbed his coat and headed out the door and down the stairs to his car.

He no more than got out of the parking lot and onto the street when he realized he'd left the paper with all the A.R.E. information on it in his apartment. Turning the car around and parking on the curb in front of the building, he jumped out and sprinted in the front doors and up the stairs. Just as he opened the door at the top of the stairs leading into the hall, the elevator doors opened, and a man he'd never seen before stepped out. He was wearing a tan trench coat with a matching winter hat pulled down low, but Ty caught a glimpse of nearly black hair and a full beard that looked a little peculiar. The man froze in his tracks when he saw Ty. For a few seconds they stopped and stared at each other. Then the man, somewhat awkwardly, stepped back into the elevator then rushed to push the button to make the doors close behind him.

Ty stood there for a moment without moving, not knowing what to do or think. It seemed as though this stranger had just deliberately dodged him. Furthermore, it was almost like the man was surprised to see him there. As Ty thought about it, there was something familiar about the way the man was dressed. He didn't recognize the face as so little of it was exposed. Usually nobody was moving around on the floor at this time of day, especially on a Sunday. He thought about running down the stairs to confront the man, but he was a little spooked and confused by the whole situation and decided against it. His dad had instilled in him a long time ago to always assume your adversary was armed and willing to use it. *Adversary?* he thought. What made him think this guy was an adversary? As far as Ty knew, he didn't have any enemies. Hell, he hardly ever even disagreed with anyone.

He tried to rationalize what had just transpired with several other theories. Maybe the man just happened to realize he was on the wrong floor. Ty looked at the elevator to see it was now on the first floor. Maybe one of his neighbors was having a secret affair with the guy. Whatever the case, he couldn't help but feel like the stranger was surprised to see him there and acted as though he'd been caught doing something wrong, but maybe Ty was just being paranoid. After thinking the situation over, he went into his apartment and grabbed the paper he'd left behind and double checked that his door was locked. Getting back to his car, he looked around, but the stranger was nowhere in sight.

Once on the road, traffic was light—just as he'd expected— and his imagination was running wild with everything that had come to light in the past few days, including what had just happened with the stranger from the elevator. Even though he realized there was a good chance there was nothing to it, he had a strange feeling there was. He felt something wasn't right when he made eye contact with the man, but he couldn't quite put his finger on it.

Turning his thoughts back to the story of Atlantis and the Bible, Ty reflected. Most of the stories in the Bible were considered to be true by millions of people, but was there really any proof to back them up? There was evidence all around the world that the surface of the earth had drastically changed over the eons, including fossils of seafaring creatures in high mountainous terrain, but that wasn't proof of a worldwide flood such as the one mentioned in the Bible. It wasn't as though anyone had ever found Noah's Ark. And what about the creation story of Adam and Eve itself? Was there any proof to back up that story? Other than the fact that we are here, no. So why not give a pervasive legend, such as Atlantis, at least a closer look? Before he knew it, he was almost to Virginia Beach.

THE MAP HE'D printed led him right to the parking lot of the Edgar Cayce Foundation Visitor Center. With only a few cars in the lot, there were several open spots left. The building looked like a fairly modern structure and was three stories tall. There were several long vertical windows covering the square concrete building. Up a hill to the left were stairs leading to another, much older-looking structure.

He entered the main entrance to find a couple of ladies sitting at a counter to help with questions. Ty visited with them for a while and found out that the building up the hill was the hospital that Cayce had built in 1928 to help people with medical problems, which was still used for health services and a spa. They also told him about the daily activities at the foundation, which included lectures, tours of the building, a film about Edgar Cayce, and even meditation up on the third floor. On the second floor was the library—the country's largest metaphysical library consisting of over 66,000 volumes—along with transcripts of all Cayce's readings, which numbered over 14,300, they said. Of the 14,300 readings that Cayce gave, to people ranging from commoners to wealthy businessmen to the president of the United States, 10,000 of them were related to health issues, with the remainder about different subjects including ancient Egypt and, yes, Atlantis. Ty was shocked at how many people believed in this man and his readings. Even Thomas Edison had a reading.

He thanked the two women and proceeded to check out the place. It didn't take much time to figure out Cayce was world famous. Ascending the stairs to the second floor, he was amazed at the vast extent of the library. With the overwhelming amount of literature, he had to ask for help to narrow down the subject of interest. The librarians were more than happy to help him, and it didn't take long for them to steer him in the right direction. Of all his readings, Edgar Cayce had mentioned Atlantis over 700 times.

Time flew by as Ty poured over the Atlantis-related information. The more he read, the more fascinating it became. The ancient world Cayce was talking about was so amazing that it almost sounded like a fairytale. It was obvious that Cayce wasn't retrieving this information from any of the history books Ty had read. The stories involving Atlantis talked about an advanced civilization that began almost 200,000 years ago when spiritual beings descended onto the planet and materialized into human forms. There were eventually two groups of people occupying Atlantis known as "The Sons of Belial" and "The Children of the Law of One." They were familiar with the forces of nature such as solar power, electromagnetism, particle physics, astronomy, astrology, and had even mastered gravity. The feats they were reportedly able to accomplish with these forces were utterly amazing. It sounded as though the Sons of Belial were wicked in their ways and were maybe even fornicating with flesh-and-blood beings, which was against the beliefs of the children of the Law of One.

When Ty read this, he had an eerie feeling come over him. Was this referring to the same verse in Genesis that had started this quest? Was it possible that the Sons of Belial were the same as the Sons of God mentioned in the Bible? The few short verses in Genesis, chapter six, were very vague about life on earth in that time period, but it was very clear that something incredibly strange had taken place so long ago, something that was bad enough to cause the Creator to flood the planet and wipe it clean. The story in the Bible made it sound as though Noah and his family were the only survivors of this deluge, but the book of Enoch had told a slightly different account, with ten percent of the *Nephilim* surviving as well. Ty read on to see if any of Mr. Cayce's readings about Atlantis might refer to this time period and, surprisingly, one of Mr. Cayce's readings specifically stated just that:

> *These were the periods as termed in the scripture when, "the sons of God looked upon the daughters of men and saw them as being fair."*

Damn! Ty thought, *talk about ask and ye shall receive!* He continued reading and after another hour of poring over the information that referred to Atlantis, he had to take a step back to digest everything he'd just read. If this stuff had any truth to it, the history of mankind would have to be rewritten. Obviously, the dates given by Cayce, as far as the age of the earth and mankind, were drastically older than what traditional Bible scholars thought (about 6000 years), but Cayce's dates were more in line with what we were learning from modern science today.

As far as survivors from the cataclysm that brought about the destruction of Atlantis, according to Cayce, there were some. Where did they go? Just a few places such as Peru, the Yucatan, and Egypt. Interestingly enough, all these places were riddled by ruins and unexplainable megalithic structures with dates of origin so controversial that, if true, would rebuke conventional history. Could there possibly be a grain of truth to any of this? It was sure starting to seem so. If Mr. Cayce's ability to diagnose and treat medical problems were as accurate as history had noted, then how could his readings regarding man's past be totally inadmissible?

Then something else dawned on Ty. The Sons of Belial? He reached into his pocket and took the paper out of his wallet with the two names that were found in the crate with the machine that his dad's friend, Will, had shown him. The first word was the name of a Tibetan god Ty had yet to research, but the second? None other than Belial! The dots were definitely starting to come together, but Ty had no idea where they were leading.

CHAPTER 11

GRANT LAY IN bed pondering what he'd just read and the events that took place since his son left. It had only been a little over twenty-four hours, and in that time he'd found out way more about Enoch than he ever could've imagined, especially since he'd just heard about him for the first time. He had time to read both The Book of Enoch and The Book of Jubilees, both of which went into much more detail of life on earth before the Great Flood than the Bible did.

What had really caught his attention was the story in which Noah's father, Lamech, thought his wife had been unfaithful to him with one of the Watchers because of the physical traits Noah had as an infant. Apparently Noah's appearance was in such resemblance of the Watchers that Lamech went to Enoch for council on the matter, who reassured Lamech of his wife's faithfulness. Grant was both fascinated and confused as to why this was the first time he'd ever heard any of these stories; after all, his own father had been a Bible scholar.

Ty's research had definitely piqued Grant's interest, but for now his main concern was to find out who and why somebody was following his son. In an effort to cover all the bases, he had Will visit the Ethiopian Church to find any leads, and according to the agents who were keeping an eye on Ty, there was no doubt that he was being followed.

Whoever was behind the operation appeared to be organized enough to be untraceable. So far, that is. Just like the phony license plate on the car that had been parked on their street, the same was true of the car now tailing Ty in Alexandria. Not only were the Virginia plates fake, but they were good enough that if the driver was pulled over by a patrolman, the fact they were fake wouldn't even show up. It was only with a much more detailed search (such as Grant did with the computer at the Agency), that the fake plates would ever be noticed.

The level of expertise behind whoever was following Ty made Grant nervous, but he couldn't let Ty's tail become aware that *they* were being watched and risk losing the upper hand. Grant's knowledge that someone inside the Agency had used their computer system to run his plate made this operation even more difficult, with only a trusted few aware of what he was doing. It seemed obvious that whoever was following Ty wasn't intending to harm him as no acts of aggression of any kind had been attempted yet. While that was still Grant's primary concern, he still couldn't figure out what possible reason they had for following him and that thought alone was unsettling enough. Grant was going to have to investigate every aspect of his son's life to find out. He felt bad not being able to let Ty know what was going on, but he thought that would just be too risky.

The information Will found so far was pretty benign. The people he talked to at the church were very helpful as to what their beliefs were and they went into great detail about the Ark of the Covenant when asked about it, but he didn't learn anything that would help Grant.

As for the two agents Grant had watching Ty, it was still too early for them to get a good idea of what was going on. One thing they knew for certain was that there was definitely more than one person involved. Usually whenever something like this happened, sooner or later someone was more than likely to slip up and leave a clue. Taking all precautions, Grant decided to set up two surveillance cameras: one to monitor his son's apartment building and one to monitor the inside of Ty's apartment. It was crucial that they found out who they were dealing with and why before their cover was blown.

As usual, Grant couldn't tell his wife anything, and, in this case it was probably for the best. He quietly reached over and shut off the light trying not to wake her, for had she not been sound asleep, the look on Grant's face would've certainly tipped her off that something was wrong.

CHAPTER 12

TY STAYED AT the Edgar Cayce Foundation looking over as much information as he could and talking to several other people who were interested in Cayce's work until almost closing time. It seemed as though Cayce had almost achieved a rock-star like status throughout the entire world. Over 300 books were written about him and his work and there were "Edgar Cayce Centers" in thirty-seven countries and members of the A.R.E. in more than sixty. To say that he had a large fan base would be an understatement, and yet Ty really hadn't heard anything about him before yesterday.

The medical diagnoses were impressive enough. Cayce's ability to tap into a person's body somehow and know what was wrong and what they needed to do to fix the problem sounded like an impossible feat, yet he did it over 10,000 times! That alone had to give some merit to his *other* readings like those pertaining to the history of mankind. According to what Ty was finding out at the foundation, he learned that when Cayce was in a hypnotic trance, he was able to tap into what's known as the "Akashic records." These records were comparable to a "psychic library" of anything that had ever happened throughout time. So, if Atlantis did in fact exist, then someone with Cayce's ability would more than likely be able to access information about it.

Ty found that Cayce believed some people fled Atlantis to either Central America or Egypt. Cayce also said the Great Pyramid and the Sphinx were actually built by the Atlanteans who arrived in Egypt after the final destruction of Atlantis. Mainstream archeologists believe that the Great Pyramid and the Sphinx were built about 4,600 years ago, but according to Cayce, they were built long before that, somewhere around 12,500 years ago. These dates seemed outlandish at first, but according to several geologists who have looked at the weathering of the Sphinx, they have become convinced that it must be much older than previously thought. This belief was based on the fact that the weathering appears to be from years of rainfall, and that part of the world hasn't experienced that kind of weather for 9,000 years, just after the last Ice Age.

Another eerie thing that Ty found during his visit was how the pyramid was built. According to Cayce, the massive stone blocks weren't pulled up ramps by thousands of workers, but were instead made to float through the air with some advanced technique. When he heard this, all the stories of levitation that he'd read about in the past few days came to mind once again.

Might all this circumstantial evidence he was uncovering be proof of an advanced ancient civilization? And could they possibly have been capable of such achievements, as Cayce had suggested? If not, it was definitely enough to keep him interested and searching for more clues. If there really had been such an advanced civilization, despite being wiped out by a flood, there would certainly be some physical clues left behind to prove their existence, but maybe all the construction with the huge stones was just that. After all, it was still unknown how all of the ancient megalithic stone construction had been accomplished, not to mention that some of the stones were so heavy that even with the largest cranes modern man still couldn't move them. Somehow or somewhere there had to be more evidence, and Ty was bound and determined to find a smoking gun if at all possible.

Everyone had been very friendly and more than helpful with Ty's questions and he actually hated to leave, but it was closing time and he had a three-hour drive ahead of him, so he thanked the ladies one last time and exited the building.

He was walking across the parking lot to his car when he remembered the oil stain in his parking spot back at the apartment and realized he hadn't checked to see where the leak was coming from yet. Crouching down in front of the car on the side where the spot had been, he was delighted to see there wasn't a drip to be found. After a moment of feeling relieved, he began to feel a sinking suspicion. This was odd, these kinds of problems don't fix themselves, instead they usually just get worse. He unlocked his car and popped the hood open. Maybe the oil level had dropped low enough to be below where the leak was coming from, he thought. However, when he checked the dipstick, he found to his surprise, it was dead even with the "full" mark. After thinking about it for a second, he wondered if maybe someone else who lived in his building had used his spot. That didn't seem likely, though, since the tenants were assigned their own numbered parking spaces, and they all respected each other's spot. *Oh well, no harm done,* he thought as he closed the hood, although still not shaking the feeling that something peculiar was going on.

Turning around, he was startled to find a short pudgy man wearing a long, dark gray trench coat with a black scarf and hat— which kind of resembled something Sherlock Holmes might wear—standing only about four feet behind him. Ty stepped back until he was against the hood of his car and stared at the newcomer.

"Sorry for startling you, but I couldn't help but overhearing your questions concerning the pre-flood civilization that Mr. Cayce had talked about time and time again. Is this something you're going to pursue further?"

Ty thought this was an odd question to ask. He tried to get a quick read on the man before answering. The stranger looked as though he was sincere and harmless enough, so Ty decided to be open with him. "Actually, I would like to find out as much as possible on the subject. In fact, that's the whole reason that I drove down here today, although to be honest with you, I find everything about Mr. Cayce fascinating. It would've been something to actually have met the man, but yes, my main concern right now is just that. Why do you ask?"

It appeared that the man took a second to do the exact same thing that Ty had done with him, and then replied. "Are you familiar with Cape Charles?"

Ty thought for a second then answered, "No, I don't think so, why?"

"It's not far from here; I can tell you how to get there if you're interested."

Ty was puzzled. "Uh, well, what's in Cape Charles?"

"Oh, I'm sorry, sometimes I talk without thinking," the man replied. "I have a... well, let's just say an acquaintance of mine lives out on the peninsula. You might want to talk to him."

Ty was more than a little confused. "Is he an Edgar Cayce enthusiast?"

The man gave a short laugh. "No, no, not as far as I know, but he's a... well, let's just say he's somewhat of a specialist on some of the people who lived before the Great Flood."

The man was definitely a little strange, but he had Ty's attention now. "Really? A specialist in what way?"

"That's something that he'd have to tell you, but if you're interested, I can tell you where he lives."

This was an awkward situation, to say the least, and Ty's knee-jerk reaction was to say thanks but no thanks, but instead his curiosity got the best of him. "Sure. Except, do you think it's okay for me to just drop in? Should I call him first to see if this is a good time?"

"No. If you did, I'm sure he wouldn't answer the phone anyway. Just tell him what you're interested in and I'm sure he'll invite you in. You have a pen by any chance?" he said as he pulled out a folded up flier from inside the exhibit and began unfolding it. Somewhat awkwardly, Ty inched out from against his hood, went to the backseat of his car, and fished a pen out of his backpack. The stranger scribbled something down quickly, returned the pen and now slightly crumpled paper, and with an expression that almost looked like a sneer, the man wished Ty good luck and turned to leave.

Ty thought for a moment, realizing the man never told him the name of the so-called specialist he was about to visit. "Excuse me, sir, but who am I going to see? His name, I mean."

The stranger paused and turned to face Ty again. "I think he likes to be called David," the strange little man said with an odd sort of chuckle that continued as he turned and walked off.

He thinks? Ty thought as he watched the man walk away. Here he was going to drive into the middle of nowhere to see someone who had no idea he was coming, and he wasn't even sure of the man's name? This sounded like the opposite of a good idea. He thought it over for a minute. Odds were there wouldn't be a problem, but there was always a chance that things might go sour. At least, under the influence of his father, he always traveled with a pistol under the seat. This was by no means a guarantee it would save him in a bad situation, but it might just even the odds a little if need be. He got into his car and sat without starting it for a moment while pondering the situation.

After looking at the map, it wasn't going to be much out of his way, anyway. There was about a fifteen-mile bridge he'd have to cross to get to the other side of the Chesapeake Bay. From there it would be another ten miles or so. After quickly doing the math in his head, he deduced it would add about another hour or so to his drive home, and depending on how long he was at "David's" house (if he didn't chicken out), he probably wouldn't get home until sometime after 11:00. At least he could start down the road toward "David's" house and just see what it looked like before he made his final decision.

It wasn't long after he got on the road that the sun started to disappear. The sky was clear, and the moon was beginning to emerge for the night. It was beautiful to see the whitecaps of the ocean swell and crash into the supports of the bridge; he wished he'd been able to see more of this during the daylight.

As he drove across the long bridge, the excitement began to wane and the uneasiness set in again. As though to match his emotional state, the moonlight began to fade as a result of low-lying clouds rolling in. There was still time for him to change his mind and turn around, but his curiosity was getting the best of him. Not only that, but if this guy could save him some time on his research, it'd be well worth it. The closer he came to the mainland of the peninsula, the darker it became. What had started out as a clear moonlit night was now turning into a dark and stormy one.

CHAPTER 13

NO SOONER HAD Ty gotten off the bridge and back onto land that the rain began. A slow drizzle had quickly turned into what seemed like the floodgates of Noah's day opening wide. Ty's windshield wipers on high were barely adequate to allow him to see well enough to stay on the road, and if there had been more traffic, he probably would've pulled over to wait for the rain to let up; thankfully the traffic was light. Had he known the weather was going to change like this, he never would've ventured on this little side trip, but he was almost to the house now and decided he wasn't going to turn back.

With the rain still pounding down, the street signs at the intersections were a little challenging to make out. According to the map, there were a few small towns he had to go through first, and after about twenty minutes, he finally came to the turnoff he was looking for. Now all he'd have to do was follow this lane to the end, which appeared to be about two miles. It looked as though the surrounding vegetation was trying to choke out the road, which was barely wide enough for two cars. He hoped he wouldn't meet any traffic, but that seemed unlikely on a night like this.

Just as soon as that thought ran through his head, a car came racing around the corner, forcing him into the ditch and almost into the trees. *Jerk!* he thought as he took a second to regroup. Luckily he was able to steer himself back on the road, although he noticed his hands were shaking a bit as he maneuvered through the underbrush and up the slight embankment that led back to the highway. Maybe people who lived out here weren't used to meeting oncoming traffic, but the driver could've pulled over or slowed down a little. Ty didn't care about getting scratches on his car, but wrecking it in the middle of nowhere was a different story.

Still a little shook up after the close call, he figured he must be getting close; hopefully he wouldn't meet any other cars in such a hurry. He took one last corner and with the rain still pouring down, he saw lights in the distance. As he got closer, he could start to make out the shape of a building and saw that there was a light coming from an upper-story window. The rest were night lights that surrounded the entire circumference of the property, creating an almost eerie glow over the place.

As he got even closer, it became obvious this was the end of the road, so this must be the place, although it didn't look like any house he'd ever seen before. It appeared to be a three-story structure that was maybe forty feet square. What was so strange about it was it had absolutely no widows on the bottom two stories; the only windows were on the top floor. There were no trees in the yard, which was rather large, and encircling it was a tall security fence with only one small entry gate, just big enough for someone to walk through.

Ty pulled up to a small parking area next to the gate and sat there for a minute to assess the situation. Here he was, somewhere across Chesapeake Bay in the pouring rain, on some side road in the middle of nowhere, looking at a house that appeared to be a small fortress, going to see someone that he'd never met who didn't know he was coming, and absolutely no one knew where he was (except the strange little man he'd met about thirty minutes ago). Although he never liked to worry his dad, he thought maybe he should at least give him a call to let him know where he was. He took out his cell phone and, of course... no service. Somehow, that didn't surprise him.

Well, he wasn't going to stop now. The man who'd sent him out here seemed harmless enough, a little weird sure, but harmless all the same and very sincere. Just in case, Ty reached under his seat and pulled out the holster carrying his pistol and shoved it into the front of his pants, securing it to his belt.

Ty still hadn't gotten his concealed carry permit yet—thanks to his procrastination—and although it was legal for him to have the pistol in the car with him, tucked into his pants out of site was a different story. If he got caught, he'd probably blow his chances of ever working for the CIA. Regardless, he was willing to take that chance if it meant staying safe and not winding up in some crazy man's freezer, or worse. And from hearing some of his dad's stories... there definitely was worse.

Of course he didn't have an umbrella, but there was a chance he had a hat somewhere in the car. He looked on the backseat and on the floor with no luck. None too thrilled at the thought of getting soaked, he looked out his window to assess the situation. There was a little overhang next to the gate where there looked to be a phone, which must be the way to contact the house. He shook his head in disbelief of what he was doing and thought, *All right, let's do this.* Ty opened the door and sprinted through the pouring rain to the overhang.

The phone didn't have numbers on it, just the receiver. No sooner than he was reaching for it did it start to ring. To say he was startled would be an understatement, which is why he probably stared at it, letting it ring about five times before he realized it must be for him. Finally coming to his senses, he picked up the receiver, but before he even had a chance to say anything, a faint but gruff voice barked from the other end. "What do you want, why are you here?" Ty was so caught off guard that he just stammered a little not really knowing what to say. The voice growled at him again, "Speak up! What do you want? Why are you here?"

By this time Ty had his composure back and responded, "I'm looking for David."

The man was quick to reply, "Who said my name was David? Who are you?"

Now Ty was starting to question if he was even at the right house. "I might be at the wrong house, sir. My name's Ty Larson, and I was at the Edgar Cayce Foundation doing some research on an ancient civilization when I met somebody who said you might be able to help me out a little. He said you were a specialist on the pre-flood civilization. I'm sorry I didn't call first, and I apologize if I'm at the wrong house."

Suddenly the gate unlocked and swung open and the voice on the phone was quick to say, "You're at the right place. Hurry through, the gate won't stay open long."

Ty looked at the gate, stared at the receiver in his hand for a split second, then hung it up and stepped through the gate. Almost as soon as he was through the gate, it slammed shut, and Ty heard the click of the locking mechanism. Had it not been raining so hard, he would've stopped to think if this whole thing was really that wise a decision, but with the rain pounding down on him, he took off running toward the house. Normally Ty could do this distance in about five seconds in his track clothes, on a nice smooth surface and in dry conditions, but these conditions weren't quite so perfect.

As he reached the house, he almost expected to see an oversized front door that would be fitting of a castle, but instead the door was abnormally small. It was then that he noticed the walls of the house appeared to be made of solid concrete about two to three feet thick. Who and why would anyone build a house like this? A three-story house, made of thick concrete with barely any windows and only one door that a full-grown man could barely fit through, all surrounded by a twenty-foot iron fence? This is definitely a story he'd probably not tell his mother if he wanted her to ever get any sleep again.

Just before he could knock on the small door, it swung open, and the same voice he'd heard at the gate came over a speaker telling him to come in. Somewhat hesitantly at first, he ducked and started through the door, then picked up the pace halfway through remembering how fast the outside gate had slammed behind him. Once he was inside, the door swung shut, and he heard the clunk of an even bigger locking mechanism.

And there he was, standing inside a locked concrete house waiting to meet a man he knew absolutely nothing about. The only thing that made him feel a little at ease was the reassuring pressure of his pistol inside his waistband, concealed by his shirt and jacket.

CHAPTER 14

ONCE THE INITIAL shock of hearing the latch on the door lock faded a bit, Ty started to look around the enormous room. It was definitely not what he expected after seeing the odd structure from the outside. The bright and warm glow of the room was the first thing that caught his eye; he had anticipated it was going to be dark and dreary.

Instead of having the decor of an old castle, it was actually quite modern. The only thing that looked like an antique was the chandelier hanging from the ceiling in the center of the room. By itself it probably would've given off enough light, but there were several other lamps on as well. (Ty tried to imagine what the power bill was like.) There were pieces of leather furniture scattered throughout, and each one had a matching padded footrest. He was surprised not to see a TV in the room, only small coffee tables. The walls were painted a warm maroon color with various pieces of artwork on them, most of which looked like something that Picasso might do. It looked as though the room took up most of the first floor, and there was one other door at the far end. To the right of the chandelier was a spiral staircase that led to the upper floors. The view from the inside of the room made it impossible to tell that Ty was inside a concrete building.

Just as he was looking at the grand staircase, thinking what good shape someone would have to be in to live in a house like this, an elderly man with a well-groomed beard and a full head of gray hair came slowly down the stairs. Carrying a towel in one hand, he was cursing the staircase under his breath, but loud enough for Ty to hear. After hearing his voice on the intercom, Ty was expecting him to be a little crotchety. He tensed up as he waited for him to speak, thinking he might be angry for stopping by unannounced.

"I'm sorry you had to stand there so long in the rain. You must be freezing."

Ty had almost forgotten that he was drenched, and with his adrenaline running high, he hadn't even felt the cold until now. Once the man was all the way down the stairs, he came over to Ty and handed him the towel. "Here you go, son, you can dry yourself off with this, and we'll get you in front of the stove so you can warm up."

Ty was pleasantly surprised by how nice the man was. "Thank you. This weather came out of nowhere. It was gorgeous when I left Virginia Beach, but the rain started just as I was getting off the bridge."

"Let me take your wet jacket, and we'll go hang it by the fireplace."

The fireplace? That was the one thing in the room he hadn't noticed because it was behind the staircase. Following the man, he could start to feel the heat radiating as they got closer.

"I haven't seen one of these in a while, but there sure is nothing like wood heat. And thank you for the towel." Ty was already a lot more at ease with the situation, but that didn't mean he was going to let his guard down.

The man hung Ty's jacket on a hook by the fireplace and turned to face him with his hand outstretched. "Forgive me for not introducing myself, Mr. Larson. I'm Victor Blackwell."

Ty reached out and shook his hand. He must've had a confused look on his face, but before he could say anything, Victor said, "So you were told my name was David? Well, it's not! Some of the locals like to refer to me as that even though they know it displeases me."

Ty stammered a little. "Well I'm sure sorry if I offended you. I didn't know."

"Oh, I know it's not your fault. But from now on, I'd prefer you call me Victor. Anyway, you said you were doing some research on the pre-flood civilization. Tell me, why are you interested in it? What have you found out so far?"

Ty proceeded to tell him about the class he was taking and that after reading Genesis, chapter six, and the Book of Enoch, he was starting to become somewhat obsessed with what was going on back then. He told him about his theories on the worldwide megalithic construction and how his journey had taken him to Virginia Beach to the Edgar Cayce Foundation and Mr. Cayce's readings regarding Atlantis. Ty was amazed how effortless it was to talk about his wild ideas, although it was easier when he was talking to someone that he'd probably never see again.

Victor had listened intently the entire time and when Ty finished, Victor looked at him and said, "I don't know anything of Mr. Cayce, but I do have something that I think you'll be interested in. Come, and I'll show you." Victor turned and headed for the only other door in the room.

Although Victor's demeanor had put Ty somewhat at ease, in the back of his mind he was thinking, *Please don't be going to the basement, please don't be going to the basement.* Then Victor took a key out of his pocket and unlocked the door, swung it open, and sure enough… stairs going down to the basement! Ty's awareness of his surroundings was higher than ever now as he looked around to make sure that no one was behind him. Victor turned on a light and started down the stairs asking Ty to watch his step. Assessing the situation quickly, he thought, *Well, if you can't trust an old man who lives in a locked up concrete fortress out across Chesapeake Bay, then who can you trust?* Ty followed him down as the stairway hit a ninety-degree turn, which led to another door that Ty figured was probably locked. Thankfully the door behind them didn't automatically slam shut like the other ones had.

Victor fumbled around with the keys a little before finding the right one. After a few seconds, he unlocked the door, opened it, and turned on a light. Ty was amazed at what he saw. Even though he didn't really know what he was looking at, it was obvious that someone had been very meticulous in setting up all of the displays. The room was almost the same size as the one upstairs, but instead of being full of furniture, it looked like a museum. It was full of glass cases with artifacts and bones of some kind, and the walls were covered with newspaper clippings.

Ty looked around and noticed that the displays all had something in common: everything was exceptionally large. Then he noticed the display in the far corner. By now he'd become somewhat mesmerized and had slowly walked over to get a closer look without realizing what he was doing. Under a glass case about five feet wide and five feet high were three skulls that looked very, very old. All were extremely large, two of them had odd, elongated shapes, and yet they all appeared to be human. Ty just stood there and stared. They looked so real, but could that be possible? And, if so, where'd they come from?

"Your reaction is quite common for those who see this place

for the first time. And yes, they're real, if you were wondering. Utterly amazing, aren't they?"

Ty was so caught up in the moment that he didn't even try to hide his excitement. "How can they be real? They're so big, and the shape... who or what are they? Where'd they come from?"

Victor smiled through crinkled eyes and gave a single laugh. "Tell me again, son, why are you here?"

Ty thought for a second, trying to grasp what he was looking at, and then it hit him.

"The *Nephilim!*" he blurted out, instantly feeling ridiculous and yet excited for suggesting it.

Victor could see Ty's obvious exhilaration. "Correct! Just as described in Genesis six, four. '*The mighty men which were of old, men of renown, Giants!*'"

Ty's imagination began to run wild. "So they actually did exist?"

"Oh, yes, they did indeed exist," Victor seemed to share the enthusiasm, "just as they've been written about by countless civilizations. The legends, the folklore, all of the stories that have been told about giants are based on truth."

Ty was in a state of shock. "But how, where... where'd you get these?"

Victor squinted his eyes. "Let's just say a collector has his ways and we'll leave it at that, shall we?"

Ty looked around the rest of the room. Now these displays made a little more sense: an enormous ax, a gigantic sledgehammer, large bones, and many other objects that he couldn't readily identify.

Then he noticed something else that was odd that caught his eye from across the room. Seemingly captivated by the object, he walked over to the display to get a closer look. Inside the open case, was the only thing in the room that was of normal size. It was a dagger, a very old dagger. Nothing fancy, just a simple small dagger with a worn bone handle. Ty bent over to get a closer look. On the blade, he could just barely make out the initials S.O.J. etched in the side. He turned to ask Victor about the small weapon, only to see he was now standing right behind him. Ty was somewhat startled and before he could ask his question, Victor looked at the dagger, then to him with a questioning look on his face. "That's odd. In the midst of all these things, not many would pay attention to a common dagger. What drew you to this display?"

Ty looked back at the open case and stammered. "I... I'm not sure. It just seemed out of place, maybe... I guess."

Victor closed the case to the display. "Never mind. There's plenty more for you to see here. Look at what has been hidden from us for years." Victor said, changing the subject and pointing to the wall.

Ty looked to where Victor was motioning. Covering the walls, were articles. Lots of articles. The wall had clippings from *The New York Times* and *The Washington Post* about giant skeletons being unearthed right here in the U.S.

"How can this be? Why haven't I heard of any of this before?" Ty's mind was focused on the wall now.

"Oh, it's no accident, son. That's the truth. This is one of the longest ongoing cover-ups in existence today." Victor was still just as serious.

"But why? Who would possibly have anything to gain by keeping this quiet?" Ty asked.

"There are some very powerful people in charge who want to keep the current view of the history of mankind intact. They'll do whatever it takes to see that it does. As you can see from these articles, that was not always the case. Once the white man sent the Native Americans from their homelands and started to expand westward, they began to unearth evidence of an unknown race of people of "gigantic proportions" all over the country. The Natives knew of their existence; take a look at this article over here." Victor walked over to one of the newspaper clippings. "Here, here's a prime example of both the Native Americans' knowledge and the cover-up of a race of red-haired giants in Nevada."

Ty walked over to read the article. Apparently in 1911, a place known as Lovelock Cave had undergone a mining operation for bat guano (excrement). Throughout the cleanup, the artifacts and skeletons that were found were routinely tossed aside. Then, after thirteen years had passed, some archeologists were contacted to sort through the findings that hadn't been destroyed. Along with approximately ten thousand artifacts were two mummified humans with red hair... both very tall, one was over eight feet. Then again in 1931, two mummified skeletons dressed in strange clothing were found in the dry Humboldt lakebed near Lovelock. Both of those remains had red hair, and one was over ten feet tall! As the story goes, the skeletons were sent to a museum out east and "mysteriously" were lost.

What made the story even more creditable was the myth the Paiute Indians had. According to legend, when their ancestors came to the area some 15,000 years ago, it was inhabited by a race of red-haired giants who stood over twelve feet tall. The giants were fierce and constantly warring with the Native Americans, eating their flesh for food. After this went on for many years, the different tribes banded together to get rid of the evil giants once and for all. They chased the giants into the cave, filled the entrance with brush, and set it on fire. The giants who tried to escape to get air were shot and killed with arrows; the ones that stayed inside were killed from asphyxiation. The incredible thing was that when the Lovelock Cave was excavated, arrows were found and there was evidence of a fire, substantiating the story.

When Ty had finished reading the article, he looked around the room at the rest of the newspaper clippings in disbelief. How could there've been so many stories yet none of this was common knowledge? He looked at Victor and was at a loss for words.

Victor looked at Ty and nodded his head. "Absolutely none of this is in any of the history books. What else, do you think, might they be keeping from us?"

Ty shook his head, trying to grasp everything. "What happened to all of them? The giants I mean? How is it they weren't the dominant race?"

Victor took a moment before he said anything, then looked Ty in the eye. "You already know the answer to that question, my friend."

What was he talking about? He already knew what? Based on Victor's little museum, Ty didn't know anything because all of this was new information to him. Prior to this exact moment, Ty viewed his research still leaning more toward folklore or myth. Until now. Now, all of a sudden, fantasy was becoming reality. The circumstantial evidence had been piling up, and here was a room full of tangible evidence. Every piece in the room had a story behind it, and Victor was more than happy to tell each one. His passion was obvious, and he enjoyed sharing it with someone on the same path; all the questions Ty had now were the same ones Victor once asked years ago.

Ty lost track of time as he poured over Victor's collection, picking the man's brain as he went. He came back to earth when he finally looked at his watch and saw that it was almost midnight, realizing he still had a long drive ahead of him. He turned and said, "Well, Victor, I can honestly say this is an experience I'll cherish for the rest of my life. This is amazing; I don't even know how to take it all in. I really appreciate your hospitality, and the knowledge you shared with me is sure to help my research. Maybe someday I'll get a chance to repay you somehow."

Victor responded with apparent sincerity. "You do not owe me a thing, Mr. Larson. All I ask is that if you do come across something someday that supports any of the stories I've shared with you, I'd appreciate it if you'd let me know."

"You have my word. I just hope the opportunity will arise," Ty said as he thought about the possibilities of what he might yet uncover.

"If you look hard enough, my boy... I assure you it will," he said with a peculiar tone of sincerity.

They went back upstairs where Ty grabbed his coat, which was dry now, and thanked Victor again. Victor walked him over to the door, wished him luck, and told him to come back anytime. Just before he closed the door, the old man firmly grabbed Ty by the shoulder and looked him in the eyes; then with a grim look that consumed his face said, "Remember my boy... the Almighty is with *you*." Victor took his hand from his shoulder and quickly closed the door, leaving Ty to contemplate his closing remark.

The Almighty is with me? What an odd thing to say, and why did he wait until I was out the door before he mentioned it? Ty thought almost out loud.

Standing there confused by what had just transpired, he realized the rain had finally stopped. He walked across the grounds back to the gate, thinking about what Victor had just said, when it dawned on him. Why might Victor live in a fortress like this? Was he trying to keep someone, or maybe *something* out? Did Victor actually think that the *Nephilim* were still around?

The gate swung open just as soon as he got to it, shutting just as quickly once he was through it. After he got in his car, he stared at the entire complex for a bit, just thinking. If giants did exist, this complex of concrete and fencing would probably keep them out. *Wait a second,* Ty thought...

"Aha!" he shouted out loud, unable to contain the excitement. He couldn't believe it took him until now to figure it out: "David! David, the Giant slayer, of David and Goliath!" he exclaimed to the steering wheel. That's why people in town called him that. When he gained some sense again, he realized that maybe Victor was watching from the house, and he decided he should get going. He turned the car around and started down the road, passing the point he'd been run off, when he slammed on the brakes and came to a stop. There hadn't been any other roads between here and Victor's house! According to Victor, he hadn't had any company in a long while, but whoever ran him off the road must've, in fact, come from Victor's. Ty looked over his shoulder to the dark, overgrown road toward where he had just come. What was going on? Something was starting to stink, and it was time he found out what it was.

VICTOR WATCHED TY Larson pass through the gate and get back into his car from the handheld monitor he'd had in his pocket. While watching the boy, he reached over and picked up the telephone that was fastened to the wall and dialed a number that he had known for the last thirty years. It only rang once before someone on the other end answered.

"It's me, Blackwell, in Virginia." As he listened to the voice on the other end, he continued to watch the Larson boy just sitting in his car. "I think I may have found a possible recruit for you. I assume you are always looking?"... "Tyler Larson." After listening for several seconds Victor replied, "I thought that Nazi bastard was dead?"... "No. The boy doesn't know anything, but I think you should know, he was drawn to the dagger."... "I don't know," Victor was a little defensive, "the case was accidentally left open. The point is, he was drawn to it from across the room!"... "I know, it is interesting, very much so."... "Okay then." Victor looked at the monitor as he hung up the phone to watch his late-night visitor drive off.

CHAPTER 15

VICTOR'S PLACE WAS on Ty's mind the entire drive home, which made it seem to go by in a flash. It sure seemed as though there'd been giants who roamed the earth in the past and for some reason, their existence had been covered up. Victor had been so nice, yet the strange question regarding the dagger display and his parting remark was also weighing on Ty's mind. Maybe he's just a paranoid old man who's lived by himself too long, but it was a little creepy nonetheless.

It wasn't until he was almost to the elevator in the lobby of his apartment building and saw his neighbor, Rosie Miller, waiting for the doors to open that he realized he'd been driving most of the night. Rosie had lived in the apartments for several years and was Ty's favorite neighbor. She was in her eighties, which meant she'd seen a lot over the years and was always very enjoyable to visit with.

Rosie saw him coming and was the first to speak, "Good morning, Tyler. I knew you got up early, but isn't this a *little* early, even for you?"

Ty looked at his watch and saw that it was 4:30 a.m. He let out a tired chuckle. "Good morning, Rosie. Actually, I've been on the road all night, but you're right, it's too early... even for me."

They chatted while waiting for the elevator, and then the slow ride to the top began.

"Did you have a nice visit with your friends yesterday?" Rosie asked.

Ty was a little confused as to what she was talking about, but responded, "Actually, I was gone all day doing research for a paper I have to write."

She looked at him with a puzzled look on her face. "Oh, I guess you must've had visitors before you left then?"

"No, I left pretty early."

Then Ty remembered the stranger he'd seen coming out of the elevator when he'd come back to his apartment to get the address for the Edgar Cayce Foundation. So much had happened since then, he almost forgot all about the bizarre encounter.

"Was it a guy with a beard wearing a long trench coat?" he asked.

The elevator came to a stop and the doors opened up. "No... there were two of them, and they were nicely-dressed and clean-shaven."

Ty couldn't think of who it might've been. He wondered if maybe it was a couple of his classmates.

"It might've been some friends from school who dropped by."

They were now at Rosie's door, and as she opened it, she looked at him somewhat bewildered, "Tyler, whoever it was, they were in your apartment. You didn't leave your door unlocked, did you?"

Ty's heartbeat accelerated as his adrenaline started to pump. "Are you sure they were inside my apartment and not the one across the hall?"

"No, I'm sure I heard your door shut, and I looked out the peephole and saw those two men leaving. Do you not know them?"

Although some perplexing things had been happening lately, Ty didn't want to cause Rosie to worry about anything. "I bet it was some friends from school and come to think of it, I think I did leave the door unlocked," Ty said, knowing that he hadn't. Again, trying not to alarm Rosie, he said, "Now remember, if there's ever anything you need help with, just let me know." He watched her enter her apartment then said goodbye.

As soon as he was in his own apartment, he looked over the entire place to see if anything was missing. Not having much to start with, it didn't take long to see that nothing was gone or even out of place. He checked the door lock to see if it was working properly, which it was, so he went and checked both of the windows, and both were latched. The superintendent had keys to each unit, but he'd always coordinate with the tenants first if he needed access, which was extremely rare. It was possible that Rosie was mistaken, but along with everything else that had been happening, he wasn't going to take any chances. It was time to call his dad.

NORMALLY HIS DAD wouldn't go into the office until 9:00 a.m., but Ty couldn't wait any longer and tried calling him at 8:00. He was surprised to hear him answer the phone. Something else with his dad seemed peculiar, too: how his dad reacted when he told him that Rosie had seen two men leave his apartment while he was gone yesterday. His dad simply told him that in his experience, older people can get their facts mixed up easily, and he should really take their observations with a grain of salt. Not that they intentionally try to mislead anyone, but they can be wrong about things, whether it was what they saw, the time they saw it, or even the actual day they saw it. He went on to say that if nothing appeared to be moved or missing, she must've been confused or maybe even dreaming, so not to be alarmed. If, on the other hand, something turned up missing, to let him know.

On a different topic, Grant told Ty that he was going to be in Alexandria on business later that day and asked if he'd have time to get together for lunch. Ty liked the idea and said he wasn't planning on going anywhere. His dad told Ty he'd give him a call a half hour beforehand, which would give him enough time to get ready. Agreeing to his dad's plan, he hung up his phone and crawled into bed, hoping he'd be able to get some much-needed rest while he waited for his dad's wake up call.

The next thing he knew, his phone was ringing. He rubbed his eyes and looked at his watch; it was 1:00 p.m. He reached over to answer his phone in disbelief that he'd slept so soundly for the past four-and-a-half hours.

"Hey, Dad, you must be getting hungry."

"Oh, you know me, son, I can always eat. How about you?"

Ty yawned a little as he was still waking up. "Actually, I'm starving. Where do you want to meet?"

"Why don't we go to that little pub you like? They serve food, don't they?"

By now, Ty was awake enough to sit up on the bed. "Oh yeah, and it's pretty good too. How soon will you be there?"

"I'll be there in about twenty minutes or so. I could swing by and pick you up if you'd like," his dad offered.

"Oh no, I'll throw my sweats on and jog over. I'll see you in about twenty," Ty said.

"By the way," his dad said before he hung up, "your mother and I are going to celebrate our thirtieth wedding anniversary this year, and she wants to make sure you have a nice suit to wear. So after lunch, she wants me to take you out to find one, if you have time."

"A suit?" Ty wasn't really into suits. "Okay, I'd better jump in the shower first then." Stretching a little after he hung up, he slowly got up then made his way to the shower.

He was still a little shocked that his dad had been so nonchalant about what Rosie said she thought she saw. As far as he could tell, nothing was missing or seemed to be disturbed, and even though Rosie was older, she still seemed to be pretty sharp. And how could she mistake one guy for two? Still, his dad did have a lot of experience with this kind of thing, and Ty always respected his opinion, both personally as a father and professionally as an agent.

Making sure the windows were locked one last time, he left and then double checked that the door was locked behind him too. Although his dad had pretty much told him there was nothing to worry about, he was still going to be a little more cautious.

The slow ride down gave him more time to ponder the events of the past few days. Even if Rosie was confused about what she'd seen and heard, there was no doubt about the man Ty had seen get back into the elevator yesterday morning.

As soon as the elevator got to the lobby and the doors opened, he glanced at his watch and saw he'd have to pick up the pace if he wanted to be on time to meet his dad. It was a sunny day, and the temperature was perfect for running, not too cold but cool enough that he didn't break a sweat, which was probably a good thing if he was trying on suits later. As he spotted his dad's car parked in front of the pub, he remembered just how punctual he always was.

Walking through the door of O'Rielly's, it took his eyes a few seconds to adjust to the dim lighting. He didn't have to scan the place, because he knew where to find his dad. He was the one who taught Ty to always sit near an exit with his back to the wall where he could see the entire room. True to form, there he was, back by the rear exit, facing the entrance.

His father got up and gave him a hug as soon as he got to the table. Even though it had only been a couple of days since they'd seen each other, they were close and enjoyed each other's company. By now he felt well rested and was ready for some food, so it didn't take him long to figure out what he wanted to order.

While waiting for their food, Ty told his dad about his trip down to Virginia Beach to the Edgar Cayce Foundation and about what Mr. Cayce had said about the ancient civilization of Atlantis and its demise. His father had never heard of Edgar Cayce, but seemed pretty intrigued. Ty wanted to tell him all about Victor Blackwell, and at first he was a little hesitant but eventually told him anyway.

"Good God, Ty! What if that man had been Jack the Ripper's brother?" his father said seemingly alarmed.

Ty tried to ease his dad's concern by continuing with the fascinating story about the old man's house. He could see his dad was extremely interested in what he'd had to say about Mr. Blackwell's strange collection. Ty figured if his dad were in his shoes, he'd probably be doing the exact same thing with the same enthusiasm. For some reason though, he left out the part about the dagger and Victor's strange remark when he left.

It wasn't long before their lunch arrived, and while they ate, they talked a little more about what Rosie had said. He was still stunned at how his dad seemed to be blowing off the entire situation, as if she didn't know what she was talking about. It even seemed as though he was trying to change the subject by bringing up their thirtieth wedding anniversary again. It just wasn't like his dad to act like this.

Once they had paid the bill and were walking out, Grant said,

"Now let's go see if we can find you a suit. I noticed a small clothing store a couple of doors down, so let's step over there real quick to see if we can find something."

Ty thought for a second. "Oh yeah, I knew I took a shower for something."

"And believe me, we all appreciate it, son," Grant said to Ty emitting a look of gratitude.

They walked down the sidewalk past the pharmacy and came to "Stichies," a small clothing boutique.

A small bell rang as they opened the door and they were met by a tall, elegantly dressed woman with long dark hair wearing a pinstriped suit.

"Hello. Can I help you find anything?"

Grant asked the clerk if there was somewhere Ty could try on a couple of suits.

She replied, "Sure, the men's suits are all in the back, and the dressing room is right there as well. I think there's a customer in the dressing room now, but I'm sure he won't be long. Just let me know if I can help," she said, then pointed them to the rear of the store.

They walked back to where the clerk had directed them and found the rack of suits. Grant went up to the rack and started thumbing through the different sizes. "Let's see now... you look like you're still the same size as I am. I hope you like grey. It's your mother's recommendation."

Ty shrugged his shoulders. "Sure, I'm easy."

Grant found a very nice European cut jacket and slacks amidst the masses of material, steely grey in color. "Okay, give this one a try then."

Just then, the dressing room door swung open, and a well-dressed man who looked like he was in his early forties came out, closing the door behind him. Ty was just about to open the dressing room door when Grant beat him to the punch. "Allow me," he said as he pushed the door open for Ty.

"Ah, thank you, James. I'll ring for you when I'm finished," Ty joked with raised eyebrows, before noticing the serious look on his dad's face.

Straight away, he knew something wasn't right. Before he could say anything, his father handed him the suit and said, "Try this on, and let me see what it looks like on you." His look was stern, so Ty just said okay, and went in the dressing room while his dad closed the door behind him. He was momentarily confused about his dad's sudden change of demeanor, but then he noticed a sheet of paper taped to the inside wall of the dressing room that said:

Ty, don't say anything. Hang the suit up and get undressed. Pile all your clothes on the bench, including your shoes. Hang your jacket up and leave your cell phone in the pocket. Once you have done that, put on both the suit jacket and pants. Then, in the right inside pocket of the jacket, there's an electronic device. It's a bug sweep and it's already on, you will see a green light. Hold it up next to everything you took off, sweeping it back and forth and watch the light. If the light stays green, I want you to say the suit feels a little tight through the shoulders when you come out. If it turns red, I want you to tell me it seems to fit okay. When you come back into the dressing room, take this note down and put it in your pocket along with the bug sweep and bring it with you. One more thing, try to act natural. We are being watched!

CHAPTER 16

IT TOOK TY a moment to digest what was going on, then it all made sense. That's why his dad was blowing off what Rosie had said; he must've thought he was being bugged. Doing exactly as the note had directed, he put on the suit and found the electronic device in the pocket. This was crazy: one minute he was having a leisurely lunch with his dad and the next he was running a bug sweep over his belongings. It seemed as though he'd just fallen into the middle of a James Bond movie. The light stayed green as Ty followed the note's instructions. He assumed that was a good sign, but figured he wouldn't know for certain until he had a chance to talk to his dad, when the time was right.

He opened the door and came out of the dressing room. Before Ty had a chance to say anything, his dad asked, "How's it feel?"

Without missing a beat, Ty responded, "I like the way it looks, but it feels a little tight through the shoulders."

His father nodded with his eyes slightly squinted and handed him another jacket to try. "Well you're the one who has to wear it, so let's find one that fits better. Here, try this one; it's the next size bigger."

Ty swapped jackets. They were both pretty similar in fit, but he knew they weren't really there to try on suits. With a similar exchange regarding the fit of the second jacket, he glanced at his dad a couple of times for reassurance he was playing this little game correctly.

"Well, I guess we'll have to get one tailored to fit," his dad said, providing them a convenient out.

Ty went into the dressing room and changed, took the note off the door and along with the bug sweep, hid them away in his coat pocket. They returned the jackets to their rightful places, thanked the clerk and left.

Once safely in the car, Ty began to speak. Grant, however, gave him a sharp look and replied under his breath. "Not yet. Once we get moving, then we can talk."

Ty didn't respond and busied himself by putting on his seat belt and checking his cell for any texts. Only once they had driven a few blocks from the boutique did Grant finally speak, "Okay Ty, now we know you're not bugged, but we're definitely being followed. It's incredibly important that we act as though nothing's wrong. Don't look behind us too much, no fidgeting, none of that. What I need you to do now is to slide the note and bug sweep over to me."

Ty nodded and did as he was told, trying to look casual, although that was the opposite of how he felt. "What the hell is going on, Dad? Who and why would anyone be watching us?"

His dad kept his eyes on the road as he answered. "First things first, Ty, I'm afraid to say that it's you they're watching, not us. And second, we still have no clue who's behind it or why. In fact, I was hoping you might be able to shed some light on that," he said, though he didn't pause for Ty to actually try to answer. "Now I can tell you what we do know. We know that whoever it is, they're very well connected. We know they seem to cover their tracks extremely well. We know they've been inside your apartment, and though they haven't bugged it yet, the security of your computer has been compromised, and everything you do on it is being monitored. We also know you've been under their surveillance at least since you came to D.C. the other day. Whether they were watching you before then is something we have no way of knowing. Oh, and by the way, the two men your neighbor saw yesterday were my guys; I just had to play dumb until I knew if you or your cell phone had been bugged."

Ty was having a hard time internalizing anything his father was saying. In a flat tone that gave away his shocked state, he began to try to think aloud. "Why would... I don't understand...why would anyone care what *I'm* doing?"

"That's what we need to find out, and you have to be totally honest with me. There's gotta be something. People like this don't just decide to track someone for nothing. Now, can you think of any possible reason—and I mean anything at all, no matter how remote or trivial you think it is?"

Ty tried to think, but was too stunned by what his dad was saying. Somebody was following him? Slowly some of the odd things that had taken place over the past few days came to mind. He then started to tell his dad everything—from the flier for the Edgar Cayce Foundation being left on his windshield, to the stranger in the elevator at his apartment, to being run off the road on his excursion to Victor Blackwell's house.

Grant continued driving as he listened to all that Ty had for him until they came to a stop several blocks from where they had started. Ty looked out to see where they were. The sign on the front of a small building read *Bordello's Tailoring*. It was then it dawned on him how good his dad was at his job. Looking over at him, but before Ty could say anything, his dad spoke up.

"We have to play this thing through, Ty, but we have to be careful so we don't tip them off that we're onto them. We need to find out who they are and what they're after. In the old days, we'd just grab one and then water-board it out of them." His dad paused in thought, then continued. "Hopefully it won't come to that, for a couple of reasons. The first being: water-boarding is frowned upon these days, and the second: it's never a guarantee the information obtained that way is accurate anyway."

Hearing his dad even mention the term water-boarding (whether he was joking or not) made Ty realize just how serious this whole situation was. His head was spinning, but he obviously had no choice and would have to play along. They went into the tailor shop—and after forty minutes at least he knew what size he was and that he'd have a new suit in six to nine business days, complements of his dad.

They went out to the car talking and laughing as though everything was normal. Once inside and on the road again, they were able to talk freely. Grant told Ty he had two of the Agency's men tailing him, assuring him he wasn't in any danger. He also told him he was able to get the Agency's help, which was because someone inside had accessed the computer to trace the license plates on the car they were now sitting in.

"Even though this is technically a job for Internal Affairs," his dad began, "I was able to pull a few strings to oversee the operation, at least for the time being."

"Wow..." Ty said as he thought about the situation, almost as if he was becoming excited, "Thanks, Dad."

As they drove through the neighborhood back to Ty's apartment, about the only thing they figured out was, ironically, that they had absolutely no clue why anyone would have a reason to follow him. His dad told him it was crucial to continue as though everything was normal. He also reminded Ty about the two men who would continue to follow him for his own safety.

They pulled over to the curb, and his dad told him it was time to put on the act again.

"If you need to talk about this, just call me like it's a routine conversation, but ask how Uncle Dale is doing," he said with a look that indicated that it was cloak-and-dagger time again. His dad told him he'd take it from there and meet with him in a similar fashion as they did today. Ty nodded in acknowledgment and began to open the car door to get out when his dad stopped him with a hand on his arm, handing him a manila envelope.

"Oh, by the way, son, Will did a little research on what you were talking about the other day and printed up some stuff he thought might be helpful for your paper."

Ty took the envelope. "Oh, right. I've been so distracted by everything else, I'd almost forgotten about that. Tell him I said thanks."

They both got out of the car and said their goodbyes, ending with a father-son embrace. His dad waved one last time as he drove off.

Once his dad was out of sight, the harsh reality of the situation began to set in. Was he going to be convincing with this act, now that he knew his every move was being watched? As he turned and began walking to his building, he wondered where his "admirers" were watching from. He was in such a daze that he really didn't even remember deciding to take the elevator rather than the stairs until the doors were opening and he was walking out onto his floor. *Wow,* he thought to himself, *what the hell?* But as the overwhelming feeling of what was going on vibrated throughout his body, he realized… he was actually enjoying it, the familiar rush of adrenaline he had come to know and love over the years with the competition at track meets.

He unlocked his door wondering how many people had been in there the last few days without his knowledge. Casually, he walked around just to see if he was alone, which he was, and then he sat down to see what Will had put together for him. Although his dad told him he wasn't in any danger, he still decided to grab his pistol and put it under the couch cushion while he read what was in the envelope. Inside were several printed pages, with the exception of the first which was a handwritten note that read:

Ty, I looked into those two names that were on that piece of paper and printed out some info for you. I also ran across a couple of other things in the process that you might find interesting. Hope this is helpful.
Will

The first two pages were an article about Yar-lha-sham-po, which they already knew was the name of a Tibetan god. The next page was an article about Belial. Will had already mentioned he was a demon figure from the Bible. What intrigued Ty even more about Belial was that Edgar Cayce had mentioned the "Sons of Belial" in his stories regarding Atlantis along with the "Children of the Law of One." According to Cayce they were the same civilizations that were mentioned only briefly in the Bible in Genesis chapter six. That's what had sparked Ty's interest in this whole thing to begin with. He glanced over the next article. It was about Tibetan Monks and levitation, which was something he hadn't seen yet in his research, but also fueled his hunger for more proof.

The last couple of pages were an article about someone else he'd never heard about, a man by the name of Edward Leedskalnin. He skimmed more of the article to see what this Edward Leedskalnin had done that Will thought was of interest, and it didn't take long to figure out what it was: apparently, he claimed to know the secrets of how the pyramids of Egypt were built.

CHAPTER 17

TY PACED HIS apartment, conflicted and overwhelmed. His mind felt as though it might explode soon, and he couldn't help but think that perhaps humans were not built to be able to process so many things at once. Deciding to focus on the lesser of the two battles raging in his head, Ty temporarily erased the alarming news he'd gotten from his dad and returned to the newest developments on his research project.

There were several theories floating around about how the Egyptians built the pyramids, but they were just that, theories. For someone to make the claim they knew the secrets of how they were built was nothing new, but after reading the article Will had given him, it looked as though a man named Edward Leedskalnin just might've been telling the truth.

Edward (Ed) Leedskalnin was born in Latvia in 1887. Though not a whole lot is known about his early years, it's documented that his family wasn't very wealthy and Ed only had a fourth-grade education. Due to his poor health at an early age, most of his time was spent inside, reading books. He didn't drop out of school because he couldn't keep up; it was actually just the opposite, Ty learned from the article. Ed had a thirst for knowledge, and from his own study he'd easily surpassed the level of his classmates. Later on, he apparently had a girlfriend he was engaged to marry; she was only sixteen and Ed was twenty-six. She apparently broke off their engagement the night before their wedding, which not only broke Ed's heart, but most likely sent him over the edge as well. Ed eventually moved to North America, working in lumber camps in various places, and took up more permanent residence in Florida around 1919 for the warm climate after coming down with tuberculosis. Some of the locals saw Ed riding around on his bike, looking for the *right spot* and muttering something about his sweet sixteen. He finally must've found the *right spot*, and bought a piece of land in Florida City where he began construction of what's now known as Coral Castle.

Within a few years' time, at just five feet tall and only weighing around a hundred pounds, Ed had singlehandedly quarried over one thousand stones—with the largest one weighing near thirty tons—and constructed what he called "Rock Gate Park." Rock Gate Park consisted of walls surrounding all the various things Ed made out of stone, including carvings, furniture, and even a bathtub and his living quarters. The most famous piece is the eight-ton revolving gate he built that was so well balanced a child could open it with the push of a finger.

The strangest thing about the whole story was what seemed to be the same reappearing question of all megalithic construction of the past: how was he moving these enormous blocks of stone? According to the article, Ty learned, Ed always worked alone and usually at night so nobody could watch. When asked how he was moving the large stone blocks, he was quoted as saying, "I have discovered the secrets of the pyramids and have found out how the Egyptians and the ancient builders in Peru, Yucatan, and Asia, with only primitive tools, raised and set in place blocks of stone weighing many tons." There were photos of him lifting a huge block he'd quarried with a tripod consisting of cables and pulleys. The extraordinary thing about that was, when the experts did the math with the number of pulleys he had hooked to the tripod, there weren't enough required to lift the enormous weight of the carved stone. However, there were also a couple of wires coming from his work shed, running to the top of the tripod, and disappearing into a box that covered it. What was under the box? No one knows because Ed never shared his secrets with anyone.

Ty kept reading, completely fascinated.

Another article was a story about two young boys who were secretly watching Ed work one night and claimed they saw him making the heavy blocks float through the air like balloons… but were they telling the truth? There was yet another claim that Ed was heard singing while the stones levitated. This reminded Ty of that form of acoustic levitation that was at the root of so many other legends.

Yet another strange story with a witness was when Ed decided to move his rock park to a different location. He'd hired a truck to haul the heavy stone blocks and when the truck driver showed up, Ed asked him to leave the truck and come back later. The driver did as he was told, but returned in just a few minutes, for what the account didn't specify, and found there were already several blocks loaded on the truck. How could Ed possibly have done this without any heavy equipment? And why wouldn't he ever let anyone watch or even tell them how he was able to pull off these seemingly impossible acts? Although there'd been the story of the boys watching him make stones float through the air, supposedly whenever someone tried to sneak up and watch him work he'd stop, look into the dark and say, "How are you doing tonight?

When you leave, I can go back to work." It was almost as if he had a sixth sense and could feel when somebody was watching him.

Ed also designed a magnetic generator, a kind of perpetual motion device, which apparently was missing a crucial piece for it to operate properly (Ty thought this echoed familiarity with Mr. Keely's machine). Among other things, he authored a book titled *Magnetic Current*. Was he able to move those enormous stones with a magnetic current? Ty remembered another form of levitation he'd read about involving this principle. Maybe Ed was using a combination of acoustic and magnetic levitation. Was it possible that they might be closely related? Why did people always seem to take these kinds of secrets to their graves? Or are all these stories just a bunch of hoaxes? It seemed the more Ty found out, the more questions he had. He wondered if there would ever be an end to all this or would he be left hanging? Ty thought he'd have to read Mr. Leedskalnin's book someday, but for now he was going to have to concentrate on getting his paper done. The deadline was looming closer.

Ty thumbed through the other pages Will had printed for him to the one titled "*Yar-lha-sham-po.*" What connection, if any, did a Tibetan god have to do with what he was researching? He started reading the article. Yar-lha-sham-po was the Tibetan's second highest of several gods. Yar-lha-sham-po in particular was portrayed as a white yak that could transform into a white man in order to father children with human women. *Now why doesn't this surprise me?* he thought to himself. The parallels with Genesis seemed to keep popping up everywhere, first with the Book of Enoch, then with the Roman and Greek mythology, then with Edgar Cayce's stories, and now with this. Yar-lha-sham-po was also capable of causing great floods. Was there really any connection between these stories, or could it all just be one big coincidence? And what did this have to do with Mr. Keely? Had he stumbled onto the same secrets that Ed Leedskalnin had? Was it possible the two of them had found an unknown force of nature that was common knowledge in the distant past? As for the piece of paper that was left in the crate with Mr. Keely's invention, its connection to this was certainly a mystery, but one thing was certain: someone at some point had known its significance. Maybe if there were connections to a secret society the knowledge might still be alive somewhere today, known only by a select few.

There was more reading about the Tibetan god that Ty thought he would save for later. Right now there was one more article in the packet that Will had dug up for him (oddly, it came from the same part of the world). As with all the stories he'd read lately, this one was no different as far as provability, but along with the Edward Leedskalnin story, it was the most recent.

Apparently in 1939, Dr. Jarl, a Swedish doctor who had studied at Oxford a few years earlier, was traveling in Egypt for the English Scientific Society. A messenger of a Tibetan friend who he'd become acquainted with at Oxford found Dr. Jarl and requested he accompany him back to Tibet to give medical attention to a high Lama. Dr. Jarl did as asked and eventually reached the monastery where his friend and the Lama were living. Dr. Jarl ended up staying there for quite some time and became a close and trusted friend to the Tibetans. Because of this friendship, Dr. Jarl became exposed to many of the local events, customs, and traditions.

As the story went, one day his friend took him to an area below some cliffs where there was a cave about 250 meters up from the base. The monks were building a rock wall in the opening of the cave, but the fascinating aspect of the story was how they were getting the stone blocks up the face of the cliff to the opening. At the base was a polished rock slab shaped like a bowl, which was about a meter across. Precisely sixty-three meters behind the bowl-shaped slab were nineteen monks next to each other, splayed out in an arc that was exactly ninety degrees from the bowl-shaped slab. Six of these monks had trumpets and the other thirteen had drums: eight large ones, four medium, and one small. Behind each monk who had an instrument were more monks standing in single file. In all, there were two hundred monks arrayed near the slab. A stone was dragged to the bowl-shaped slab by yak oxen, and then, with all the instruments pointed directly at it, the monks would play their instruments, while the ones without instruments would sing and chant. As this "symphony" became louder, the stone would flutter around a little and eventually start to float in the air toward the cave. After about three minutes, the rock would float the entire 250 meters up to the cave. The measurements where each monk would stand during this entire operation were very precise.

Although some people had heard of this type of levitation—including Dr. Jarl—he was the first foreigner to witness it. But even after he saw it for himself, he was understandably baffled, so he made two films to confirm the event. When Dr. Jarl returned home, the English Society confiscated both of the films and declared them classified; they still haven't been released for public viewing, the article stated. Obviously the confiscation didn't help to validate Dr. Jarl's story, but some research has shown that with the precise measurements given, optimum harmonic reaction in that situation was achievable. Was this just a coincidence? Might the monks really have been able to manipulate gravity through sound?

Ty was amazed at the amount of bizarre stories he'd heard and read about the past few days, but which was more absurd: these wild stories or the fact that somebody was following him? Then he thought about it for a second... which happened first, the strange stories or someone following him? Laying the papers on the coffee table, he stared out the window thinking back. Last Thursday when he visited the church was when he first heard about the Book of Enoch and the fallen angels from the deacon. According to his dad, the first known signs of anybody following him weren't until the next day, after he'd left the Ethiopian Church. He had a feeling all these things were connected... but how?

CHAPTER 18

TY RUBBED HIS eyes as he rolled over and looked at the clock: 7:30 a.m., which was kind of nice considering he was usually awake by 5:30. He'd gone to bed early last night, but it took him a little while to finally nod off. Thinking there was probably someone outside in the shadows watching him didn't help, but he trusted his dad's assessment of the situation, so between that and his .357 Magnum under his pillow now, he must've felt comfortable enough to eventually fall asleep.

Today was Tuesday—class day—but that wasn't until 1:00. He still had plenty of time to relax a little before he had to get moving.

With that in mind, Ty remembered that today they were going to discuss the Olmec civilization, and he hadn't really prepared for it. *So much for relaxing a little,* he thought to himself as he made his way to the computer. How was it that he only had one class, but yet the only spare time he experienced in the last few days was at his parents' and the evening at the pub with Tom? In both cases, most of the conversation had been spent talking about what he was researching. He hoped he was getting closer to some answers, if indeed there were any.

Once at his favorite chair in front of his computer, Ty settled in and started to read about a civilization that had intrigued him since he first heard about it in high school.

The Olmec were a civilization discovered in southern Mexico and were once confused with the Mayans. That was until around 1860 when the first colossal head was discovered. When the mystery of this long-lost civilization began to unfold over the next several decades, a total of seventeen giant stone heads were found throughout southern Mexico. The enormous heads—which were up to eleven feet tall and weighed as much as forty tons—were their trademark. Maybe the most interesting aspect about the giant heads, Ty thought, was the faces that were carved into them. At first glance, they didn't appear to resemble the indigenous people at all. Ty saw from the photos on the internet that all the carved faces portrayed different, clean-shaven males with thick lips and wide noses and wearing some type of helmet. Although the giant heads had this appearance, there were also photos of smaller statues that seemed to have much different appearances, some even having beards.

All the faces were carved from single boulders of basalt, which was extremely hard volcanic rock that was mined more than one hundred miles from their resting sites. Ty thought how this was starting to sound like a broken record: ancient people moving huge chunks of stone of such immense weight over vast distances.

Once the scholars realized the artifacts being unearthed were of an entirely different civilization than the Mayans, it became obvious that whoever they were, they not only predated the Mayans but also much of what the Mayans had been recognized for: their numbering system, basketball game, and most likely even their famous calendar. All of these were later credited to the Olmec.

The dates mainstream archeologists give to the Mayan culture range from early 500 BC to around 900 AD, with the classic Mayan culture not really coming into existence until somewhere around 250 AD. The Olmec were in existence somewhere between 1,700 BC to around 400 BC, although Ty had become a little cautious about accepting timelines of events from so long ago. He'd already seen too many discrepancies in the ages of past civilizations to make him a little apprehensive. With the different theories of who the Olmec were and where they came from, from the article that Ty was reading, it seemed like the majority of the people seemed to think they may have come from Africa. If this were the case, then maybe the history books should be rewritten as to whom the first settlers really were in the Americas.

The giant carved heads made him think about the statues (known as Moai) scattered across Easter Island in the South Pacific. He opened up another tab on the internet browser to refresh his memory of the Easter Island statues. They, too, were monolithic statues carved out of enormous slabs of stone, but that's where the similarities ended. The Olmec heads were portraits of different individuals with varying appearances, but the Moai all seemed to have the same features: long heads, thin lips, sharp noses, and abnormally long ears. Their chins were also very sharp and looked as though they may possibly be bearded, but owing to erosion over the years, it was hard to say. Strangely enough, with the exception of a very few, all of the Moai faced toward the center of the island. One of the legends of how they reached their resting spot was by priests who made them float through the air. Oddly enough, it was said they could only move in a clockwise path out of the quarry around the island to where they sat now.

Unlike the Olmec heads, the Moai also had bodies, which were buried almost to their necks in soil from the passing of time. This also was something that Ty found puzzling; supposedly,

Easter Island wasn't settled until around 700 AD. If this was the case, could erosion alone have been enough to bury a statue almost forty feet high? And how long would it have been before the islanders would've had any statues to move anyway? Surely they would've spent a little time checking out their new home before they got bored and spent their time carving huge statues out of volcanic rock and lugging them across the island. Unless... well just who were the statues portraying? And why were most of them facing toward the center of the island?

Ty dug deeper into his research. Apparently when Dutch Captain Jacob Roggeveen discovered the island in 1722 on Easter Sunday (hence the name), there were three different groups of people living on the island: red skinned, dark skinned, and people with pale skin and red hair... red hair? That seemed odd. What about the red-haired giants found in the Lovelock Cave in Nevada? Might there possibly be a connection? He thought back to all the different articles Victor Blackwell had.

Ty's train of thought was broken when he heard a noise coming from the hallway. Just as he got up to see what was going on, the screeching of tires outside diverted his path to the window facing the street. He pulled the curtains open enough to see two cars stopped in the middle of the intersection. It looked as though the driver on Fourth Avenue probably didn't yield to the driver coming down Main Street. This wasn't the first time he saw this happen, and probably wouldn't be the last, as a large lilac bush obscured the view of the drivers on the side street.

Ty saw that nobody was hurt, and then at the same moment, he noticed that a light-haired man in a parked car across the street seemed to be looking directly at him. Ty stared back for a moment, trying to deny the man's gaze, but with both Ty's curtain and the man's window being open, it was initially a straight view that proved impossible to deny. The man in the car suddenly focused his attention to the rearview mirror, to where the accident had occurred and where the occupants of each car were now bustling around in the street, talking loudly of fault and insurance. Distracted by the altercation, Ty looked to the commotion as well, only giving them his attention for a moment. When he turned back, however, the car and the mysterious man behind the wheel were nowhere to be seen. The reality of the situation that Ty was somehow tangled up in hit him once again. He backed away from the window and the curtains went back into place, obscuring his view to the outside and the outside's view to him. Frozen, he began to truly realize just how much his world had changed, literally overnight.

Just then there was a knock on the door, which reminded him of the noise he'd heard in the hallway, which was why he'd gotten up in the first place.

CHAPTER 19

TY STARED AT the door, unsure whether to go to it or not. Another knock. It was too hard a knock to be Rosie. After a pause, there came a familiar voice.

"Dude, you in there?" It was Tom.

"Yeah! Yeah, I'm here. Just one second." Once he was at the door, he looked through the peephole by habit, seeing nothing but black. "Funny, man. Are you giving me the finger?" Ty asked as he opened the door.

"Actually, it's the thumb," Tom said. "I thought you were going to reverse your peephole so you could see if anyone was waiting in your apartment to ambush you. Did you give up on that idea?"

Ty laughed. "Well if I remember right, it didn't work out too well for Kramer, so I changed my mind." The two of them had truly become friends when Tom had found out in class that Ty had never seen the show Seinfeld, Tom's longtime favorite show. Under the pretense of free beer, Tom had gotten Ty to come over and watch a few episodes, and he was instantly hooked.

Tom looked at Ty and had a surprised look on his face. "What the hell, dude? Are you going to the gym in your pajamas?"

Ty had been so preoccupied that he'd completely forgotten he hadn't changed yet. They usually went to the gym together before class on Tuesdays, so this was nothing short of embarrassing.

"Oh, crap! I completely forgot. I've been researching my paper and totally spaced it out. Sorry man."

"Hey, no problem." Tom's next sentence was interrupted when he came to a pile of Ty's clothes on the floor. "Because, I mean, its obvious you didn't ditch the gym to clean. It looks like your closet blew up. It didn't, did it?"

"Like yours is any better. Oh, wait, no, that's right, they have people to clean rooms at the old folk's home, don't they?"

"Whatever. Get dressed and we'll see who's feeble at the gym."

With a roll of his eyes, Ty went to his bedroom to dress and grab his class supplies.

When he came out of his room, Tom was at his desk reading off his computer. "I see you've been preparing for Dr. Eisenberg's class. I was up late last night doing the same."

"Yeah, I have to admit, this is all pretty interesting stuff. It's amazing what people used to do with their free time. I still can't get over the weight and size of the stones they were using back then. Their artwork was pretty mind-boggling, too." Ty wasn't trying to hold back his enthusiasm.

"I know," Tom agreed. "That's what got me into the whole archaeology thing to begin with. I'm pretty pumped to actually get outta class and see what it's like hands on."

"I hear you there. If I ever decide that criminal justice isn't for me, I think I'd probably try for a degree in archaeology as well."

"Well, I'm starting to lose motivation, so let's get rolling before the mood wears off," Tom said as he backed away from Ty's desk.

Ty agreed, shut down his computer, and they left the room, Ty taking special care to make sure the door was locked. They decided to take the stairs down this time, and because Tom lived too far from the school to walk, they would always take his car, and Ty would walk home after class. As they exited the lobby to Tom's car parked out front, Ty had to make a conscious effort not to look around to see where any of the men watching him might be lurking, but at the same time, still be aware of his surroundings. In the back of his mind, he wondered if he would ever be able to look at a stranger again without being suspicious. It seemed as though the naivety that came with adolescence was most likely a thing of the past.

It was a short drive to campus, and even with all of the leaves nearing their peak of the vibrant colors of autumn, everything seemed a little different now. It was still beautiful, but now he was noticing all the imperfections for some reason, like the patches of broken concrete in the sidewalks, the weeds scattered around, and even the scars on the trees where limbs had been cut off. And everything seemed to be almost running in slow motion; the drive seemed longer than usual; the walk from the parking lot to the gym seemed to take forever; and the normal hour-and-a-half stint in the gym seemed like three.

Tom noticed Ty was a little distant and commented on it after their workout. "Everything all right, Ty? You don't seem like your normal self today."

It was then Ty realized he was going to have to brush up on his acting skills. "Oh yeah, I'm just starting to feel the crunch a little on our paper. Ever since I was in grade school and had any writing to do, I'd always dread it so much that I'd put it off until the last minute. I still hate to do any writing. I guess some things never change."

Tom looked at Ty as if he was trying to get a read on him. "Are you sure that's all? If you ever need to talk about anything, just let me know. Don't forget, I used to do a little bartending in my past life and got pretty good at pretending to care."

Ty laughed. "At least I know that your concern is genuine then. What do you charge?"

"Hey, buddy, for you it's free... as long as you don't freak me out too much. Then it might cost ya a beer or two."

Ty wanted to change the subject. "Seriously, how much have you worked on your paper?"

"Well, unlike you, I don't wait until the last minute. About the only thing I have left to write is the conclusion and the citation page, then it's done."

"Well, aren't you the overachiever? Me... I usually get mentally constipated anytime I have to write anything."

"Mentally constipated?" Tom laughed while shaking his head. "Dude, where do you come up with this stuff?"

Ty was happy they were off the "what's bothering him" subject as they grabbed their bags and started the walk to the archaeology building, which was on the other side of the campus.

The campus was sprawled out over two square blocks of well-manicured lawn and dotted with elms and maples between buildings. All of the buildings had been built sometime in the late twenties—shortly before the great depression—were constructed of red brick, and most were four stories high. Ty had always found it comical that, to the students from out west, this seemed like an old campus. To the locals, anything built in the 1900s was usually considered somewhat new.

He was doing his best to act normal, but in the back of his mind he was still wondering who was following him and why. Were they somewhere in sight right now?

As they approached the building, his train of thought was broken by the sight of a classy-dressed blonde who was disappearing through the doors. Tom noticed right away what had caught Ty's eye as he made no attempt to hide it. "Damn, did you see that, I mean, her?"

"Yeah, looks like she got all dressed up for you, dude."

Ty was a little confused. "What are you talking about? Who is she?"

Tom sounded as though he couldn't believe what Ty had just said. "What do you mean 'who is she'? Do you really not recognize her?"

Ty thought about it for a second then realized who it must've been. "That wasn't Celeste, was it?"

"Bingo!" Tom replied, "She was fixed up pretty nice the other night when you stood her up, too. I think she's into you, dude."

Ty scoffed. "Yeah right, and I'm the King of England." They were at the door to the building themselves now as were several other students.

"Okay, Your Highness, we'll see," Tom said as they walked in.

Dr. Eisenberg's classroom was the first one on the first floor, leaving the rest of the upper floors for the less important classes (at least that's what Dr. Eisenberg always said). Tom and Ty walked into the classroom and went around the back to their usual seats, put their bags on the floor by their desks, and sat down. Celeste sat in the far corner in the front, so in order for Ty to make eye contact with her, she'd have to turn around. Sure enough, they had no more than sat down when she turned around and smiled at him.

Tom nudged him a little and whispered under his breath, "I told you so!"

Ty felt like he was probably turning a little red in the cheeks by now and ignored Tom's comment. He'd been very attracted to Celeste from the first time he saw her. It's rare that a guy sees a girl who has every desirable trait, yet here was Celeste, maybe the first girl Ty had ever seen who met the physical traits he was attracted to. Until now, he wasn't really sure if she was interested in him… and who knows—a smile doesn't mean anything—but after listening to Tom, maybe she *was* interested. When he laid eyes on her for the first time during fall registration, they made eye contact and she gave him a smile then, too.

Dr. Eisenberg walked in, closing the door behind him. He always looked like a man on a mission and every move he made seemed to have purpose. Judging by his lectures, it was obvious that he took his work seriously and considered archaeology an extremely important part of mankind's continued perseverance. He stressed the fact that if the rise and fall of previous civilizations were studied in the right light, we could possibly prevent making the same mistakes and, consequently, not suffer the same outcome.

He walked over to the podium. "Afternoon! We're a little bit behind on where the syllabus says we should be, most likely because of my uncanny ability to spend an entire lecture on an unrelated rant, but that's neither here nor there. Just means we might need to pick up the pace a bit. Now, who has heard of the Olmec civilization?"

Dr. Eisenberg turned on the PowerPoint that overtook the front of the room. "Most of you will recognize the colossal heads that've been discovered in southern Mexico as relics of the Olmec civilization, but there's much more to their culture than that."

Photos of several artifacts, including the gigantic heads, were presented on the next slide. They were all very familiar to Ty, as these pictures were attached to every website he had gone to this morning. Then he noticed at the bottom of the screen two artifacts known as the "Twins" that he'd never seen before. Not only that, but there was something odd about them, something that reminded him of one of the Edgar Cayce readings.

According to Mr. Cayce, before the final destruction of Atlantis over some 12,000 years ago, some of the Atlanteans escaped the deluge by fleeing to Egypt while others fled to the Yucatan Peninsula taking their knowledge with them. Now according to the mainstream archeologists, there wasn't any connection between the old world and the new one until the Spanish arrived in the late 1400s, but there Ty was, staring at a photo of two stone statues of children found in the Yucatan area suspected to be at least 3,000 years old. That wasn't the odd part, though. The strange thing was that they were wearing something on their heads that was very out of place... undeniably, they were wearing *Egyptian* headdresses.

CHAPTER 20

DURING THE SAME time Ty was at class, Grant was in his office and realized he'd missed lunch again. Having been poring over a stack of papers since 6:00 a.m., he still didn't know why his son was being followed, and a growling stomach wasn't enough to suspend his progress just yet. It was a good thing he'd been with the Agency long enough to delegate some of his daily tasks to others without any question as to why he needed to do so. Whatever his son was involved in was more extensive than he ever imagined, especially since discovering that Ty's apartment had been compromised.

Adding further confusion and conflict, Grant's men reported that each time they had tracked one of Ty's hounds, they'd discovered that it was never the same person. While the same car was spotted often, the men following Ty were always different. So far, the agents counted at least six different goons (some of whom appeared to be wearing fake facial hair or other disguises) and four different cars.

The first opportunity for one of Grant's men to follow one of these "shift workers" was the previous night. The agent tailed the car all the way into the heart of D.C., where it disappeared into a parking garage at the 1090 Vermont Avenue building. Grant then researched the intel to learn about the twelve-story site: it was constructed in the late '70s and early '80s and was now owned by a giant Japanese real estate firm. The office space was leased to different entities, all of which were checked out by Grant for plausible connections.

So far he hadn't found anything that seemed out of the ordinary—it was possible he might not—but it was a job he had to do nonetheless to find a potential motive behind Ty's situation. Because of the involvement of someone inside of the Agency with the license plate trace, Grant couldn't use his office phone for anything to do with this case. He couldn't do any research on his computer either, which made everything a little more difficult. All the information about the different companies who were leasing space at the Vermont Avenue building had to come from an outside, secure source. Even then, he knew that he couldn't be too careful. It would only take one little slip up and the wrong person might be tipped off, causing what little leads he had to dry up as fast as the juices of a squashed bug in the middle of the Sahara Desert.

With limited resources, especially for a job that really didn't involve the CIA, Grant had to call in a favor from a longtime friend and retired former agent, Butch Colton. Butch's job was to stake out the Vermont Avenue building to try to catch a glimpse of one of the "shift workers" leaving and hopefully find out more about what was going on and who was involved. So the next time there was a shift change, one of Grant's men would call Butch on a secure line and tell him which car was returning to the parking garage. Butch would take it from there.

Grant and Butch went way back to when Grant worked for the Border Patrol in Montana. Grant never told the story to anyone of how they met, but the circumstances that had caused their paths to cross had created a very unique relationship between the two. They never really talked much, but whenever either one needed help of any kind, the other would drop whatever he was doing and be there without question. Grant never even told Marion the story, but she seemed to understand that whatever it was that had happened between the two men had created a bond for life.

Grant's stomach let out another growl. Just then, his pager vibrated. Several people had his cell phone number, but there was only one person who had his pager number... Butch. Finally some progress! Eager to find out what it was, Grant quickly shuffled papers from his desk into his briefcase, picked up his phone, and alerted the receptionist that he was stepping out for some lunch and would be back around 2:00.

His drive to Athens—a small Greek restaurant he'd visit every once in a while—appeared normal, but once he was inside the door, a man in a back booth by the corner with dark hair and a short beard wearing glasses and a baseball cap got up and disappeared into the adjoining bar, without returning. Grant proceeded over to the booth where the bearded man had been and sat down. On the seat in the corner was a small notebook which Grant slid into his pocket. He really didn't think anyone was following him, but to be on the safe side, he'd have to play a little cloak and dagger until he knew for sure.

The waitress came and took his order, and it wasn't long before he could finally settle his stomach's cravings. His gyro was as good as he remembered, but the entire time he was eating he was wondering what was in the notebook. Whatever Butch found out was, with any luck, something that would shed some light on a few things. Grant had no doubt that Ty had been honest with him and, hopefully, whatever was going on didn't mean his son was in any danger.

After finishing his lunch and paying the bill, he went out to his car and drove back to the office. Letting the receptionist know he was back from lunch as he passed her desk, he went down the hallway toward his office, stopping in the restroom. Ascertaining that he was alone, he went to the far stall. Closing the door behind him and taking the only seat in the room, he took the notebook out of his pocket and read what Butch had written down. After he'd read everything (which was only a few sentences), he washed up and went back to his office. He sat down at his desk and stared at his blank computer screen with a disheartened expression.

BUTCH HAD BEEN across the street from the parking garage when the car and driver he'd been waiting for finally showed up. Although that same car never reemerged from the building, he was lucky enough to recognize the same posture of the driver of a different car leave the garage shortly after. Interestingly enough (although not surprising in the least), the driver who entered the garage had light-colored hair going in, but was bald as a cue ball on the way out. Butch not only got his license plate number, but was able to follow him home without being noticed. Thanks to modern technology and Butch's resources, he found out everything there was to know about his target in only a couple of hours. Butch wrote it down for Grant:

Although he has a name, it's surely unimportant. He's just an average Joe, with an average family, with an average job, and an average background. Everything indicates these qualities are not fabricated.

BUTCH NEVER SAID anything more than necessary to convey his point, and this time was no different. Grant knew the assessment was ironclad and accepted his results as gospel; Butch was the best at what he did, and he knew he wouldn't have reported his findings to Grant unless he was absolutely sure. It was the certainty of Butch's cryptic note that was so befuddling. Grant had originally expected it would help, but having an average Joe tailing his son made no sense. It only made the water even murkier.

CHAPTER 21

WHY WOULD STONE statues found in Mexico that were most likely over 3000 years old have Egyptian headdresses on them? The rest of the time in class, Ty's thoughts wandered to Cayce's readings about Atlantis and its inevitable destruction. Might these stories have a grain of truth embedded in them? At first, they'd sounded so far-fetched that Ty was doing everything he could not to give them any merit, but with little things popping up like this, Cayce's stories were becoming more and more credible. Although this was just more circumstantial evidence at best—and maybe even a strange coincidence—it was still a little eerie, in light of everything else. If there hadn't been a connection between the new and old worlds until the Spanish arrived in the late 1400s, then what could possibly explain this?

The two-hour class went by in a blur as he pondered the possibilities. He'd totally forgotten about the little flirtation episode with Celeste at the start of class until he happened to glance in her direction and caught her looking his way again. She gave him another smile and looked away as she picked up her books and got up to leave the classroom. Then, all of a sudden, it hit him. If someone was following him with their intentions unknown, should he be concerned about others that were close to him? Might their safety be jeopardized because of him? With this new thought and the potential outcomes racing through his head, he intentionally drug his feet as he put his books into his bag. The timing of this epiphany was horrible, but what choice did he have?

Tom had been watching the interaction between the two and appeared somewhat confused when Ty started to take his time gathering up his stuff.

"Hey, dude! What are you doing? Now's the perfect time to talk to her," he said as he nudged Ty.

Ty felt like he was caught between a rock and a hard place. He desperately wanted to get to know her better, but if his little situation of being followed might potentially put her in danger, that was something he wouldn't risk.

Tom looked at him in disbelief. "Quit playing hard to get. It's obvious she's into you."

Ty really wanted to talk to her, but now was not the time. "Hey, I don't want her to think I'm a pushover. Besides, I'm still not convinced that she's all that interested."

Tom shook his head and replied, "Well, I wouldn't wait too much longer if I were you. I'll bet she has lots of guys chasing her around."

Ty shrugged his shoulders, and Tom looked as if he took the hint.

"Okay, but I think you're making a mistake. Anyway, are you going back to your place, or are you going to hang here at the library for a while?" Tom asked.

"I think I'm going to go straight home today. What about you?"

"I think I'll go to the library and do some studying for my next class, so I probably won't see you until Thursday then," Tom said.

"Okay, see you then. Don't study too hard," Ty said as they went their separate ways.

On the way home, Ty wondered if he did the right thing about Celeste and maybe losing his opportunity with her. If he was in a potentially dangerous situation, he obviously did the right thing, but if there was no danger involved—like his dad said... the more he thought about that, the more it started to make him a little mad that he'd blown his chance. Initially, when he'd heard his dad bring up water-boarding one of them, he couldn't believe something like that would ever have been an option. Now, as he thought about maybe losing his chances with Celeste, the more he felt it might not be a bad idea. Hopefully his dad was finding some answers and getting to the bottom of this so he could put it all behind him and move on with his life.

As he was getting closer to home, he saw a statue of a Union soldier in front of the local park that shifted his thoughts back to the pictures of the two Olmec children wearing Egyptian head-dresses. As crazy as it sounded, it seemed as though Edgar Cayce's view of Atlantis would be one possible explanation of why there were similarities between the Egyptians and the people living in the Yucatan region in the same era. However Cayce was getting his information, if he was always right about his medical diagnoses, why would his other readings, such as those regarding Atlantis, be wrong?

Ty was so caught up with his thoughts again, that he didn't even have to force himself not to look to see who might be watching as he was walking home. It wasn't until he was inside his apartment building and starting up the stairs that he remembered he most likely had a fan club outside, observing him as he came home. He thought about calling his home phone and letting anyone who might be there know he was on his way, but it was probably something his dad wouldn't think was too funny. Anyway, it was likely whatever they needed to do was probably already done by now, and he wouldn't have to worry about surprising any intruders with his presence.

Once upstairs, he unlocked the door and opened it cautiously. It was obvious that if anyone had been here while he was out he or she still didn't bother to clean up the place. Looking around, it was apparent his housekeeping skills were lacking, and putting off his paper made it obvious that his writing skills weren't on the top of his list of favorite things, either. The big question was… which one of these daunting tasks was he going to put off the longest?

More than two hours later, Ty sat at his computer staring at a blank page one on his word processor, tapping a pen up and down on his desk. The one thing different now was the furniture and countertops seemed to have come alive, as though they could, at last, breathe again. Finally the entire apartment was brightened by a shine on surfaces that hadn't been seen since a week after he'd moved in.

MEANWHILE, A CONTINENT away in what looked like a room in an ancient dungeon, a large, shiny, bell-shaped object with strange markings etched in its side sat soundly on the floor. In the background in an adjoining room, under the banner of a swastika, an aging man lay motionless in a coma-like state, hooked up to a life support machine that was keeping a vigilant watch over his lifeless body.

CHAPTER 22

TWO DAYS HAD passed since Ty had holed up in his apartment to write his paper. Even though several games of solitaire, Black Ops, and more episodes of Seinfeld than he cared to admit had come and gone, he had once again shown that if one waits until the last minute to get something done, it will get done. Since he'd started the assignment and after finding out all the bizarre myths and legends so many people believed to be true, he'd almost forgotten the premise of the paper was to try to prove a connection between the Bible and the ancient megalithic structures scattered across the earth. Now staring at his completed paper, with the title being the only thing missing, it came to him what the most fitting, yet simplistic title should be:

Tyler Larson
Archeology 287
Semester Paper
University of Alexandria

PROOF

To be able to prove anything from the distant past is almost an insurmountable task, if not an impossible one. Although there will be clues left behind from any past civilization, the further back in time you go, one would think the clues might become much fuzzier, but do they? Should one consider a carved stone that weighs 2,370,000 pounds a fuzzy clue? Although the clues themselves may not be fuzzy, the knowledge we have about the people who left them is another story.

Legends and myths have survived eons, but how much validity do they have? Then again... what is a myth? One definition describes a myth as a story passed down orally that is thought to be true. Even large portions of the Bible were passed down orally for years before being written down, but how many people would refer to the Bible as mythology? As amazing as the stories of mythological beings such as the Titans are, could there possibly be any truth to them?

Then again, what about the stories in the Bible? A flood that engulfed the entire world with only one family surviving because they were tipped off by the Creator who also told them how to build a boat that was large enough to carry two of every animal on the planet to safety is a remarkable story as well... yet millions of people today believe it to be fact. What about the story in Genesis of the creation of all things including mankind and the universe itself? Would the story of the Titans be any more fantastic than this? After taking a closer look at some of the stories in Genesis, it becomes apparent that some details are left out. For example, Genesis 1:26 states:

And God said, "Let us make man in our image, after our likeness; and let them have dominion over the fish of the sea, and over the fowl of the air, and over the cattle, and over all the earth, and over every creeping thing that creepeth upon the earth."

Who is the us and the our that God is referring to? Then again in Genesis 3:22, after Adam and Eve have eaten the forbidden fruit:

And the LORD God said, "Behold, the man is become like one of us, to know good and evil; and now, lest he put forth his hand, and take also of the tree of life, and eat, and live forever—"

Then, several years pass and in Genesis, chapter six:

[6:1] And it came to pass, when men began to multiply on the face of the earth, and daughters were born unto them,
[6:2] That the sons of God saw the daughters of men that they were fair; and they took them wives of all which they chose.
[6:3] Then the LORD said, "My spirit shall not always strive with man for that he also is flesh; yet his days shall be an hundred twenty years."
[6:4] There were giants in the earth in those days; and also after that, when the sons of God came in unto the daughters of men, and they bare children to them. The same became mighty men which were of old, men of renown.

Who could these sons of God possibly be, and how long were they here? And for that matter, how much time passed between the creation of mankind until the sons of God arrived? The math through the timeline of the generations can be done to come up with a number, but is this really an accurate method? Using this method, the earth would only be a little over 6,000 years old, but time after time, through modern science, we are coming up with numbers much older than that.

For some reason, not much is written about the sons of God in the Bible, but they are undeniably mentioned. If they were part of the "us" and the "our" that God referred to on more than one occasion, then what would they know about the secrets of the universe? Would it have been possible that they might've even helped the Creator with the daunting task of creating the complex world we live in? If they did and even if they didn't, they would know much more than mankind about how the forces of nature work and, quite possibly, how to manipulate them to their advantage. If this was the case, then it would surely be one explanation of how a stone weighing 2,370,000 pounds was shaped and moved to its current resting spot.

Another explanation might be through the sheer brute strength of the *Nephilim*, the offspring of the sons of God and the daughters of men (who were thought to be giants). Along with many other ancient civilizations, the Maya and Inca civilizations thought there was a race of giants on earth before a Great Flood. The Bible mentions giants on more than one occasion as well. The only strange thing about the giants in the Bible is the fact that they are here *after* the Great Flood. The Great Flood that (according to the Bible) only one family survived. Did one of the survivors possibly have *Nephilim* DNA tucked away somewhere in his or her genes, or might there be more to the story than the Bible reveals?

That brings us to Enoch. Besides being the son of Jared and the father of Methuselah, who was Enoch? According to the Bible, he was a man who walked with God, but hardly anything else is written about him, that is... in the Bible. In November of 1946, near the Dead Sea, a Bedouin shepherd stumbled across a cave and found seven ancient scrolls inside. Since then, eleven more caves were discovered and a total of 972 texts found, which include the Hebrew Bible and other extra-biblical documents that date from between 408 BC and 318 AD. Among the extra-biblical documents found in cave number eleven was a copy of the Book of Enoch. That's right, an entire book dedicated to Enoch. Now this was not the first time that the Book of Enoch was known about.

The Orthodox Ethiopians had the book all along, but it wasn't until 1773 when the famous Scottish traveler James Bruce returned to Europe bringing back three copies written in the ancient language of Ge'ez. Obviously, at one time people put as much value in the Book of Enoch as they did in the rest of the Bible, but for some reason it, along with several other books, was never included in the Hebrew or Christian Bibles.

Why is the Book of Enoch important in regard to the quest for proof? Genesis, chapter six of the Bible only briefly mentions the sons of God taking the daughters of men and producing a progeny known as the men of renown, but the Book of Enoch goes into much, much more detail about this long-lost civilization. The sons of God are referred to as fallen angels or the Watchers, who (out of nothing more than pure lust) descended upon the earth and took human women for wives bearing their children and teaching mankind all the evils that plague the human race, even unto this day. It was this, and of the malicious actions of the half-breeds themselves, that caused the Creator to flood the earth and wipe it clean to start anew. The account of this civilization is also elaborated on in the Book of Jubilees, another of the texts found in the Dead Sea Scrolls.

With so much more written about such a fascinating civilization, why would it be glossed over so lightly in the Bible? Was it simply a period in history that was lost to the sands of time, or could it possibly be a cover up of, literally, Biblical proportions?

There have been over 500 documented flood legends from around the world... most all eerily resemble the account of Noah given in the Bible. From continent to continent there are legends of a worldwide flood where one family is warned and spared by building a boat. Several of these stories also include the salvation of the animal kingdom on the boat as well. One that stands out the most is probably from one of the oldest known civilizations in human history... the Babylonian flood story found in a Sumerian poem about the Epic of Gilgamesh.

The Epic of Gilgamesh parallels the Biblical flood story of Noah with uncanny similarities and is thought to predate it as well, but there is another Sumerian legend not as well known that also has an eerie parallel to another Biblical story... the *Anunnaki*. *Anunnaki* translates into "those who from heaven to earth came." According to ancient Sumerian text, the *Anunnaki* created hu-mankind some 400,000 years ago only to return after the human race had grown and found the human women irresistible and even though forbidden, took human women as wives who bore their children.

Countless stories across the globe reiterate this theme, but is that proof? Might it all come down to someone in the distant past with an overactive imagination or could it actually be a rec-ord of events that humanity would just as soon forget? Scattered across the globe are the unexplainable remnants of a long-lost culture who were using enormous stones that were cut with such precision and fit together so precisely that even with today's mod-ern technology would be considered an almost impossible feat.

In Sacayhuaman, Peru, there are stones that show evidence of what is known as vitrification. Vitrification is a process done to the surface of a stone to give it a mirror-like finish. There are a few ideas of how this was accomplished, but the most popular theory is that it was achieved with extreme heat. There appears to be a molecular change on the surface of the stones that would not be evident if the finish was done only by polishing, but what kind of heat source could possibly have been used? Temperatures required to melt rock vary with the type of stone, but it is in the range of 1,300 to 2,400 degrees Fahrenheit. How on earth could these kind of temperatures have been created and how could anything that would create these temperatures be controlled? One theory is that the stones were somehow being molded to make the perfect fitting seams (and there were several that did have the appearance of coming out of a mold), but how would that have been possible? Was it possible the ancients somehow manipulated matter at its very core? Recently there have been successful experiments where scientists have turned energy into matter... maybe we are just now rediscovering what the ancients knew all along.

In Peru there are other places like Ollantaytambo and Machu Picchu, in Bolivia there is Pumapunka and Tiahuanaco, in Egypt there are many including the Osireion, and of course the Great Pyramid itself with unexplainable stonework. These are only a few of many, but one of the most interesting may be in Lebanon.

In Baalbek, Lebanon, beneath the Roman Temple of Jupiter, are three colossal carved stones that weigh in at a mere two million pounds apiece known as the Trilithon. No one on earth can explain how anything so heavy could've been carved, transported, and stacked so precisely that a knife blade can't even fit in the seams, but yet there they are. Another interesting thing about the structure is the different layers of stones used. The Romans are undoubtedly responsible for the top layer of smaller stones somewhere around 2000 years ago. Then we come to the much older layer, which includes the massive unexplainable stones. Something that might even be more interesting is the next and final layer of smaller, more manageable stones again. The top layer is rather easily explained as they match what the Romans were doing at the time. And for obvious reasons, the middle layer with the enormous 2,000,000 pound stones leaves everybody scratching their heads, but what about the layer they are stacked so neatly on? What could possibly explain those? To go from a bottom layer of small manageable stones to a layer of enormous stones that seem humanly impossible to move back to a layer of small manageable ones doesn't really make sense... or does it?

Could the walls of the Temple of Jupiter in Baalbek, Lebanon possibly be a timeline of human history here on earth? Might the first layer have been built eons ago by the civilization that was here before the sons of God came and took the daughters of men and produced the *Nephilim*? This could explain the use of the smaller stones for the first layer of the construction. The appearance of the Watchers and the *Nephilim* might also explain the use of the enormous stones that came next, and if a worldwide flood came before they could finish, this too could explain why the megalithic construction came to a halt.

If a worldwide flood did occur and wipe out most of humanity, how long would it take for civilization to regroup and be able to begin construction again once the waters had subsided? It most likely would've been at least several hundred years before mankind would be in any kind of shape to pick up construction on a project the size of the Temple of Jupiter. Although this is obviously all circumstantial evidence and in no way proves anything, it does, however, pose one possible explanation of the construction at Baalbek that would fit into the timeline of man here on earth if the theory is correct.

To be able to prove anything such as this, which happened so many eons ago would only be surpassed in magnitude by finding weapons of mass destruction in Iraq or being able to prove beyond a shadow of a doubt how humans came into existence in the first place. No matter what angle you take, whether it be the theory of creation or the accident theory (Darwinism) and follow the trail backwards, either one is impossible to prove. Take creationism, although it makes sense to some, you will always be faced with the age old question... where did God come from? Impossible to answer. Then let's look at the accident theory and the Big Bang. The theory does make some sense until the question is asked... where did the Primordial Particle from which the Big Bang originated come from? Another impossible question to answer. In fact, when you look at both options, anyone of any intelligence at all will only be able to come up with one possible conclusion... that it is impossible for us to exist, yet here we are.

So in that comparison, to prove a connection between any ancient civilization and their scattered debris left around might not be such an unattainable task. Is it possible that a Biblical, almost superhuman race roamed the earth eons ago? Maybe... maybe not... yet the proof seems to be everywhere.

CHAPTER 23

Ty FELT THE vibration of his phone. He quietly pulled it from his pocket to see that his good friend Tom had sent him a text.

"Dude, bored at the Pub. Come and join."

He silently laughed to himself while shaking his head. Here it was, a Saturday night, and he was holed up in the local library in front of a computer with a couple of unopened books on top of the desk, one of which was his Bible. Several weeks had gone by since he'd handed in his paper, and he still had no idea how he did. Dr. Eisenberg said he was going to announce the winner of the contest in class next Tuesday, and Ty was actually kind of excited to see what his professor thought of his ideas. He wasn't very optimistic about winning the contest and going to the Middle East, but it was a hope that was nestled in the back of his mind.

One change recently was that whoever had been keeping tabs on him had suddenly lost interest, or so it seemed. According to his dad, he hadn't been tailed in the last three weeks, and it was as though the interest in him had been turned off like a light switch. Although he was relieved that whatever had been going on was apparently over, he actually sort of missed the excitement. The whole thing was still baffling to him all the same; what reason would anyone have to follow him? His dad told him he thought it was probably some kind of mistake, but Ty knew there was a good chance that his dad wasn't telling him everything. He knew all too well how tight lipped his father had been over the years and figured this most likely was no different.

Not only had the excitement with the cloak and dagger situation cooled off, so had the flirtation (as little as it was) with Celeste. He still hadn't followed up with her, and now she didn't seem as interested as she once had been. That didn't surprise him at all, but he was hopeful that he still had a chance before the semester was over, or he may never see her again. Tom and a few of his other classmates had gone to O'Reilly's a couple more times in the last few weeks, but no Celeste.

In the meantime, Ty was starting to lose interest in the ancient civilization he'd been so diligently researching. Now he was thinking about getting resumes out, and applying for an internship with the Agency, possibly speeding up the process of securing a position there.

As boredom was ever so slowly getting the best of him in the library, Ty reached for his phone to respond to Tom's request. Just then, a gust of wind came through an open window from across the room. At that same moment, a chill went through his body followed by a strange feeling that something wasn't right. He slowly turned to see what might be the cause of the feeling, and as soon as he did, a light went out between the two bookshelves directly behind him. He couldn't help but get up and walk to the row where the light had been extinguished. It was as though he was being drawn there for some unknown reason.

The shelf was against the wall and was the only one in the library that had a top row too high to reach. Something made him look up there. All the titles seemed to be blurry, except for one. Maybe that was what caught his eye, the title. It was the same one he used for his paper... *"Proof."*

The proper protocol was to get the librarian to use the stepstool to retrieve the books off that top shelf, but Ty couldn't help himself, he just had to get a closer look. Without taking his eyes off the book, he dragged the stool over with his foot and stepped up; he was just high enough to reach it. The book was tightly wedged between the others, so he had to use more force than he'd wanted. As the book began to slide out, he could just start to see the cover. It was a strange cover and one that captivated him. Below the title was an image of an open Bible, but that wasn't what had his attention. It was what was tearing its way out of the open Bible that kept his focus.

He continued to pull it out the rest of the way, but before he could see who the author was, one of the legs on the stool broke. Ty, along with several of the books came crashing down. Everyone in the library was now staring at him and the pile of books that were strewn about.

The librarian came rushing over in a panic. "Tyler! Are you all right? You know I'm supposed to do that."

Ty crawled back to his feet. "I'm so sorry. The book was jammed in there so tightly and the stool just collapsed I guess." He hadn't felt this embarrassed in a long time.

"Oh, it's all right. I'll get another stool and you can hand the books up to me."

"No problem." Ty was more than willing to do anything to help, especially since he made the mess.

The librarian was only gone a few seconds before she returned with a new stepstool, and Ty quickly cleared a spot in the pile of fallen books for her to put it down. As he was handing her the books one at a time while she was putting each one in its place, it wasn't until he'd handed her the last one that he realized he still hadn't seen the book that had drawn him into this debacle. He bent down to look under the shelves, only to see bare floor. He looked around the entire area, only to see more of the same. Thinking maybe he handed it to the librarian without noticing, he looked up at the ones she'd just replaced... it wasn't there, but there *was* enough space left for one more.

"It looks like one's missing," Ty pointed out.

She looked around, then nodding her head in agreement said, "It sure does. Are you sure it's not on the floor?"

Ty looked around, but it was nowhere to be found. That was strange. How could a book have just disappeared into thin air? He looked around at the patrons who had gone back to their work. Could someone have picked it off the floor without him noticing? That didn't seem likely. Then the same eerie feeling came over him once again along with a burning thought... *"numbers mean something."*

Almost sounding as though someone had whispered it into his ear, he spun around, only to see nobody there. What an odd feeling, but the thought... *numbers mean something?* Where the hell did that come from? It meant absolutely nothing to him in the least. Then he glanced over at the desk he'd been sitting at and noticed something was different. One of the books he'd stacked on the desk was wide open, yet he was sure he hadn't opened any of them. Walking slowly back to his desk, he glanced around the room then back to the open book. As he got closer, he could see that the one that was open was his Bible. Almost in a trance like state, he bent over to get a better look. The chapter it was opened to was... Numbers! What was going on? Was it possible the wind was responsible for flipping his Bible open? Or was someone playing a trick on him? He looked around the room again suspiciously. Was this somehow connected with the missing book he'd just pulled off the shelf? His gaze went from the fellow patrons down to the open Bible and his eyes seemed to focus on one specific verse... Numbers 13:33:

And there we saw the giants, the sons of Anak, which come of the giants: and we were in our own sight as grasshoppers, and so we were in their sight.

There it was again. The same thing that started his obsession only a few months ago... giants. It was hard to believe he'd missed this verse before, but the strange course of events in the last few minutes had rekindled his interest in this long-lost civilization. Just when things were getting back to normal, it appeared as though he'd stepped straight into the *Twilight Zone*.

Reading through his Bible with a renewed vigor, it was apparent to him that Moses had more than one encounter with the *Nephilim*. Once again, Ty was imagining what kind of world it might've been when his trance was broken by an incoming text.

"If you get here in 10, I'll buy."

Ty had already forgotten about Tom's message earlier, but it didn't take long for him to decide. "Ok. Twist my arm then. Be there in a few."

Ever since the suit scenario with his father, Ty wasn't the biggest fan of having too much on his mind at once. Although he had been instantly intrigued by this new information in the Bible, he decided he'd come back to it later... for the sake of his mental health. Anyway, there wouldn't be a whole lot of opportunities to see Tom when they both went their separate ways after class was done, so a couple of drinks together sounded more significant.

He gathered up the books on his desk and shut down the computer, making sure to clear the browser history in the process.

He'd gotten in the habit of erasing the history after all the strange events started happening, especially when he found out his home computer had been compromised.

He still couldn't get over what led him to reading about Anak and the giants in Numbers. It was almost like he'd been steered through some kind of mystical force, but that didn't explain the disappearance of the book called *"Proof."* Was it possible that somebody had been lurking around and picked the book off the floor without him noticing? That didn't seem likely, but it would justify the weird feeling he had, as though he was being watched.

With his copy of the Elizabeth Clare Prophet book, *"Origins of Evil"* still in his possession, he remembered it was finally due back. He looked at the cover one last time before putting it in the book return slot. The librarian he'd become acquainted with over the past few years (which was probably why she'd been so under-standing when he made the mess with the books earlier) just happened to be retrieving the books right then and noticed the book Ty had dropped in.

"I have to say, it's funny that in the past ten years this book has only been checked out about twice, and now, since you've had it, all of a sudden it seems like everybody wants it," she said as she read the cover. "It must be good. I think there are five people who have a hold on it."

"Really?" Ty was definitely surprised, but then again, this was the only book he could find that had a copy of the Book of Enoch. "Any chance you can tell me who has it reserved?" he asked somewhat jokingly, thinking probably his request would be denied.

The librarian thought for a moment, then glanced around the library and walked over to the computer. She turned the screen slightly toward Ty and said, "Sorry Ty, I'm not allowed to do that, so if you'll excuse me, I better put these books away now."

She winked at him, then turned and walked away. Ty stood there for a second, and then leaned over enough to read what was on the screen. It took him a couple of seconds to focus, but as he glanced more closely, he started to reach for his pen to jot down the names when he came to one he recognized. He froze in his tracks, staring at the screen in disbelief. Three lines down, the screen displayed a name he'd seen countless times yet wasn't someone he thought he'd associate with the mysterious shambles his life had become: his good friend, Tom Bruiner.

CHAPTER 24

THE TEMPERATURE WAS much colder outside now, after spending four hours in the library, but the cold was the last thing on Ty's mind. It *could* just be a coincidence Tom was waiting for the book that Ty had found so fascinating. After all, it was the very class they shared that had led him to the Book of Enoch. He thought *maybe* he'd mentioned it to Tom in passing and he had developed a curiosity, but Ty sure didn't remember telling him anything. He had never even told Tom what his paper was about. It just seemed strange that Tom still had the book on hold, especially since he never even used the local library. Furthermore, who were the other four people waiting for the same book? With everything else that had happened lately, just another strange coincidence didn't seem to quite cut it.

The more he thought about it, the more questions started to pop into his head. Ty started to think back about some of the strange events that had happened, like the fact that it was Tom who told him about Edgar Cayce in the first place. Just then he remembered. The weekend that he had taken the train to D.C., only to return to find the flier about Edgar Cayce under his wiper, Tom was the only one he'd told where he was going, so who else would've known where to find his car? But, on the other hand, what reason would Tom have to steer Ty down the road to Mr. Cayce by giving him the flier secretively?

Ty tried to muster up the gall to keep his plans with Tom, but his resolve was fading fast. Initially, he had thought this would be a good chance to get the upper hand, find out why Tom had wanted to check out the book and to find out this was just a big misunderstanding after all, and Ty could have his friend back. Just the thought of Tom being the reason all of this had happened made his hands shake. It was then Ty realized he wasn't going to be able to face Tom at the pub. He'd have to come up with some excuse why he had to cancel, but his mind seemed to go blank. The only thing he could think to do was call his dad. He didn't need to use the "Uncle Dale" code his father had set up because he wasn't worried about being followed, but he also knew he probably couldn't say anything over the phone about this situation, either, just in case. He could simply tell his dad he needed to come back to D.C. to finish up some research and go from there. Although it wasn't too late to call, it was definitely odd for him to come home without more notice, so he was sure his dad would pick up that something was going on.

Ty fished his phone out of his pocket and called his dad on his private cell. Grant answered on the second ring.

"Hey, son. How's the soon-to-be graduate?"

"I still have two days left, so let's not count the chickens before they hatch. You never know, there's still a chance they could turn into scrambled eggs yet."

His father laughed. "Okay, okay, we'll hold off on the celebration for a while longer. What's up?"

"Well, it looks like I have to be in your neck of the woods again in the morning so I was wondering about coming up tonight so I could get an early start. That okay?" Ty asked.

After just a slight pause, his dad replied with an enthusiastic "Sure!" And Ty knew that his dad had caught on. "What time are you getting in?"

"Oh, I should be there in around an hour-and-a-half or so."

"No problem, son. You have a key if we're already in bed, but we'll leave the light on."

"Thanks, Dad, see you in a bit," he said before he hung up.

While he still had his phone in his hand, he began to text Tom. As simple as the lie was, it took him much longer than it should have before he felt confident enough to hit send.

"Duuude, I'm so sorry, I gotta ditch. My parent's anniversary is coming up, and I was supposed to go home this morning. I completely forgot, so I'm catching the next train out. Next 2 on me."

Tom replied a few minutes later, which was more than enough time to have convinced Ty that Tom had surely caught onto the lie.

"You forgot you planned an entire trip? Maybe it's a good thing you only take one class at a time. Next two is a deal, have fun in DC!"

Ty breathed a deep sigh of relief and turned to make way to his car. Before he had gotten too far, he remembered something else that'd been in the back of his mind for a while now—the oil stain left in his parking spot. At the time he never thought too much about it, but it had been needling him ever since he found out he was being followed. With a sinking feeling in his stomach, Ty began to wonder if Tom's car might have a leak. Until now, he had no idea if he could match it up to anyone's car, but that might've just changed. Since all of this weirdness had started, every time something strange had happened, he'd tried to rationalize it.

Where had that gotten him? Someone had been playing him for a fool and that was going to stop. Since he knew where Tom always parked when he went to O'Reilly's, now was the perfect opportunity to check if his car had an oil leak.

As he got within a block, he transitioned from the dimly-lit main street to the dark alley that ran behind the bar. Hopefully Tom wasn't going to be coming out anytime soon. After all, it was just a couple of minutes ago Ty had told him he wasn't going to join him. The closer he got to where Tom's car should be parked, the more he tried to analyze the situation. There hadn't been any reason to be suspicious of his friend all this time, but all of a sudden there seemed to be a tie between Tom and the wild set of circumstances Ty had somehow gotten tangled up in. A very loose tie was all it was, but from now on, he was going to err on the side of caution until whatever the heck was going on was in the rearview mirror.

Ty was now close enough to see Tom's car. As he approached, the softer he walked and the louder his heartbeat became. His awareness was at its peak, and the adrenaline was flooding his veins. Although he didn't think this was any kind of life-and-death situation, it'd be extremely awkward if Tom caught him snooping around his car, especially after Ty just told him he wasn't going to be able to meet him.

Stopping two cars away to assess the situation, Ty reached into his pocket to retrieve a key chain that held a tiny flashlight his father had given him when he got his first car. Even though he'd only used it a couple of times, it had been worth its weight in gold. With his flashlight ready, he looked around again, paying particular attention to the area Tom would be coming from if he'd be leaving. Then after taking a deep breath, he quickly walked up to Tom's car and looked around one last time to see that no one was coming. He crouched down and aimed his flashlight under Tom's car. Sure enough, there it was, the exact same oil slick that had been in his parking spot when he returned from his parents' a few weeks ago. Just to be sure, he directed the light up to see if the oil slick was coming from Tom's car, or if, by coincidence, it had already been there.

Just then he heard the sound of footsteps coming toward him. Shutting off his flashlight and staying crouched down, he quickly maneuvered around to the front of the car that was parked in front of Tom's. With nowhere to go now without being seen, he was going to have to wait. If it was Tom who was coming, Ty would stay in his hiding spot until he pulled out and drove away. Ty's heart was racing as he waited to hear if the footsteps were stopping at Tom's car. If they didn't, he was going to have to do something quickly or he'd be seen for sure. Just as he was trying to come up with a plan, the footsteps stopped and he could hear Tom's car door open. Ty felt a sigh of relief that he wouldn't be caught, but his heart was still thumping as he waited to hear the sound of the engine break the silence.

It seemed like an eternity as he waited, but Tom still hadn't started his car. *What could be taking so long?* he thought. As he waited, he finally heard Tom's voice. It sounded like he was talking to someone on his phone. Now, instead of wishing Tom would hurry up and leave, he wanted to hear the conversation. Even though the neighborhood was quiet this time of night, Tom's voice was muffled just enough that Ty couldn't quite make out everything he was saying, but he thought he heard the words, "He's not coming."

Ty had a gut feeling he knew who Tom was talking about. There was silence for a few moments, either Tom's conversation was over or he was listening to whoever was on the other end of the phone.

Ty started to get a little nervous. He had no idea what he would do if someone from the other direction came along and saw him hiding there. What was taking him so long to start the car and get the hell out of there? What seemed like an eternity was probably less than a minute, then, finally, the sound of Tom's engine broke the late-night silence. And not a moment too soon, as Ty saw lights from the opposite direction turn into the alley.

Just as he was grateful for the good timing, Tom shut his engine off. *Are you kidding me?* Ty thought as he looked around for some kind of exit. There was none, and if he got up now, Tom would see him for sure. The only thing he could possibly do was crawl around to the curb side of the car he was hiding behind, lie down, and hope he'd somehow go unnoticed. He quickly slid around to the side of the car, lowering himself onto his belly on the pavement. Trying to wedge himself into the space under the car as far as possible, he crammed himself into the gap and froze.

As he lay there on the cold asphalt, the approaching car's lights suddenly disappeared, but the sound of the engine seemed to be getting closer. *Now what?* Ty thought as the oncoming car was almost next to the one he was hiding behind. It must be a cop on patrol, who else would be driving with their lights off down a dark alley? From his vantage point, he could see the car pass by him, and then once it was next to Tom, it stopped. It was apparent that whoever it was, the person was specifically there for Tom.

The engine noise of the stranger's car made it impossible for Ty to make out what they were saying, but he could hear the tone of their voices, and there was no doubt that they knew each other. He tried desperately to listen to the conversation, but it was no use. The car was just too loud. At least Ty's hiding spot was safe for now, and as long as nobody came walking down the sidewalk, he'd remain unseen. Not only was there no hope of Ty hearing what was being said, but lying on the ground made it impossible for him to see any part of the stranger as well.

After what seemed like another eternity went by, the muffled conversation finally came to an end and the car drove off. Then

Tom started his engine back up and drove off in the opposite direction. Ty continued to lie in his cold hiding spot until the sound of Tom's car faded into the silence of the night. Slowly uncorking himself from the frigid spot he'd been wedged into for the last several minutes, he stood up as the blood in his body once again started to flow freely. Looking both directions down the now empty alley, he couldn't help but wonder who the man he thought was his friend really was.

CHAPTER 25

TY SPENT THE weekend relaxing at his parents' house, enjoying the company of his mother and trying to see through the smoke of what was happening back in Alexandria with his father. Before any of them knew it, though, it was Tuesday and time for Ty to get back for the last week of school, hopefully coming out of it with a diploma. He didn't have to be back at class until 1:00 in the afternoon, so he was able to have breakfast with his parents before his dad went to work and, because it was her day off, have a nice visit with his mother before it was time to leave.

After he was halfway into his drive home, he realized he'd been so caught up in thinking about the situation he was tangled up in that he didn't remember the last few miles. He shook his head to snap out of it and tried to pay attention to the road instead of his thoughts.

His dad had informed him that the Agency could no longer foot the bill for his safeguarding, but not to worry because he still had a lot of favors that he could—and would—cash in. Tom had already been checked out in the prior weeks along with other acquaintances of Ty's with no red flags showing up, but his dad was now in the process of doing a more thorough check. Even though his dad had told him not to let his suspicions get the best of him, the more he thought about the situation with Tom, the more wary he became. Not only was he the only one who knew where his car would be to put the Edgar Cayce flier on the windshield, but Tom was also the one who first broke the ice with Ty when their class first started. Looking back now, it almost seemed like Tom had gone out of his way to see to it that they became friends. Even the other night at the library with the eerie feeling and the missing book now seemed to somewhat point to Tom… nothing else seemed to make any sense.

Before Ty had started his drive back to his apartment, he thought he should send Tom a text that he might not be back in time for their session at the gym, but changed his mind. His dad had given him some pointers on how to interact with people he didn't think he could trust without tipping them off. "Son, it's kind of like playing poker," he told him. "If you know what your opponent's hole card is, you can't let them know that you know." What was going to make it a challenge, in Tom's case, was that Ty had thought of him as a friend, and a close friend at that.

Trusted friends were hard to come by in his father's business, and maybe that was the reason why he and his father had always been so tight; maybe his dad had needed a confidant, and Ty was one of the few he could really trust. Whatever the reason, he was glad they were close and wanted to make his father proud of him, which he knew that he was.

Keeping his mind on the road was proving to be really difficult, especially knowing he'd be seeing Tom in class soon and would have to put his acting skills to work. The weather was nice, though, and the traffic was light and before he knew it, Ty was pulling into the parking spot at his apartment complex. As he sat in his car for a moment, he realized it'd only be a couple more weeks and he'd be moving out of the place he'd called home for the past four years. With class finishing up this week and Christmas being a mere two weeks away, this wouldn't be his residence much longer. Even though it'd only been a temporary dwelling, he had good memories and would surely miss it after he was gone.

Once the sentimental moment had passed, he remembered about the oil stain. He restarted his car and backed up to take another look. Not surprisingly, there it was in exactly the same spot as under Tom's car. It still could all be a coincidence, but he was done looking the other way when it came to those.

Taking the stairs to his apartment to get everything he needed for class, he couldn't help but wonder why anybody, especially Tom, would've been stalking him. There was obviously something going on that he was unaware of, but what was it?

Taking a deep breath, he opened the door to see everything appeared to be as he'd left it. Without bothering to shut the door, Ty went inside to get his bag and thought about checking his email, but decided to do so after class.

With his bag in his hand he turned to leave, but stopped in his tracks as he was suddenly facing a silhouette of a man slightly taller than himself standing in his open doorway. With the glare from the sunlight through the window in the hall and all of Ty's curtains closed, he couldn't make out a face. Here he was again, feeling vulnerable and unsure what to do. Several thoughts of different strategies ran through Ty's head in the split second before the man spoke.

"Everything okay, Ty?"

It was Tom, and Ty wasn't sure how to react. Had it been three days ago, he would've been glad to see him, but now it was a different story.

"Hey, Tom. I didn't hear you come in. You had me freaked for a second."

"Sorry about that, Ty, I just stopped by to see if everything was okay. I texted you a few times and never heard back from you, so I got a little worried. I thought maybe something might've happened on your drive home." Tom let himself in and hugged him, patting Ty's back sharply a few times. "I'll try not to lurk in dark doorways anymore, man. Now, loosen up, stop looking at me like I'm Hannibal Lecter."

Before Ty responded, in the back of his mind he wondered if Tom was aware that he'd been snooping around his car the other night. He was pretty sure no one had seen him, but there was a slight possibility that whoever had stopped to talk to Tom may have.

"No, it's all good. Sorry, man, I haven't really checked my phone lately. I just got back from my parents' place and haven't checked my messages yet. I had my phone off the entire time." He could see Tom's face now that he'd come into the room a little further.

Judging by the look, for only a brief moment, it almost appeared as though Tom thought he was being lied to, then in an instant, his face lit up and he said, "Well, I suppose you're going to wuss out and skip the gym then."

Ty was definitely uncomfortable, but as he looked at his watch, he replied, "Yeah, sorry about that, Tom, but we only have enough time to get to class."

Tom now appeared to be the Tom of old. "Yeah, I know, I'm just screwing with you. Can I give you a ride?"

He wasn't ready to be locked in a car with Tom so this was the perfect opportunity to avoid that. "I think I'm gonna run it. I didn't get any exercise in this weekend, so I really need to get back into it. Wish I had gotten back sooner so we could've gone to the gym, though."

Tom nodded, appearing to be understanding. "I don't suppose you heard who the lucky winner is who wrote the best paper and gets to go on the trip with Dr. Eisenberg is, did you?"

Ty looked up, temporarily putting aside his distrust of Tom. "No! Did he announce it?! Who?"

Tom must've been able to tell by the look on Ty's face that he was hopeful it might be him. "I hate to burst your bubble, buddy, but it ain't you or me, but I'll give you one guess."

Although he was visibly disappointed, deep down he knew he didn't really ever stand a chance. "I give up. Who?"

"Well, if you got to pick someone in the class to go away with, who would you take?"

Ty immediately knew who he was talking about. "Not Celeste?"

"Bingo!" Tom answered.

"Are you sure about that?" Ty said hoping there was some kind of mistake.

"Yeah. Sorry, buddy. Hopefully she doesn't like the grandfather type, or you're in trouble."

"I thought he wasn't going to say who the winner was until class today. How did you hear about it already?" Ty asked as he started toward the door.

Tom backed into the hall out of Ty's way so he could close and lock the door. "I guess there was a problem with the travel arrangements so they have to leave after class today. He told her ahead of time so she'd be ready to go then, and just sort of decided to email the rest of the class while he was at it since the surprise had already been ruined."

"Damn! Good thing Dr. Eisenberg made sure we all had our passports in advance. It looks like I might've missed my opportunity with her after all" Ty said, as his voice trailed off with disappointment.

"Don't worry too much, buddy," Tom appeared consoling. "It's not like she won't be coming back. They're only gonna be gone two weeks."

It was then that Ty realized what a good friend Tom had been to him, and if he'd been faking it, he'd done a convincing job. Ty sure hoped he was wrong about Tom, but in the meantime, his guard was staying up. Not feeling comfortable about turning his back on Tom, he waited for him to start for the stairs, then followed behind.

The more they talked as they descended down the eight flights of stairs, the more Ty realized he'd be able to pull off the act. It seemed easy to tuck away his feelings of distrust and focus on the traits that he knew he liked about Tom, making their conversation flow as smoothly as it always had before.

Once downstairs, Ty remembered to look at the asphalt where Tom had parked. Although he felt a bit bad lying to his friend, if that really is what he was, he told Tom he needed to get something out of his car and said he'd see him in class. Tom left through the front door and Ty pretended to exit the back, then returned to the lobby so he could see when Tom's vehicle was gone.

Exiting the front of the building, he could hear the sound of tires screeching a few blocks away. He looked down the street to see Tom long gone and walked to where his car had been only to confirm what he already knew: another oil spot.

CHAPTER 26

IT WAS EARLY Tuesday afternoon and the driver of the car that followed Tom Bruiner to Tyler Larson's apartment had parked a half block away to watch as Mr. Bruiner got out and went inside the lobby doors at the front of the building. Mr. Bruiner had only been inside for a few minutes before reemerging through the front door with the Larson boy. After they had a brief conversation, the Larson boy went back inside and Mr. Bruiner went to his car, but before he opened the door, he reached in his pocket and took out his phone that had begun to ring. Just a few seconds later, Mr. Bruiner put the phone to his ear and slowly swung his head around, glancing directly at who'd been following him all morning, then casually looked away as if he was totally unaware that he was being watched.

The on-looking driver in the parked car had been on many such stakeouts before and he knew when he'd been made. It wasn't much of a signal, but just enough to let him know he was no longer an invisible observer. Whoever had called Mr. Bruiner somehow knew and must've informed him that he was under surveillance. Unfortunately for Mr. Bruiner, his ever-so-discrete glance at the parked car halfway down the street was enough to tip off the driver.

Mr. Bruiner got in his car and pulled out, diligently watching his mirror. Once down the road a little, the car he'd just been warned about eased back onto the street in pursuit. Not being used to these kinds of situations, Mr. Bruiner became uneasy and when he got to the next intersection he quickly made a hard right turn, speeding up as he went. What Mr. Bruiner didn't know was that the man in pursuit had strict orders not to let him get away, so as soon as he sped up, the car following him also sped up, which made the situation for him all the worse.

Mr. Bruiner was driving a 2000 Honda Civic with a four-cylinder engine that was very dependable and got great gas mileage, but it was never designed for racing. On the other hand, the car that had been following Mr. Bruiner apparently was built for speed as the gap between the two closed in an instant. The car in chase almost seemed to be shot from a cannon as he rounded the corner accelerating past Mr. Bruiner. In the blink of an eye, the car cut off Mr. Bruiner, forcing him to come to a screeching halt with absolutely nowhere to go. As soon as Mr. Bruiner's car came to a stop, he slid over and jumped out the passenger door in an attempt to make a break for it through the alley.

His assailant calmly opened his door, stood up, and out from under his long trench coat covering his broad burly body, he pulled a Ruger .454 Casull revolver with an eight-inch, custom-made silencer on the end of an already long, seven-and-a-half-inch barrel. The only good thing about the situation for Mr. Bruiner was that the man who was about to squeeze the trigger of the ferocious weapon also had strict orders not to do him any permanent physical harm.

Even though a rubber bullet is considered to be non-lethal, it doesn't mean it comes without pain. As Mr. Bruiner made it about three strides into his escape, he felt as though someone had hit him with a sledgehammer right between the shoulder blades. All of the air was expelled from his lungs as he fell to the ground, first to his knees with a quick pause, then continuing the rest of the way, landing face first on the pavement.

Mr. Bruiner lay sprawled out and gasping for air, feeling like his back had been broken in half. Just when the air started to refill his lungs, he tried to force himself off the ground. The last thing he remembered was a powerful arm grabbing him around the neck and a large hand covering his nose and mouth with a cloth that reeked of a strong chemical odor. Mr. Bruiner's limp body was quickly stuffed into the trunk of the assailant's car by the burly figure wearing the long trench coat.

The entire incident transpired in only a few minutes, and in a neighborhood where most of the inhabitants were at work, no one heard a thing. Not only was the driver in a hurry to leave, but he knew that whoever had tipped off his subject must be close; that was something he did not want to deal with right now. After driving several blocks and making numerous turns, it was obvious no one was following him, which was probably a good thing for them... judging from what had just happened to Mr. Bruiner.

CHAPTER 27

WALKING THROUGH CAMPUS, it looked as though Ty was going to be right on time as waves of students started to emerge from the immediate buildings, indicating the end of the previous class. By the time he got to the Archaeology building, the outgoing flow had subsided to a trickle. Most of the class had already claimed their seats by the time he sat down, but oddly enough, no sign of Tom. Soon it was time for class to begin, and still no Tom. Ty wondered if he had decided there was no point in showing up, but they were supposed to get their papers back today as well, so that didn't really add up. Checking his phone, he saw that Tom hadn't texted him either.

Dr. Eisenberg was the last to come in, as usual, and closing the door behind him, said, "Good afternoon! We've got a short and sweet class today. I'm sure by now many of you have gotten the email, but I want everyone to know that it wasn't an easy decision to make at all. Some of you made some very convincing arguments that...well, let's just say some of you have taken a very interesting view on your topics, but I guess when dealing with antiquity that is almost unavoidable." He paused and looked around the room with his gaze momentarily stopping at Ty before moving on. "I truly wish I could take all of you with me, but unfortunately that's not possible, so without further ado, let's give a congratulatory round of applause to Miss Celeste Peterson."

Celeste seemed to blush a little as her fellow classmates clapped spiritedly for her. Dr. Eisenberg smiled proudly, and just as the applause began to wane, he interrupted, "Unfortunately, because of some complications with our travel itinerary, we have to leave this afternoon so we'll regretfully have to miss our last class together," he said. "Yes, yes, I know, getting out early – such a tragedy. Maybe I should have called a sub. Your grades will be officially posted soon, and your papers are up here for you to take at the end of class. I can honestly say it's been my pleasure to have had the chance to enlighten each of you this semester."

Almost in unison, the class thanked the professor with big smiles on their faces. It was apparent that the professor had touched the lives of the entire class, and not just Ty's.

Dr. Eisenberg returned the smile then walked over to the podium in the front and center of the room. "Thank you," he said humbly. "Now let's turn our focus to something Miss Peterson touched on in her paper. It's something that she agreed to let me share with you." The look on the professor's face was once again all business as he continued.

"The search for Noah's Ark has been an undertaking of many scholars and explorers throughout history, and if you ask a hundred different people where the Ark is or even if it was real, I guarantee that you'll get enough different responses that you may even begin to question your own beliefs. There've been several people who've claimed to have seen it, and some even claim to have been to it, yet the mystery continues. In my opinion—and in the opinion of the Turkish government and that of Miss Peterson as well—Noah's Ark was rediscovered in modern times in the year 1959."

Of course this was a topic that had Ty's interest. After all, it was the Great Flood that wiped out the civilization he'd been researching so diligently over the last few weeks. As soon as Dr. Eisenberg mentioned the date of 1959 though, he knew he'd heard this story before. In all actuality, he'd already dismissed it as false and maybe even a hoax, but if Dr. Eisenberg believed it to be true, then maybe there was something to it after all. No matter what, his professor had his full attention. It was apparent Dr. Eisenberg knew this subject well, as he had no notes or opened book to reference as he spoke. He did, however, have several slides for the class to view on the PowerPoint as he continued. Although the evidence that Dr. Eisenberg presented over the next hour was most certainly circumstantial, it was still bewildering to say the least.

In 1959, a Turkish Captain by the name of Llhan Durupinar was going over some survey photos taken in eastern Turkey near the Iranian border about eighteen miles south of the famous Mt. Ararat. What jumped out at him that seemed rather odd (especially at an elevation of 6,524 feet above sea level) was what appeared to be an enormous boat-shaped formation embedded in the ground.

It was no secret that Mt. Ararat had been searched for years as the resting site of Noah's Ark, but according to the Bible the ark came to rest in the mountains of Ararat, not necessarily on the mountain of Ararat itself. If the Bible is accurate, the flood took place at least 6,000 years ago, so what could possibly be left of the ark today? Maybe exactly what lies some eighteen miles south of Mt. Ararat.

Soon after the formation was discovered and officials in the U.S. had studied the photo, Dr. Arthur J. Brandenburger (an expert in photogrammetry) was quoted as saying, "I have no doubt at all that this object is a ship. In my entire career, I have never seen an object like this on a stereo photograph." Shortly after, an expedition set out to eastern Turkey to study it firsthand. After a visual inspection was made of the area without the use of any scientific methods whatsoever, they decided it was just an odd geological formation and left it at that.

Seventeen years later, a man by the name of Ronald Wyatt grew interested in the site. After numerous trips to the area over the next fifteen years, he thought he'd proven that the formation was indeed Noah's Ark. The mountain where it lies is known to the locals as Doomsday Mountain, and the valley below has always been referred to as the Valley of Eight (supposedly referring to the eight survivors of the Great Flood).

The structure is 515 feet long which, according to the Bible, the Ark was 300 cubits. If the Egyptian cubit was used—which is twenty-point-six inches—surprisingly enough, that's exactly 515 feet!

The professor had just told the class the dimensions of the anomaly when one of the students from the far side of the room interjected. "But why would the Egyptian cubit have been used? I know Moses wrote the Book of Genesis, which is where the account of the flood is written, but I thought he was an Israelite."

"Well, you're right about the fact that Moses was an Israelite and he did write the Book of Genesis," the professor explained. "But you're forgetting where Moses was educated."

Almost immediately it hit the student. "Egypt!"

"Precisely... Egypt!" It was as if the professor was just as excited.

Dr. Eisenberg then went on to explain how ground-penetrating radar had been used to see if there was any sign of a manmade structure in the belly of the formation. The radar readouts corresponded with what looked like a regular pattern of possible petrified remnants of timbers used to make the hull of a boat. Apparently, Mr. Wyatt found a rock that seemed to be a piece of petrified wood with laminated joints and glue oozing out the seams. A few other strange items found inside were remnants of ancient rivets composed of metals that don't occur naturally, along with petrified animal dung and an antler.

More evidence nearby included large stones with manmade holes in the top that resembled anchor stones. These were commonly used in the Mediterranean on ships to steady the boat, and as Dr. Eisenberg said with great emotion, "These are several times larger than any anchor stone ever found. If indeed these huge stones are anchor stones, they would obviously have been for use on an *extremely* large ship!" he paused, only for a second, then continued. "On an extremely large ship that had been floating on waters a few thousand feet above what we now know as sea level!"

All the evidence was apparently enough to convince the Turkish government to declare the site "Noah's Ark National Park" in 1987. A visitor's center was constructed that displayed various artifacts found at the site. Although it seemed this could in fact be Noah's Ark, there were a lot of critics who said otherwise. Was it possible there was something the skeptics overlooked? Obviously Dr. Eisenberg thought so, along with several others, but what was it?

Something else the professor told the class that Ty had never heard before were the different words in the neighboring countries used to describe Mount Ararat. In Armenia it was *the landing place, those who descended, mother of the world,* and *the planting of the vine.* In Turkey, *doomsday, painful, the raven won't land,* and *anchor. The eight* in Iran, and *flood* in China. This only added to the circumstantial evidence that Noah's Ark landed somewhere in the area, but at this point, that's all it was, circumstantial evidence.

Another thing that didn't make sense to Ty was how this had anything to do with the megalithic structures they had been assigned to write about, although he presumed this was probably not everything Celeste included in her paper. Maybe he was just suffering from a case of sour grapes.

Fifteen minutes into their already shortened class, the professor's cell began to loudly buzz on the podium. With a furrowed brow, he murmured something about excusing himself and left the room through a seldom-used door near the front of the room.

It was obvious there was something wrong when he returned a few minutes later. "Sorry, class," he said in a wavering voice, "I've just received some troubling news." After a short pause he continued, "My sister has been in a serious automobile accident, and I'm going to have to leave." He then looked at Celeste, "And I truly apologize to you, Miss Peterson, but I'm afraid I'm going to have to cancel our trip."

It was hard for Celeste to hide her disappointment, but at the same time it was apparent she felt sorry for Dr. Eisenberg, as it was for the rest of the class who were all now dead silent.

Dr. Eisenberg walked over to his desk slowly and slid into his chair. After a couple seconds of speechlessness, he snapped out of his state of shock and apologized again to the class.

"Forgive me class, but we're going to have to quit a little early. I truly am sorry we have to end the class like this, but sometimes the unexpected will force us on a detour around what we've planned."

After a few more seconds of silence, everyone little by little gathered up their stuff and started out the door in single file giving Dr. Eisenberg words of encouragement as they went to the front to collect their papers.

Just as Celeste was almost to the door, Dr. Eisenberg called out asking if he could speak to her for a moment. The rest of the class stood in the hall speculating about the crash that the professor's sister had been in. It was apparent that everyone was very fond of Dr. Eisenberg, as nobody really wanted to leave. Slowly, the remaining students started to disperse, making their way outside.

Under the circumstances, Ty wasn't in a hurry and really wanted to talk to Dr. Eisenberg along with congratulating Celeste. Even though her trip had been canceled, it was still an opportunity to try to talk to her. After several minutes, Ty began to think that with the bad news his professor just received and the fact that he was still busy talking to Celeste, maybe this wasn't a good time to talk to either one, so he started to walk away instead.

He was partially down the walkway when he heard, "Ty... wait, Ty!" He turned to see that Celeste was trying to wave him down. By the way she was dressed, it was obvious that she'd been ready for the prized trip, although he'd never seen her when she didn't look anything but utterly gorgeous. To see her running after him calling his name was something he thought would only be in his dreams. Actually he'd only heard her say his name a couple of times, and he really liked the way it sounded coming out of her mouth.

Being so caught up with the view before him, he had a little trouble coming up with something to say as she approached him, but luckily he didn't have to.

"I'm glad I caught you," she said, breathing a little hard after having to rush after him. "Dr. Eisenberg wants to talk to you."

It took him a second to get his mind off her heaving chest and her labored breathing before he realized he needed to say something. "Me? What for? Is everything okay?"

"He'll have to tell you. Do you have time to see him now?" She said as her breathing was starting to slow down.

Ty had to laugh a little to himself—he had nothing but time. He didn't want to seem too eager to jump, though, so he glanced at his watch before saying, "Sure, but are you sure everything's okay?"

"Well, he's pretty broken up about his sister, but he wants to see you about something else."

They were already walking back toward the Archaeology building, and it wasn't until they were almost there that he really started to wonder what Dr. Eisenberg wanted to see him about. Until now, all he could think about was seeing Celeste running toward him and calling his name. This was actually what he'd hoped for when he left class, to talk to Dr. Eisenberg about his paper and have one last chance to talk to Celeste. From the tone of her voice, he could tell that whatever Dr. Eisenberg wanted was somewhat urgent, which started to spark his curiosity even more.

Dr. Eisenberg was still sitting at his desk, but instead of staring off into space, he was now going through some papers in his briefcase. Ty didn't quite know what to say, but started to speak anyway when the professor looked up and interrupted, "Tyler, I apologize for bringing this to you on such short notice, but time is of the essence with this matter."

What matter could he be referring to? Ty wondered, but before he had a chance to say anything, the professor continued, "As you know, Miss Peterson and I already had to change our travel arrangements and now with my sister in critical condition, unfortunately I'll not be able to leave at all. In good conscience, I cannot possibly send a student off on her own. I would much prefer that at least two make this trip, even with a guide on the other end. With both tickets prepaid, I think we may be able to pull the trip off after all. I've made the necessary calls and can have my ticket changed to your name, as your paper was the second best of the group. If you're interested in accompanying Miss Peterson, the trip is yours. However, I'll need to know right now to be able to make everything work out."

Ty stood there wanting to ask someone to pinch him, but refrained. Originally he was prepared to head back to his apartment to pack up some things and get ready to move out, but now he had a choice between that or packing for a two-week trip to the Middle East with the most beautiful girl he'd ever laid eyes on... if only all of life's choices were this easy!

CHAPTER 28

GRANT HAD JUST returned from lunch when a text came through on his private cell. It was Butch and his message was short. *"Game time has been moved up."*

He cleared off his desk and called the receptionist to let her know he'd be out for the rest of the day, then unlocked the bottom file cabinet drawer and grabbed a folder that he'd buried at the bottom of the pile titled "Miscellaneous," and put it into his briefcase.

The thought that there was someone inside the Agency who was somehow involved with this whole deal had been bothering him for weeks now, but he still had absolutely no idea who it might be and how his son was involved. Even though he thought things had cooled off a little, obviously they were picking back up again. Needless to say, as he walked down the hallway and out the lobby, he found himself regarding everyone he passed as a suspect. His circle of trust had shrunk down to one person outside of his family and that was Butch.

Although he still had no idea what was going on, he'd found out a little more about Tom Bruiner since his son had told him of his suspicions. It's amazing the kind of clues that can go unnoticed when looking into someone's background at first glance. It wasn't until the second time of digging into Tom Bruiner's past Grant noticed something that he'd missed.

Tom was originally from Montana, just like he'd said, and he had been to all the schools he said he'd attended, his birth certificate checked out, and he'd been working at a concrete company in the Houston area for the last nine years, confirming everything. A career change at thirty years of age wasn't all that uncommon, but what didn't quite add up was that there were several schools that offered archaeology degrees in and around the Houston area, and they were probably even better than the one in Alexandria. So why would he move 1,500 miles to go to school instead of attending one in his own backyard and pay out-of-state tuition? Also interesting was that he'd gotten an academic scholarship; it was highly unusual for anyone to obtain that specific type of scholarship after graduating from high school so long ago.

That's what eventually prompted Grant into doing some research into Tom's scholarship. At first glance, everything appeared to be normal: the funding for his scholarship came from a private organization by the name of The Indigenous Foundation. Doing a little fact checking on them, he found out they were a private organization focused on the continuing education of Native Americans. He also noticed a big contributor to the foundation was a company called S.O.J. International.

When Grant tried to find out anything about them, he hit a brick wall. As far as he could tell, S.O.J. International had absolutely no affiliation with anything, let alone a business. What they did (if anything at all), was a complete mystery. It was obviously a front for something, but whatever it was and whoever was behind it had an agenda covered up so well that even the CIA couldn't crack it.

Once Grant started to look into Tom Bruiner's finances, he also discovered that he had a perpetual car payment for the last nine years. This wouldn't be too much out of the ordinary, except the only car Tom had would've been paid off years ago. So where was the monthly payment actually going? Grant checked into it and found out the money was going to a company called Auto Loans Inc., which was owned by none other than S.O.J. International! This whole thing stunk to high heaven, but there was absolutely nothing illegal about any of it.

Not having much to go on, Grant decided to go after the only other lead he had: the one guy Butch had made who'd been following Ty. Grant had sent Butch back to bring him in, so he could get to the bottom of this once and for all. However, lo and behold, when Butch had moved in, the suspect and his family were gone, lock stock and barrel! Gone without a trace. Here was an average family who'd been living at the very same address for over twenty years, and now they were nowhere to be found.

Feeling completely unsuccessful at this little game, it was then that Grant realized he'd have to go after the only other lead he knew of before he disappeared too. Not feeling confident about his connections, but knowing he had no choice, Grant put in the call to capture the unsuspecting Tom Bruiner.

Grant stopped at home to change into clothes that didn't scream "CIA" before he hit the road. The drive from Langley to Alexandria was a quick trip this time of day, since most everyone was still at work. Couple that with the anxiety Grant was experiencing, and he was there before he knew it.

There were two stops he had to make before he met up with Butch. The first was to a car rental place—where he'd pick up a rental under an alias—and the second was the train depot. He remembered Ty said someone put a flier under his wiper when he'd come up for the weekend a couple of months ago (which was when he figured all of this had started), and with any luck, one of the parking lot's surveillance cameras might've gotten the whole thing on video.

With a fox in the henhouse back at the Agency, this was something that couldn't be done over the phone. Either he or Butch would have to do it in person, or else the video (if there was one), might mysteriously disappear.

Once he was at the train depot security office, it didn't take much to convince the security guard in charge to let him have a copy of the video of the weekend in question. Luckily for him they still had it. Although it appeared to be 100% intact, he wasn't going to have time to look it over until after he met up with Butch.

He was only a few minutes away from their rendezvous point, but he was still paying particular attention to the rearview mirror in case anyone was trying to follow him. After taking a long, roundabout way, he was sure he was alone.

Every city had a fair share of vacant buildings, and it usually wasn't hard to find one that fit the bill for a little field interrogation work. Although this kind of thing surely wasn't common practice anymore, it was still effective for something like this with such short notice.

Grant pulled onto the road that accessed the property, which was a half block off the main avenue down an alley in the old industrial part of town. Most of the surrounding buildings were no longer in use because of the rerouting of the train tracks to the outskirts of town some fifty years ago. There'd been some land developers trying to market the area for residential expansion, but the cost had been too high and the demand was too low to get anything started. Some of the buildings were used for storage, but other than that, the area was like a ghost town.

Grant could see it was unlikely that any prying eyes would even notice anyone driving into the parking garage and impossible for an observer to see an unwilling victim being transported from the trunk of a car to the inside of the vacant building. He pulled next to Butch's car and saw he was waiting in the shadows next to the door that adjoined the parking garage with the main building.

In all of his years with the CIA, Grant had been involved in several different covert operations, all of which were different than the last, and none of which involved his son. Of course, this was the first time he wasn't acting on behalf of the Agency. So far, he hadn't done anything illegal… other than a minor case of kidnapping. If it all went according to plan, neither his nor Butch's identity would ever be found out, and with the possibility his son's life might be in jeopardy, he was willing to take that chance.

Butch was the kind of guy who liked high-tech devices, and he always had something to aid him in most situations. This time he had a small camera, along with a motion detector that he placed on the top of his car to watch for any unwanted company that might happen along and surprise them before they were finished with their work.

Once they were inside and the door was shut, Butch unzipped a duffel bag he was carrying and took out two full-face masks. Grant quickly grabbed the Richard Nixon mask and put it over his head. Butch shook his head as Grant chuckled under his breath, seeing that he was left with the one of Joan Rivers. At six-foot-five and somewhere around 280 pounds, even wearing a Joan Rivers mask Butch still looked intimidating.

Grant followed Butch down the hallway to the stairs that led to the dimly-lit basement, where they descended the flight of stairs to the cold, underground floor. They walked halfway down a hallway and opened a door to see a weary Tom Bruiner tied to a cold radiator in the corner of the small room. His hands and feet were bound with heavy zip-ties and he had a blindfold covering his eyes and a sock taped into his mouth. Grant never enjoyed this kind of thing (Butch... he wasn't so sure about), but sometimes drastic measures were needed. They both hoped Tom would be willing to give them the answers they were looking for without too much persuasion.

Butch walked across the room to Tom and took the sock out of his mouth and slipped the blindfold off his head. He was still groggy from the chloroform that had put him out for the last couple of hours, but he was awake and becoming more coherent by the minute.

"What do you want from me?" Tom said while shaking his head as if he were trying to wake up.

"Tell me, Mr. Bruiner," Butch said in a deep, gruff voice, "What brings you to Alexandria?"

Tom started to say something but Butch interrupted, "Just remember before you answer, I don't like to play games."

"We're on the same side," Tom said with a weak voice.

Butch and Grant looked at each other then, and it was Grant who responded. "What do you mean *the same side*? What side would that be?"

Tom was still weak, but he was gradually becoming more alert. "I know who you are... at least you, Mr. Larson. I'm not sure who your ape is, but that doesn't really matter now, does it?"

Tom's response was a surprise to both of them, but didn't change their objective. "The man asked you 'what side that would be.' If I were you, I'd just answer his question," Butch said in an even deeper voice.

"Look," Tom said as he started to squirm fighting his restraints. "I know you're just worried about your son, but believe me, he's not in any danger from us."

Without looking at Grant, Butch leaned over in Tom's face and said, "Who's 'us'?"

Tom was quiet for a moment, looking back and forth between the two, and then said, "I want to see my attorney." Had Tom's comment come under different circumstances, Grant would most likely have broken into tears from laughter, but because of his son's involvement, he failed to see the humor.

It was obvious Tom wasn't going to cooperate, but this was something they'd come prepared for. Butch looked at Grant, then opened his bag and brought out a hypodermic needle and a small vial containing a clear liquid. The CIA had traditionally used sodium pentothal as a truth serum, and even though the United States Supreme Court had ruled that any confessions obtained through the use of such a drug were inadmissible in court, sometimes these tactics were still used in the field to aid in gathering intelligence.

Grant knew Butch was no stranger in the use of these drugs, although since his departure from the Agency, he'd become acquainted with a different drug, one that the KGB had been using for several years, called SP-117. There were some things Grant never asked Butch about—how he became familiar with a drug the KGB routinely used was one of them.

Butch carefully plunged the needle into the vial and filled the syringe halfway with the fluid. Tom struggled as much as he could, but Butch's powerful grasp on Tom's forehead easily wrenched his head to the side, exposing the bare skin of his neck. Butch whispered something into Tom's ear, which made him stop squirming while he plunged the needle into his skin and emptied the contents of the syringe.

The effects of the drug were almost immediate. However, after several minutes of questioning, they only had two new pieces of information. One: Tom mentioned the letters "S.O.J." once and then started to go into convulsions as soon as it came out of his mouth (as though he'd been programmed to self-destruct), so they dropped the subject abruptly. Two: while Grant recalled hitting a dead end with the company S.O.J. International from the background check on Tom, the next name he said was something that he was very familiar with... ODESSA.

CHAPTER 29

EVERYTHING WAS HAPPENING so fast for Ty (which was probably a good thing to help settle his nerves a little), and going on a two-week trip to the Middle East would've been exciting enough by itself, but the fact that he was going with Celeste made it much more exhilarating.

He'd tried to call both his parents to let them know what was happening, but he got his father's voicemail and a busy signal when he tried to call his mom. His message for his dad said that he had some great news and would try him later. Surely he'd be able to get through at some point before their flight left. It was a little unusual when his dad didn't pick up, though, so Ty assumed he must be involved in something rather important.

Looking at his watch, he realized he needed to wrap up his packing and get downstairs. He had made sure to secure his passport, first of all. Celeste had reminded him to pack it when they had parted ways. It was probably a good thing she had, considering he'd never been out of the country before. With his suitcase in tow, he made one last glance around to see if he was forgetting anything (most likely once he was on the airplane he'd remember something), but for now, everything looked like a go.

Just as he was about to leave, he heard someone quietly knocking on a door at the opposite end of the hallway. Without hesitating, he opened his door and instinctively glanced in the direction of the knocking. Standing at the far end of the hallway was a well-dressed man wearing dark glasses and a long overcoat similar to something his dad would wear. The stranger heard Ty step into the hall and turned to look.

As Ty shut his door, he decided to take the elevator, since he was dragging his suitcase in one hand and his duffel bag in the other. The man looked vaguely familiar to him, but he couldn't place where he'd seen him before.

Ty pushed the elevator button, turning again to the stranger to say hello. The well-dressed man nodded his head in acknowledgment then turned back to face the door he'd been knocking on. This was one time Ty hoped the elevator would take its sweet time, so he could try to remember where he'd seen this guy before. He was sure it wasn't from around the building, but where? It was obvious this was going to bother him, but it was time to refocus and get back to the adventure that was before him.

This was the first time he ever had a "car" come for him, to put it in Dr. Eisenberg's words, and he was looking forward to the experience.

The elevator doors opened and he walked through the lobby to the front doors to see that his ride wasn't there yet. Looking at his watch he saw it was 2:55 p.m., which made him five minutes early. It was cold outside, and with his destination in mind, he had only worn a light coat, so he thought it was best to wait inside until his ride showed up.

Not having been able to share the excitement of the impending trip with anyone close to him yet was a little bit of a downer and made him think of Tom once again. Tom had been his best friend for the entire last year and he confided in him often, but now he didn't know what to think. Despite his doubts, he still decided to call and tell him what was happening, but just like his call to his father, no answer.

Like clockwork, as soon as five minutes had passed, a black limousine pulled up and came to a stop directly in front of the building. *Wow! This is really first class,* Ty thought, never having set foot in a limo before. Not wanting to appear overanxious and wanting to make sure this indeed was his ride, he slowly opened the lobby doors and started dragging his suitcase toward the limo. Just as the driver opened his door and emerged from the car, the window opened and Ty could see Celeste waving joyfully at him from the back seat as she said, "Did you remember your passport?"

Ty smiled and waved back and answered, "First thing I grabbed," as he picked up speed by increasing his stride.

It was almost like he was dreaming... getting into a limo and sitting next to the girl of his dreams on their way to the airport to get on a plane to fly halfway around the world to one of the most intriguing and mystifying places on earth. He wasn't even sure exactly where they were going, only that it was somewhere in the archeological paradise of the Middle East.

Celeste appeared to be filled with excitement as well, which seemed to ease the butterflies in Ty's stomach a little bit, knowing that she, too, was experiencing some of the same emotions that he was.

Once the driver started down the road, Ty looked at Celeste and told her, "I think I might be able to get used to this."

She snickered a bit. "What was your degree in?"

Ty shook his head. "Yeah right, I guess I'd better savor the moment."

As they turned the corner by the famous lilac bush, Ty remembered looking out his window several weeks ago to see the stranger in a parked car staring at him. Who had been following him and why did they stop? And where had he seen the well-dressed stranger in the hallway? On top of that, what about Tom? Ty quickly decided he wasn't going to think about any of that right now.

All of a sudden he realized everything had been happening so fast that he didn't even know the itinerary. Looking at his watch he asked, "What time's our flight, anyway? And which airport are we flying out of?"

"Oh, right. You'll be needing this," she said as she handed him a copy of his boarding pass.

The last time Ty flew anywhere was several years ago and it was without the luxury of checking in from home. After looking over the boarding pass, he saw they'd be flying out of Ronald Reagan International Airport directly to Cairo, Egypt! It was hard to hold in his enthusiasm.

Then he noticed when they were scheduled to depart, which didn't leave them much time to spare. *Holy crap!* he thought. *Talk about cutting it close!* Looking again at the boarding pass and after doing a little math, he worked out that it was a fourteen-hour flight. It was hard to believe he'd soon be in Egypt.

Ty turned his attention to the interior of the limo; he was quite amazed at just how plush it was. Although he'd seen longer ones in passing (which were most likely even fancier than the one they were in), this was, by far, the coolest car he'd ever been in. There were two leather bench seats in the back that faced each other with a flat screen TV on one side and a small bar on the other. The privacy window that could be raised to isolate the back from the front was fully open.

He'd been so taken by the situation, and though he hadn't forgotten Celeste was there, he hadn't had a chance to start a meaningful conversation yet. Just as he thought he should come up with something to say, she beat him to the punch.

"I almost forgot. I told my sister I'd let her know when our flight was leaving," she said as she took out her phone.

Ty realized that he should probably try his parents again, but thought he'd wait until she was finished with her call first.

"Huh, I don't seem to be getting service here. Do you mind if I try yours?"

"Sure, I always get service here." He was more than happy to let her borrow his phone, along with just about anything else she requested.

Reaching into his pocket, he took out his cell and gave it to her, hoping her hand might touch his in the process. Just as he'd hoped, her fingers brushed up against his palm. With the phone in her hand, she looked up and gave him a smile that made his heart skip a beat. Ty could only hope he wasn't blushing noticeably as his heartbeat was racing with excitement.

With a little snow just starting to flutter through the air, Ty quickly commented on it, hoping it would help his blood flow return to normal. "Looks like we're getting out of town just in time," he said, looking out the side window.

Celeste was fumbling with his phone, then looked up and said, "I'm sorry, but I can't seem to get any service with yours, either. Are you sure you have coverage here?"

"Yeah, let me try it," he said as he took it back from her. After a few moments went by, he didn't have any luck, either. "I'll be damned. Maybe there's a problem with the cell towers in the area. I'll try it again down the road."

Just then he happened to look out the window and see a Langley, Virginia sign when it hit him where he'd seen the well-dressed stranger in the hall as he was leaving his apartment... it was in his dad's office building only a couple of months ago!

CHAPTER 30

GRANT AND BUTCH looked at each other, hoping that the ODESSA they were familiar with wasn't the one that Tom was referring to. Everyone in the CIA knew stories of how several Nazis eluded capture and escaped Germany after World War II through what was known as the "ratlines," some of which were run by the secret organization called ODESSA (*Organisation der ehemalige SS-Angehorigen*, otherwise known as "Organization of Former SS Members").

Though the ratline was a very fitting name, the existence of ODESSA had never actually been proven, but there had been insurmountable circumstantial evidence over the years that had hardly left any doubt that it, indeed, was very real. Not only did the evidence support the existence of ODESSA, but there were also rumors that the organization might still exist to this day.

When it became apparent the Nazis weren't going to hold back the allied forces' push into Germany, many were able to plan their escape out of Europe through the aid of ODESSA. Thousands of

Nazi war criminals reportedly made their escape to South America, with Argentina seeming to be the most popular destination since there was an active Nazi political movement already in place there. The Argentine leader, Juan Peron, wasn't only an admirer of Hitler, but also sympathetic to the members of the Nazi regime who were being accused of, and tried for, war crimes and crimes against humanity.

Once inside the borders of countries such as Argentina, the fleeing Nazi war criminals found a safe haven and were allowed to live normal lives, although usually under an alias. Such escaped Nazis included the likes of the infamous Adolf Eichmann and Josef Mengele.

Adolf Eichmann had been in charge of the transportation of hundreds of thousands of Jews to extermination camps to be gassed in what was known as "The Final Solution," which was the Nazis' code name for the extermination of the Jews. Although Eichmann was captured initially by the U.S. Army after the war, he was using the alias Otto Eckmann and his true identity was successfully hidden from his captors. He was kept alive until he escaped and eventually made his way to Argentina... most likely with aid from ODESSA.

There he lived a peaceful, normal life under the alias Ricardo Klement for ten years doing various jobs until he was recognized by someone. His whereabouts soon became known to the Israel intelligence Agency "Mossad." After several years of planning, Mossad agents laid a trap for Eichmann and on May 11, 1960, on his way home from work, he was captured and hidden away in a safe house from Argentine authorities until he could be smuggled out of the country to Israel, and tried for his actions during the war.

The entire operation was almost straight out of a spy novel: Mossad agents dressed Eichmann up as an airline crew member and drugged him, so he appeared to be drunk, to get past Argentine authorities. Two stops later, Adolf Eichmann was in Israel to face trial for his crimes. After a long, fourteen-week trial, Eichmann was convicted, sentenced to death, and was hanged on May 31, 1962.

Mossad also tried to capture Josef Mengele, better known as "The Angel of Death," but the capture of Eichmann alerted Mengele, and he was able to evade them. He had been an officer in the *Schutzstaffel* (Protection Squadron) commonly known as the SS and a physician at the concentration camp, Auschwitz. It was there that he earned his nickname since it was he who decided who would be sent to the gas chamber and who would be left alive long enough to endure his sadistic experiments.

Although Mengele was never brought to justice for his horrific actions during the war, the fact that his cohort Eichmann was nabbed and later hanged left Mengele constantly looking over his shoulder. Living as a hunted man but never brought to justice, he finally met his demise as he drowned while swimming in the Atlantic on February 7, 1979.

With these being the kind of candidates that ODESSA helped escape to freedom, how or what could their possible involvement be with Grant's son? Hopefully this wasn't the same ODESSA that Tom had muttered, but what if it was?

Ironically, the OSS had also been responsible for recruiting Nazis after the war. "Operation Paperclip" was spawned into action in August of 1945. The intent of the operation was to recruit German scientists to come to work for the United States and keep them out of the hands of the Soviet Union or any other country who might want their services.

When Harry Truman launched Operation Paperclip, the intent was to recruit the Germans who hadn't been Nazi activists but whose knowledge might be beneficial. Though that thought was commendable, the policy excluded several top scientists. A little cover-up here and a little cover-up there and this problem was circumnavigated. The next thing you know, the United States had Nazi war criminals on the payroll. Had Truman stuck to his original values and not recruited any of the German scientists who were indeed Nazis, some projects like the United States rocket program would've been delayed for several years.

While all of this was water under the bridge now, why would an organization like ODESSA still be in existence? And even if they were, what might be their agenda? These thoughts had Grant not only troubled, but stumped.

Tom had also mentioned S.O.J., which was obviously someone or something of extreme importance. An individual under a hypnotic program to self-destruct rather than talk about it was something neither Grant nor Butch had ever seen before. What may have troubled Grant the most though, was when Tom said something about Ty being "special." Special how? Either he didn't know or didn't say, but just that someone in ODESSA thought he was special.

As they waited for the effects of the drug to wear off, Grant retrieved his laptop from his bag and inserted the DVD of the Union Station parking lot that the security guard had been so accommodating to make a copy of for him. Ty had parked his car in the lot on a Friday and didn't get back until that Sunday afternoon, so even playing it on fast forward was going to take some time.

Making himself comfortable, Grant watched the video and matched up the date and time that he figured Ty would've arrived at the station in order get on the train to D.C. He watched for Ty's car, and after only a couple of minutes, he spotted it come through the gate. Now it was only a matter of seeing where Ty parked, and the video stakeout would begin.

As Grant watched the video on triple speed, Butch only had to tell Tom to be quiet once, which was enough to keep him from interrupting Grant's focus. Even though Grant and Butch both half expected it to be none other than Tom who was spying on Ty, there were still others who'd been involved.

The question that Grant had to keep asking himself now was, what might any leftover remnants of the Nazi war machine want with his son? Hopefully, the ODESSA that they had literally drug out of Tom was something entirely different than the infamous ODESSA of World War II. The thought that there might still be some of those war criminals left in the world was bad enough, let alone that they might want something with Ty.

Several more minutes went by, and then Grant perked up and paused the video. Rewinding it slightly, he played it again, only this time it was on half speed. There it was, what he'd been looking for: someone walking over to Ty's car. Zooming in to get a close up and expecting to see Tom emerging from the camera's blind spot left Grant scratching his head. Not only was it *not* Tom, it wasn't even a man. The person who left the flier on Ty's car was a young, blonde female.

CHAPTER 31

TY HAD ONLY slept about an hour on the long flight to Cairo, and he was starting to run low on energy. It was quickly renewed, however, as the morning sun lit up the Great Pyramid of Giza. It was even more magnificent than he'd imagined, with smaller pyramids scattered everywhere. Seeing its photo in books and on websites didn't do the real view justice.

Cairo was nestled in the lush green, just south of the start of the famous Delta of the Nile. North of Cairo the delta fanned out several times wider, resembling an enormous slice of green pizza before dumping into the Mediterranean Sea. Located on top of the desert sands of the Giza Plateau, just west of Cairo, were the three most prominent pyramids in Egypt. They're lined up in a northeast direction, with the world-famous Great Pyramid closest to the city, looming over as if it were the gatekeeper of the Delta.

Ty had read that the Great Pyramid was actually eight-sided instead of just four, but it wasn't evident from his first opportunity to view this incredible site. It sounded like the only time it was apparent was during the equinoxes, when the north and south sides would cast just enough shadow to reveal that each side was actually two, with the crease running from the top straight down the center of each side. This little known feature wasn't discovered in modern times until it was noticed in a photograph taken by a British Royal Air Force pilot flying over in 1940.

With the Great Pyramid being the only one in Egypt constructed of eight sides—and the fact that it would've been far less difficult to build with only four sides—it was even more of a mystery why the engineers chose eight. The controversies of the Great Pyramid's purpose will most likely go on forever, but the more Ty read about the oddities of it, the more he was leaning away from the idea that is was built to be a tomb. After all, if it were a tomb, why wasn't there ever a mummy or any of the kings' possessions found inside? Sure, it could've been looted, but tombs also had hieroglyphs all over the walls commemorating the dead king, yet the Great Pyramid didn't have any... why not?

There were several other theories of what its purpose may have been, ranging from a power plant to just a giant grain storage bin. Although the idea of being a tomb didn't sit well with him, neither did the theory about it being an ancient power plant or grain bin either, so... what might its purpose have been? And why would anyone go to such great lengths to construct such an imposing structure? His imagination started to run wild as he tried to visualize what might've been happening here thousands of years ago.

Looking over at Celeste, he could see she was still in a state of slumber after falling asleep somewhere over the Atlantic. During their conversation before she fell asleep, it was apparent she didn't share his fascination with who might've built some of the megalithic constructions, including the Great Pyramid. Ty thought this was a little strange considering her major was archaeology. Come to think of it, he just realized he actually didn't know what her major was. Suddenly, he was astonished that he knew so little about her or her past. It seemed as though every time he started to ask her something personal, she'd give only the vaguest of answers before adroitly turning the topic of conversation back around to him. Maybe she was simply a private person, but he had two weeks to get to know her, and he was going to take advantage of every minute of it (that is, if his obsession with the builders of these ancient wonders didn't get in the way). As it was, he was somewhat torn between looking at the beauty outside his window or in the seat beside him.

The Giza Plateau and all the pyramids which stood atop of it were still in view, but were now a little behind them. He could see that the plane was passing directly over the Nile and approaching the airport.

As the aircraft started to configure for its approach, the noise from the landing gear being extended brought Celeste suddenly back to life. It was obvious she'd been in a deep sleep. "Wow," she said as she rubbed her eyes and looked out the window, "are we there already?"

"Yeah, you just missed flying past the pyramids, but I'm sure we'll have seen them so much by the time we leave, we'll be sick of things shaped like a triangle," Ty joked awkwardly.

She smiled back and said, "I don't know, they're pretty amazing" leaning over him to look out the window.

"So, who's going to pick us up, or are we gonna have to get a car and try to navigate on our own?" Ty said curiously, thinking he should've inquired about the arrangements a little earlier.

"Oh, we'll have a ride all right," she said. "Dr. Eisenberg made all of the arrangements long ago. I don't know where the hotel is or who's actually picking us up, but I know we'll have a driver and a guide the entire time, so at least we won't have to worry about that."

The Boeing 747's wings leveled out as it turned for the final approach, and pitched down as the pilots extended the rest of the flaps. It was only a few more seconds, and finally, they were on the ground in Egypt.

Although the flight past the pyramids seemed to take Ty back in time some several thousand years, seeing the modern airport terminal brought him back to the twenty-first century even quicker. From the air, it was obvious Cairo was a huge, metropolitan city, even though it seemed somewhat secluded with the desert abutting either side of the lush Nile River area. However, once experienced from back on the ground, the sheer scope of the metropolis was staggering. It was as though they were right back in a sprawled-out mega city like Los Angeles.

The one thing that made it apparent they weren't in the States anymore was that the majority of the people deplaning were of Middle Eastern descent. There were plenty of westerners as well, and luckily the signs in the terminal were also in English, so retrieving luggage and making the trek through customs wasn't difficult.

Ty and Celeste had no more than cleared customs when they saw an Arab man with dark, curly hair and large brown eyes holding a sign with "Dr. Eisenberg students" written on it. Looking at each other, then again at the man holding the sign, Celeste was the first to speak, "We're Dr. Eisenberg's students. I am Celeste Peterson and this is Ty Larson."

"Ah, good, good, I am Murshid, you follow me, car outside." Ty exchanged a look of relief with Celeste, happy to hear he spoke pretty good English only somewhat broken but with a thick accent. The man turned to leave, motioning to them with a little universal sign language.

Ty and Celeste followed Murshid through the remainder of the terminal. He seemed to be walking at a pretty fast pace weaving in and out of the seemingly endless crowd, eventually reaching the parking lot. Waiting for them was an old, compressed-looking tiny car that appeared to be something out of the 1950s. It actually looked awfully similar to Ty's dad's favorite TV sleuth's car from the series of "Columbo," only this one had four doors. He didn't have a clue as to what kind of car it was until Murshid went to the hood—which turned out to be the trunk—and opened it, taking their bags and tossing them inside as if they were dirty laundry. When he slammed the trunk shut, Ty saw the emblem *"Renault Dauphine"* swinging from side to side, as it was only half connected. Something about the little pint-sized car made him think to himself that Napoleon had left a lasting impression in Egypt after all.

Once out of the parking lot, it didn't take long for Ty and Celeste to make sure their seat belts were fastened tight, and it was obvious the horn worked well in their car as the driver (along with everyone else on the road) had no problems using it freely as he picked his way noisily through the busy Cairo streets. After a thirty-minute ride, and with only a couple of close calls involving other motorists and one pedestrian—who literally had to run for his life to keep from being run over—they were at their little hotel in downtown Cairo.

It was on a narrow side street, which was barely wide enough for their petite car to squeeze past the pedestrians, and like any typical large city, just about every square inch of real estate had a structure of some kind on it. The location of their hotel was no exception. Sandwiched between two little shops were their living quarters for the next few days, the "Akhenaten Inn." It was a small four-story building. Nearly everyone in the area appeared to be of Arab descent and from the dress of the women most likely Muslims as well, which was to be expected.

Ty walked in the front door and could see it was obvious the building was old, but it looked clean and well cared for. There wasn't a lobby per se, just a small counter that the innkeeper sat behind. At the opposite end was a staircase and a hallway lined with rooms separating the two halves of the building.

Murshid carried in their bags and spoke to the clerk in Arabic pointing to Ty and Celeste. The clerk looked them both over nodding, reached beneath the counter, and took out two keys placing them on the countertop. Murshid handed them each a key and in his broken English, told them he'd be there at 9:00 in the morning to pick them up to begin their tour. Ty reached in his pocket and took out one of the Egyptian pounds that he had exchanged for back at the airport for their driver, but Murshid refused saying, "No, no, it taken care of... I see you in morning." With that, their only contact was out the door and out of sight.

The clerk pointed toward the stairs showing them the way to their rooms speaking even more unintelligible English than the driver. Looking at each other then back at the clerk, they thanked him and proceeded up the stairs. When they found their rooms on the third floor, Celeste looked at Ty and said, "I don't know about you, but I need to lie down and recover from that long flight. Should we just meet downstairs in the morning at 9:00?"

"Sure," he said knowing he probably wasn't going to be able to sleep right now. "I'll see you then."

Celeste smiled at him and turned to unlock the door to her room, which was across the hall from Ty's. Declining his offer of help with her bags, she dragged them into the room, letting the door close behind her.

Ty's room was small with just a twin bed, a small desk and chair, and a bathroom. There wasn't a TV, but there was a small radio on the desktop. He looked at his watch, which he'd changed over to Cairo time when the plane had landed; it was only 3:30 in the afternoon.

After taking a moment to reflect on how his spur-of-the-moment trip had transpired, he realized he still hadn't told his folks what had happened and where he was. The only message he had left for his dad was that he had some great news, not knowing at the time where they were going for sure. Not only that, he wanted to tell his dad about the man he'd seen in his apartment building. Whoever he was, he'd also been at the CIA headquarters back at Langley. Maybe he was somebody working with his dad but Ty needed to find out, so he took out his phone... only to find it was completely dead.

That was odd. It had a full charge when he left and it had been turned off the entire flight. He remembered Celeste had tried to use it before they left, but she said she couldn't get any service, not that the battery was dead. Surely whatever little conspiracy he'd been tangled up with back home couldn't have followed him halfway across the world... or could it?

MEANWHILE, INSIDE WHAT was thought to be an abandoned hanger on a deserted airstrip in the remote northwestern territory of Iraq not far from the Syrian border, a small fleet of heavy twin-engine C-123s and a CH-47 Chinook helicopter that looked like they'd been resurrected straight from the Vietnam War awaited a call that would put the mission the crew had been training for in motion.

CHAPTER 32

WITH NOTHING TO do at the hotel and still being wide awake, Ty made the short walk over to the Cairo museum. Standing in front of a display of ancient artifacts that were thousands of years old was fascinating enough, but the stonework which lay just inches away, separated from Ty's touch by only a thin pane of glass was also rather mind boggling. While the artifacts were well worth seeing, Ty read that the ancient stonework unearthed nearby had something very unique about it: machine marks, undeniable machine marks. Vases, bowls, and intricate platters made from solid granite and other hard stones had visible signs of what appeared to be lathe marks on the inside surfaces.

Other than that, all the pieces looked as though they had come out of a mold, the workmanship was impeccable. But the lathe marks? Was it possible the ancients had such tools? If so, none had ever been found… at least none that anyone had made public. The bizarre thing was, the level of craftsmanship of the older pieces exceeded that of the more recent. How was this possible?

Hadn't mankind gradually progressed over the years? It seemed as though it was just the opposite. Over and over again, like a broken record, this seemed to be the case. But how? Why?

There was one more artifact on display at the Cairo museum that he absolutely had to see before he left. After about fifteen minutes of admiring other treasures, he finally found it... the mysterious Tri-Lobed disc. Not only was the method of construction of this object unknown, so was its purpose. The Tri-Lobed Disc was circular, somewhat resembling a chariot wheel, but it was made from schist—a very fragile and delicate rock—so it was obviously not a wheel at all. It was about two feet in diameter and, upon further inspection, looked like a plate with a hole, or hub, in the middle. The "plate" was separated into thirds and the three lobes seemed to be "folded" toward the center, leaving a void where each fold had been. There was a rim around the entire perimeter, giving it a slight resemblance to a steering wheel.

Naturally there were several theories of what the object was, none of which really made much sense to Ty, so what could it have possibly been used for? In addition, it also looked as if the rock it was made from would've had to have been soft like clay before being molded into its current shape, but that wasn't possible. Was it?

As he was staring at the object, out of the blue an idea hit him. What about some kind of frequency resonator? With sound and vibrations being such a key part in his theories so far, was it possible that this object might've been used to create some kind of useful frequency?

Just then he noticed a young Arab boy watching him from across the room. Oddly enough, when Ty made eye contact with the boy, he started coming toward him as if he knew him. *He must be selling something,* Ty instinctively thought as the boy approached.

"Would you buy gum?" the boy said in broken English, looking at the disc then back at Ty with a wide eyed, questioning stare.

"How much?" Ty thought, unable to resist helping the youngster.

The boy looked around as if to see if anyone was watching then said, "One U.S. dollar, please."

Ty took out his wallet to retrieve one of the few dollars he hadn't exchanged, and he no more than opened his wallet when the boy grabbed it and took off running through the crowd toward the door. In a state of shock for only an instant before reacting, Ty instinctively took off after the boy only a few steps behind. The kid was fast and much smaller and was able to dart through the museum patrons without much hindrance. Ty yelled at the boy to stop, but he knew he was wasting his breath; the boy was out of the museum in a few seconds.

Bolting out the door in close pursuit, Ty was relieved to see the crowd outside had thinned a bit. Though the sun had gone down, the street was lit enough that he wouldn't lose sight of the child. Before he could reach him, however, the boy suddenly darted off the main street into an alley.

Even though Ty was right behind him, just as he got close enough to grab the pint-sized thief, three large men emerged from the shadows knocking him to the ground. Two of them restrained him while the third shoved a piece of cloth in his mouth and forced a burlap bag over his head. As strong and athletic as Ty was, the element of surprise (and the fact that it was three against one) was enough for his assailants to subdue him quickly. In a split second his wrists and ankles were bound, rendering him helpless.

Although he couldn't see or say anything, Ty still had his hearing. If he only understood Arabic. He could, however, hear a car approaching and come to a stop, followed by the opening of doors and more Arabic speakers. His heart was pounding faster and faster as fear was starting to overtake him at his core. Then surprisingly, and somewhat carefully, he was picked up from the ground and placed in the trunk. One of the men from the car seemed to be in charge from the tone of their conversations. Whatever their plans were for him, he was literally and figuratively, along for the ride. While they drove, the fear racing through Ty's body was immense as he wondered why he had been targeted and what their plans were for him. *Could this be some kind of retaliation with the CIA?*

Finally, the car came to a stop somewhere away from the sounds of civilization. He heard the driver speaking to someone for a brief moment, then they began moving again. The car was in motion for only a minute or two before coming to another stop, and this time the engine was shut off. He could hear the car doors open, and the sounds of the men getting out, followed by the squeak of the trunk and the rush of fresh air as it was opened. Ty's adrenaline was fueling his fear, not knowing what to expect, then once again, rather oddly, he was gently removed from the trunk. He was carried a short distance on flat ground, then down several steps before he heard a sound similar to a cell door open. They proceeded to carry him down even more stairs into what... a cave? That's what it sounded like by the way their voices were muffled.

Thoughts of other hostage situations he'd read about came to mind as his kidnappers continued carrying him, finally setting him down on a hard-packed surface. After a few moments of arguing between the kidnappers, the voice of the one Ty thought might be in charge snapped at the others, quieting them as their voices receded along with their footsteps.

Just when he thought he was alone and had heard the last of them, he heard footsteps coming closer. A voice in rather good English, but with what sounded like a thick German accent whispered in his ear. "Say anything of this and the girl gets hurt. Nod if you understand."

Ty did as the man said.

"Good, now I want you to count to one hundred, then you are free to leave. Remember, say anything, and I assure you that you'll regret it. Understand?"

Again, Ty nodded and his hands were cut free.

Just as he'd been told, he counted to one hundred then waited a little longer before he moved a muscle. With his heart still beating wildly, he sat up, pulled off the hood, and removed the cloth from his mouth. After taking a few deep breaths and seeing that he was, indeed, in a cave, he untied his feet and slowly got up, being as quiet as possible. He looked on the ground in front of him and was surprised to see his wallet lying there at his feet. Upon picking it up and after a quick look through, he was even more surprised that nothing had been taken. Whatever had just transpired, it was obvious it wasn't about his money.

Realizing he wasn't hurt, he looked around listening carefully. All he could hear over the pounding of his heart was the hum of the lighting system. Looking around, he could see that he was at the end of a long cave that appeared to be carved out of solid rock. It looked to be twice as wide as a car with the ceiling about double that in height, and there were off shoots on both sides as far as the eye could see. Although he wasn't sure where the exit was, he needed to get out, and there was only one way to go.

With his heart racing, he no more than took a couple of steps when he came to the first off shoot and was stunned at what he saw. Sunken about ten feet below the level on which he stood was a room carved out of the solid rock that was the size of a two car garage, but that's not what made him freeze in his tracks and stare in awe… it was what was *in* the room.

Sitting on the floor was an enormous rectangular box that appeared to be made out of solid granite. The box itself was approximately seven feet wide, ten feet long, and seven or eight feet tall with a solid lid that was around three feet thick. The lid was slid back a couple of feet, exposing the twelve-inch thick walls of the empty box. The sides looked as though they'd been polished smooth with hieroglyphs etched on them. The workmanship was flawless... and then the reality of it hit him. This was most likely his first actual viewing of some of the ancient unexplainable stonework he'd been reading about for the past few months. In all of his research, though, he'd never seen anything like *this* before. *What was this place?*

He walked up the main corridor to the next bay and was surprised to see another box, then another. Now the fear that had once consumed him had been pushed aside and replaced with awe. He started to walk faster to see that every bay he approached contained an enormous stone box. *What on earth were they for? And who had carved them so perfectly and for that matter, how in the world had they moved them to their current resting spots?* The cave looked barely wide enough to fit them through.

Although not forgotten, the fact that he'd been kidnapped and brought here against his will was not the foremost thing on his mind at the moment. Instead, his head was spinning with amazement at what he was seeing. *How could any of this be possible?* He progressed slowly down the cave, marveling at each humungous box that he came upon.

Finally Ty approached an empty bay followed by a long stretch of cave without bays and a path that forked. If he went straight ahead, he guessed he'd see more stone boxes, so he took the fork to the left, eager to see what other treasures might lie in wait. After a long, straight stretch of nothing but cave, he came to a ninety-degree bend to the right. Squinting, he saw in the distance some kind of obstruction—he got closer and recognized it as another stone box, seemingly abandoned in transit. There was obviously enough room for it to fit through the passageway, but there wasn't much room to spare. He barely squeezed by it to find yet another object farther down the corridor: one of the lids. That was odd. What possibly could've happened to make the workers stop midstream and leave the gargantuan objects lying in the corridor? Whatever the reason, it must've been borderline catastrophic for them to completely abandon their mission, never to return.

It was difficult to keep track of the passing of time in the endless stone corridors, but Ty thought around thirty minutes had passed as he walked steadily onward, finding more bays with stone boxes. He counted twenty-four in all, along with several empty bays as well. His awe at the sight of the mysterious objects helped to hold at bay the panic of his unknown situation. Still, it was with relief when he finally made his way up and out of the underground maze. The relief was short lived, however, as he emerged from the cave only to find he was in the middle of the dark, empty desert.

What the hell was this place? Those lids had appeared to weigh several tons, so whoever or *whatever* was put inside was meant to stay put... but why? On top of the wonder of this place, there still was the matter of: who were his kidnappers? He had many questions about the events that just occurred, but right now he needed to find his way back to the hotel.

Ty started the walk toward the glow of the neon lights off in the distance. With the equivalent of about twenty U.S. dollars in his pocket and the address to his hotel on his room key, he thought he'd be able to hail a cab as he got closer, but whoever was behind this was definitely gnawing away at him. Even though the kidnappers had let him go without harming him, what was their motive for bringing him to see this mysterious place housing the enormous stone boxes? Whatever the reason... he didn't know, but there assuredly was one. He remembered the last man had spoken with a German accent and that too was weighing heavily on his mind.

What Ty *did* know is that two things were going to be different from here on out. One: he was going to have eyes in the back of his head. And two: if anyone attacked him again, they wouldn't escape without knowing they'd made a huge mistake.

CHAPTER 33

EVEN AFTER ALL the excitement of his first night in Egypt, Ty somehow managed to get a few hours of much needed sleep and felt surprisingly rested. The question of whoever was behind his little "field trip" and why he had been chosen as the lucky participant wouldn't soon be forgotten. Hopefully his newfound sense of security would hold true. Judging by the captors' treatment of him, it seemed grossly obvious they had no desire to hurt him or the damage would've already been done. And he still hadn't figured out why they'd wanted him to see the mysterious cave in the first place. He was going to have to find a way to contact his dad, but considering the itinerary planned for Celeste and him today, getting to the bottom of his abduction was going to have to wait till they got back to their hotel.

There were several different sights as options on the agenda, and when he met Celeste in the lobby that morning, she had actually insisted that he choose what they should see. It didn't take long for Ty to find a starting point to their day. The obvious place to begin was on the horizon, the Sphinx and the pyramids atop the Giza Plateau, so that's where Murshid would take them first.

As they made the climb out of the Nile River basin and onto the Giza Plateau with the Sphinx and the pyramids coming into view, he could only imagine what a grand sight it must've been when they were first constructed. For them to still be standing after so long was incredible, not to mention the shroud of mystery that still engulfed the landmarks even to this day. What, exactly, would the site have looked like thousands of years ago? Why would some-one want to build such massive structures in the first place? Ty was consumed with questions as Murshid pulled the car into a parking spot for the Sphinx along with the Sphinx Temple and the Valley Temple, which sat at the front paws of the giant beast.

Just as he'd read earlier, the head of the Sphinx looked as though it was out of proportion with the rest of the body. It seemed to be way too small, even after thousands of years of ero-sion which had whittled the body down from its original enormous stature. This brought up another thought… the age of the Sphinx.

Most Egyptologists date it to be about 4,500 years old, but the problem with that timeframe is the weathering on the body. Sev-eral geologists examined it and have come to the conclusion that the deep cuts weren't caused by sand and wind but from heavy rainfall. The dilemma with a birth date of 4,500 years ago is there hasn't been that kind of rain in the area since around 8,000 BC—10,000 years ago! So, if indeed it was rain that caused the erosion of the Sphinx, it would have to be at least that old. Ty was no ge-ologist, but as he stood there awed by the ancient craftsmanship, it looked to him as though it was possible a large runoff of rain could've been the cause of the deep fissures on the sides.

As for the conventional theory, most Egyptologists believe the weathering was from years of sand blowing into it. However, the

Great Sphinx (otherwise known as "The Terrifying One") had been buried up to its neck in sand, so if that was the case, then how could blowing sand have been the reason for the erosion? Further, the erosion marks appeared to be the same on all sides... wouldn't the side facing the prevailing winds be much worse than the others if that had been the cause?

The fact that the human head was out of proportion to the body (being much smaller) raised some questions as well. Was the original head meant to be something else? Perhaps a lion? That was the belief of some who have studied other ancient civilizations' infatuations with astronomical alignments. If the original head was that of a lion, then might it have been constructed when it would have been staring directly at the constellation of Leo? Due to the natural wobble of the earth known as precession, the last time the Sphinx was facing Leo would've been around 10,500 BC... 12,500 years ago! If this were the case, not only would it account for it being in existence to endure the period of heavy rainfall in the region, it would also give stock to all who believed there'd been an advanced civilization years before any of the history books were willing to admit.

Another theory Ty had read during his research was that maybe the body of the Great Sphinx wasn't of a lion at all, but that of a jackal, which represented the God of Anubis. While nowhere in Egyptian texts was the Sphinx as we know it mentioned (which was one reason why dating it was so hard), there are several places where a giant Anubis was referenced guarding over Giza.

As Ty stood there wondering what the area might've looked like thousands of years ago, the hollow echo of a distant blast from the direction of Cairo reached him, followed by a plume of smoke that bellowed into the air. Some Egyptians weren't happy with the current regime and there'd been talk of changes that might usher in violence and most likely wouldn't be pleasant for visiting foreigners. Although they'd been assured any unsafe environment was months away, the blast in the distance gave everyone a quick reality check and there was a sudden push to move to the next site. Ty noticed that not only were most of the tourists a little on edge now, but their guide also seemed concerned and insisted that they skip both of the ancient temples in front of the Sphinx and proceed directly to the Great Pyramid.

Ty was still shaken up from the incident the previous night, but a plot to overthrow the Egyptian president was a situation he didn't want to get tangled up in. This thought jogged his memory that he really needed to get a hold of his father. As a force of habit, he reached into his pocket and took out his cell phone, only to realize it was still dead as a doornail. He looked over at Celeste as Murshid was leading them on the short walk to the last of the Seven Wonders of the World and asked, "Did you ever get your phone to work? Mine still seems to be dead."

She responded without taking her phone out. "Oh, my phone won't work over here. When I get a chance, I'll see if I can get that taken care of though."

Ty was about to ask their guide if he could borrow his phone, but the sight of the Great Pyramid in front of him was so surreal it seemed to suck all other thoughts right out of his head. All the pictures he'd seen of it didn't come close to what he was seeing now. The magnitude of the structure was simply overwhelming! As they got a little closer, a calmness came over him, along with a strange feeling that he'd been here before. *Déjà vu?* Probably brought on from all the research he'd been doing lately, but unsettling nonetheless.

Again, Ty drifted into a time eons ago when the civilization on the Giza Plateau was at its peak. It was almost magical imagining what it would've been like to see this mysterious culture in action: a civilization that carved and stacked millions of stones that were still here thousands of years later. Was it really possible that God-like beings had been involved in this enormous undertaking? Edgar Cayce had claimed some of the inhabitants of Atlantis had migrated here after the destruction of their homeland. Might there be some truth to Cayce's claims after all? Could it be this mysterious construction was designed and built by the people from Atlantis? It was still hard for him to believe he was actually entertaining the legitimacy of the ancient folklore that had been widely classified as nothing but pure fantasy. But fantasy or not, the wondrous site in front of them was as real as life itself... but what was it, really?

It wasn't until they were at the base of the Great Pyramid that Ty realized he'd let his guard down while his imagination had been running wild with visions of the past. Looking around, he now noticed several soldiers carrying AK-47s, and the realization of where he was gave him another shot of adrenaline, something that he wasn't only becoming accustomed to, but actually starting to like... maybe even crave. Was this the feeling that had motivated and inspired his father throughout his career at the Agency? Focusing once again, and a little mad at himself for dropping his guard, Ty spread his awareness to include everyone in sight. Was his career choice going to have him looking over his shoulder for the rest of his life? It was starting to seem very possible.

In his broken English, Murshid began unloading facts about the pyramid, all of which Ty had read before. He knew it was over 450 feet tall, 756 feet wide, was supposedly built as a tomb for the Pharaoh Cheops (also known as Khufu), and had been in existence since around 2,560 BC. Ty had his doubts about the latter two "facts." One thing was certain though: the Great Pyramid of Giza wasn't only regarded as the oldest of all of the pyramids on the plateau, but also the largest and most complex.

As he and Celeste were walking along the east side, admiring it along the way, and even though he knew the entrance was on the north side, he couldn't help but feel they were going the wrong way. Something in his core was telling him this wasn't the way to get inside. Strange, he'd never experienced these kinds of feelings—some kind of intuition—so strongly prior to the other day in the library.

Another blast echoed from downtown Cairo, causing them to pick up the pace as they now walked along the north wall. Without keeping abreast of the world news lately, Ty was uncertain if the violence was escalating faster than expected. If it was, it'd surely cut their trip short, which was something he didn't want to happen. Ty felt a thrill of excitement as the entrance loomed before him, all thoughts of violence and political unrest dwarfed by the anticipation of setting foot inside the ancient wonder.

CHAPTER 34

WITH THE RISE in violence in the area lately, not everyone was allowed inside the Great Pyramid. They were told they were fortunate, however, in that Dr. Eisenberg had made some good contacts during his travels as an archeologist. Murshid spoke only a few words in Arabic to the armed guards at the entrance before they stepped aside, allowing the three of them to pass. Grateful for the special treatment, Ty noticed the guards stop the next group of tourists behind them as they entered the ancient wonder. Odd... he had no idea his professor had such clout.

It was the breach port bored into the pyramid by Al Mamoun in 830 AD that was still used to access the inside. The monument was comprised of over two-and-a-half million limestone blocks weighing between two and seventy tons each. Al Mamoun was determined to reap the rewards of the kings' treasures that were traditionally left inside tombs, along with the mummified remains of the kings themselves. Even in 830 AD there had been tales of a north side entrance to the seemingly impenetrable structure, but the exact whereabouts of the front door was unknown. Al Mamoun thought the most logical place was in the center toward the bottom, which was where he had his men start chiseling.

Originally, the pyramid was covered with smooth, white lime-stone casing stones giving it a shiny finish that was said to have acted as a giant mirror that would've been so bright it could've been visible from the moon. Most all of the casing stones were stripped from the surface around 600 years ago by the Arabs and used to build Mosques and other buildings in the immediate area. However, nobody knew for sure what happened to the missing capstone of the Great Pyramid or even what it was made of. One theory was that it was solid gold and pilfered centuries ago, but there was no evidence to back that up.

The original entrance (which was just a little higher up the north wall and slightly off center to the left) was sealed with a piv-oting stone that was said to blend in so well with the casing stones that it was invisible when shut. Al Mamoun eventually tunneled his way into the descending passageway leading to the subterranean chamber, right at the juncture of the ascending passageway, which was plugged with three perfectly fitting granite blocks. From there, Momoun's workers had tunneled around the granite plugs giving them full access to all the chambers, but found absolutely nothing. There was no gold, jewels, statues, or even a mummy... nothing except for an empty, lidless box carved out of granite in the King's Chamber. Murshid was rattling off these facts as they worked their way through Al Mamoun's passage (that took months to dig out) toward the heart of the pyramid, droning in his broken English, which Ty was now used to.

Ty was surprised to learn when they finally made it to the junction of the original passageway, they weren't allowed access to the subterranean chamber. This really bothered him for some strange reason, and made no sense at all. Just then, he felt the same odd feeling as though he was being watched... by some kind of presence? It made no sense, but it was the same as he'd experienced back at the library only a few days ago. He gazed back into the blackness of the passageway. What was down there, and why did he have the feeling that someone was looking back at him through the darkness? Murshid reminded Ty they had to keep moving so he acknowledged with a nod, still wondering what was driving these feelings he had.

They proceeded around the granite plugs and up the ascending passage toward the Grand Gallery. Had it not been for the added handrails and the makeshift steps that were installed for the convenience of the tourists, the 124-foot climb up the steep slope would've been more challenging, something the early explorers would've had to contend with as well as carrying a light.

The thought of being inside quite possibly the oldest building on earth gave Ty the chills as he hunkered down and made his way up the backbreaking slope.

At the entrance to the Grand Gallery, they came to another juncture with a horizontal shaft taking off straight into the heart of the pyramid, which is where Murshid appeared to be taking them first.

Murshid offered lots of details as he mentioned that hidden chambers were thought to exist inside. In the five or six minutes it took to traverse the 127-foot passage to what was known as the Queen's chamber, Murshid had time to bring up all the different searches and methods used for locating hidden rooms: everything from cosmic ray probes, electromagnetic sounder, x-rays, ground-penetrating radar, electronic detectors to nothing more than hammers and chisels. There were indications of the undiscovered chambers behind these very walls, but for some reason, the Egyptian government put a stop to anything that seemed promising... except for the one that was right under Ty's feet.

In 1986, two Frenchmen with an electronic detector, found a cavity of three-by-five meters directly under the passageway he and Celeste were walking on now. The Frenchmen were allowed to drill a one-inch hole through the floor and found that the chamber was filled with quartz sand (also known as musical sand) from El Tur in southern Sinai, which was several hundred miles away. Why would they have brought sand in from that far away, only to seal it off for all eternity? Ty knew that quartz had special properties, some of which involved electricity. Could that possibly have been why it was placed here? It must've served some purpose, but what? And what else was hidden away in this ancient wonder that hadn't been found yet? If in fact it wasn't a tomb, then what the hell was it? What would've been so important that justified the time and effort to complete such an enormous project?

Just then the floor dropped down a step. They could almost stand up now, and after a little farther, they came to the Queen's Chamber. Of the three known chambers, the Queen's Chamber was the first one above ground level. The room was just a little larger than a one car garage, with about a twenty foot high double-pitched gable ceiling. There were two small air shafts about nine inches square (one on the north wall and one on the south wall), but they ended mysteriously way before the outside wall of the pyramid. On the east wall, there was a sixteen-foot high niche that was originally only three-and-a-half feet deep before some early explorers tunneled into it looking for (but not finding) a hidden room. It started out around seven feet wide at the floor level and tapered off to around three feet at the top of the indentation. According to Murshid, nobody knew what the niche's purpose was. Even the name of the chamber was misleading—the only reason for its name represented the Arab tradition that their queens were buried in tombs with gabled ceilings. Even though no mummified remains were ever found anywhere in the pyramid, over the years the name had stuck.

One strange thing Murshid told them, which Ty had never heard before, was that when the pyramid was finally broken into, there was a half-inch of salt encrusted on the walls of the Queen's and subterranean chambers, but to date it was a mystery as to how it got there. If there had been a global flood in the distant past, might the seawater have left a salty clue? What else would've caused a buildup of salt? This was something Ty knew he'd want to research when he returned home.

Although the temperature had been in the mid-seventies outside, it was quite a bit warmer inside, just as Murshid had previously told them it would be. As they were walking back to the ascending passageway toward the King's Chamber, Ty asked Murshid about the vertical shaft that went straight down from the junction of the two passageways.

"Ah yes, well shaft," Murshid said laughing a little, "Nobody know why was put there, but I think it back door put in secret by workers, so they come back and rob place."

Ty looked down the shaft thinking it made sense, but he had an odd feeling again that made him think it wasn't the whole story. Ty turned away and continued on just as the same eerie feeling of having been here before came over him again, and as strange as it sounded, he was starting to get used to it.

He looked up and recognized they were in the Grand Gallery again, halfway back to the King's Chamber. The Grand Gallery itself was an impressive hallway stretching half the length of a football field. It was close to seven feet wide and had a high twenty-eight foot ceiling. Like the niche in the Queen's chamber, the stones lining the walls were stacked with a couple inches of overhang every few feet, gradually getting narrower all the way to the top of the ceiling, giving it the appearance of an acoustic chamber.

Ty couldn't help himself. "Helloooooo," he sang in a long voice to see what kind of an effect the walls would have on sound waves.

The tone sounded perfect. The design seemed to mask his voice imperfections somehow. Was this just another coincidence or did sound have some significance with the design of the structure?

He was so caught up in the situation that the gradual increase in temperature didn't faze him in the least. Celeste, on the other hand, was visibly uncomfortable, futilely fanning her hand in front of her face like a menopausal woman at a Bob Seger concert. She was oddly not as enthralled with the moment like he was. Being able to stand up with the high ceiling made it much easier, but had it not been for Celeste's obvious discomfort he would've taken more time to study the giant hallway.

If there'd been any explosions in Cairo since they had entered the walls of this historical monument, surely they wouldn't have been aware of them. Then it dawned on him, if Armageddon was in progress at this very moment, anyone inside the pyramid would surely be safe. Was it possible this was nothing more than an ancient bunker?

As they drew near to the King's Chamber, the Grand Gallery came to an end with what was known as the Great Step, a six-by-three foot stair that had obviously been patched up recently to repair a groove worn in the center. What could've created such a groove? Murshid also pointed out that the step was *exactly* in line with the east-west axis. Metal handrails and a ladder had been fastened to the original stones to accommodate tourists, reminding him that although one might be safe from Armageddon in here, not so from the countless lawyers around the world.

They climbed up the Great Step to see the passageway leveled off, but they were going to have to duck down or even crawl to continue. After a short distance, the passage opened into an antechamber, and Ty noticed that the stone blocks used for construction had changed. He was just about to ask Murshid about it when their guide spoke up. "From here, for reason unknown, pyramid builders switch limestone blocks to red granite from quarry 800 kilometers away."

Granite had different properties than limestone. Was this the reason for the change? The antechamber also had been rigged up with four sliding slabs of granite hooked to ropes and pulleys and supposedly acted as another barrier from tomb robbers, but their real function was still being debated.

After crouching again for the remainder of the passageway they finally were able to stand up inside the King's Chamber. The room was rectangular in shape and about twice as long as the Queen's Chamber, with a flat ceiling almost twenty feet high. Like the Queen's Chamber, there were two air shafts on the north and south walls, but these actually extended to the outside of the pyramid. At the far end of the room was a rectangular box carved from solid granite.

"Ah yes," Murshid said noticing the look of awe on Ty's face. "Famous coffer. Only thing found inside Great Pyramid. There is story, when Al Mamoun's men got in, Queen's Chamber also had coffer. If true, no one knows where it go."

Something about this room gave Ty a chill as he walked over to the coffer and put his hand on the upper edge. One of the corners had been chipped out, and some of the rest of the edges were also chipped, but both the inside and outside edges were completely smooth... almost like they had been machined somehow.

As Ty examined the coffer, Murshid continued with more facts. "In 1790s, Napoleon here, he spent night in sarcophagus. It is said, when he come out from pyramid in morning, he very pale and shook up."

"Why?" Ty was curious. "What happened?"

"No one knows. He tell no one. Almost did on deathbed, but change mind at last minute and said, 'What is the use? No one would believe anyway.'"

Ty knew Napoleon had been in Egypt, but he'd never heard this story before. Murshid kept talking. "Then in 1930s maybe last person allowed spend night in Great Pyramid, Paul Brunton. He philosopher from Britain and known as *mystic*. Stay night in this room."

"What did he have to say about it?" Ty asked.

"Ahhhh," Murshid said staring at Ty. "I think he insane. He said he visited by evil spirits and *angelic-type beings* that tell him of secret chambers and that it built during *Atlantis*. Also, he had what you say... *out-of-body experience...* if you choose to believe."

Ty recalled how Edgar Cayce had also mentioned Atlantis in connection with this place. As he walked around the room he began to wonder about the probability of it... could there really have been a connection? *If only these walls could talk*, he thought. An extremely high content of quartz was just one of the unique qualities of granite. The texture of the stone still tingling in the tips of his fingers, Ty couldn't help but think maybe the memories of what went on here were actually locked into the walls somehow.

Just as he was realizing the craziness of his thought, Murshid said something that got his attention, but he had to ask him to say it again to make sure he heard what he thought.

"Is right," Murshid said as he began to repeat himself, "several early explorers all said same thing. Strike sarcophagus with hammer, sounds like bell."

A bell? Ty thought to himself. Was this a little more glue to his theory involving the properties of sound, or just another coincidence?

CHAPTER 35

IT'D BEEN THIRTY-SIX hours since Grant knew the whereabouts of his son. In that time he'd come to the realization that although Tom Bruiner wasn't who anyone had originally thought, he was definitely *not* their adversary. Grant had found out the hard way that Tom wasn't willing to discuss much of anything related to S.O.J. International, the front under which his organization operated, other than the group was very large and had members worldwide. He also didn't know why anyone thought Ty was special with regards to ODESSA's mission. But after hours of interrogation, it had become quite apparent that Tom Bruiner was actually an ally and willing to cooperate with Grant to help ensure the safety of his son.

According to Tom, everyone who'd been tailing Ty up until now had most likely been one of his colleagues and never had any intention of hurting him. There were, however, other players involved that were indeed connected to ODESSA. The one and the same that Grant had feared.

Apparently, someone with S.O.J. had infiltrated ODESSA several months before and became privy to a few details in a plan that somehow involved Ty as a pawn. Although what ODESSA's plan was wasn't known for sure, S.O.J. knew what the madman at the head of the previously thought dismantled organization's goal had once been… to find a living *Nephilim*!

Fortunately, Grant had also made headway on locating where his son had disappeared. Tom was able to point Grant in the right direction to Ty's last known whereabouts. He was in Cairo, Egypt… at least that's where he was as of twenty-four hours ago. Another bad thing for Grant (other than his son was halfway around the world) was that Tom's group, which Grant learned had members throughout the world, was now cut off from the chase. Someone (most likely ODESSA) had successfully thrown them off the trail. Even though S.O.J. knew he'd been in Cairo, this was the extent of their knowledge for now and any chance of them picking up his scent was no better than the CIA's at this point.

Although the complete details of ODESSA's plan were murky at best, what Tom thought was happening was enough for Grant to take immediate action. The information Tom had given them regarding the *Nephilim* and why ODESSA might want one sounded preposterous. There was more than enough evidence though, for Grant to convince his boss that it was time for the Agency to get involved, even if it was in a surveillance-only capacity. It wasn't until Grant had tried to track down Ty's professor, Allen Eisenberg, discovering he was nowhere to be found and that the National Archaeology Association hadn't sponsored any contest involving a trip to the Middle East, that he really started to believe the wild story Tom had told him. Grant had heard plenty of peculiar stories in his career with the CIA, but this one was by far the most outrageous. The questions now were, why had they chosen Ty for his unknown support with their quest, and how far was ODDESA willing to go to achieve their goal? And if they did… then what?

For now, the main thing was to get his son home safely, which meant contacting agents in Cairo and getting on a plane himself.

TY AND CELESTE were now in the car with Murshid heading back to the hotel, and seeing the Great Pyramid firsthand had been an exhilarating experience. It also raised more questions about the purpose of the structure. Murshid had told them the airshafts in the Queen's Chamber had been explored with a small robot in the 1990s. What was discovered wasn't only that the shafts ended before making it to the outside but that they were plugged by a small stone door with two pieces of protruding copper that resembled doorknobs. What was on the other side? In recent years the Egyptian government had placed extreme restrictions on access to the pyramid. It sounded to Ty they were trying to hide something.

In early photographs of the King's Chamber there had been a fairly large piece of broken granite lying on the floor next to the coffer. Where had it come from and why had it been removed? It had also appeared that a piece of stone in the floor had been missing. It was plugged now, causing Ty to wonder if it was covering something, another passageway perhaps. If so, where did it lead? The coffer itself looked like it had been tampered with also. Instead of sitting loose on the floor as it did in early photographs, now it looked to be cemented in place. Why? There definitely appeared to be more to the Great Pyramid than meets the eye, but what secrets was it hiding?

One of the stories Murshid told them about the coffer was that it held the Ark of the Covenant at one time. According to the measurements of the Ark given in the Bible, it would've fit all right. Might that have been the purpose of this ancient wonder... to be an enormous vault? But then again, the Ark of the Covenant was said to possess some strange unearthly powers, so maybe the pyramid's purpose was much more.

The entire time Ty had been touring the Great Pyramid, he kept getting the strangest, eerie feeling that he'd been there before. *Was that a common experience of most visitors?* he wondered.

Again he was daydreaming about the potential possibilities of what the pyramid might've been when his trance was broken by Murshid answering his phone, speaking in Arabic. After only a brief conversation with whoever was on the other end, a sense of urgency seemed to come over Murshid as he stepped on the gas pedal. He explained as he drove that his haste was because the local violence had escalated and the threat of a possible coup was going to make the city unsafe for foreigners. The strange thing was it almost sounded like he was speaking with a different accent now, not Arabic or English, but something different that Ty couldn't quite put his finger on. Almost... German? It couldn't be. It must just be his imagination... maybe paranoia from his experience last night.

Regardless, Murshid said it'd be better to leave Cairo for the time being, at least until things settled down. So for now, he told them, he'd drive them back to their hotel so they could get their belongings and travel to another archeological site. When Ty asked Celeste where she wanted to go, she shrugged her shoulders and replied, "Honestly, the pyramids were what I most wanted to see, and Eisenberg knew that, so I feel like I already got to choose one. You can pick our next place."

Oddly enough she didn't seem at all nervous about the situation with the escalating violence either. It seemed strange that she showed no signs of panic, at least none Ty could see.

She'd been hard to figure out. Back at school, she'd always been a tad flirtatious with him, but now she seemed different. She wasn't cold, but definitely not playful in the least. Maybe it was because he'd been so caught up in the archeological wonderland instead of her. Whatever it was, something had changed about her and the distance she'd created between the two of them was hard to understand.

Anyway, he had to figure out where they were going next. Murshid had given him a map of the entire Middle East and told him to pick their next locale "please try stay about 800 kilometers," he told Ty. Before Ty had a chance to look at the map very closely, they were pulling into their hotel.

Murshid parked in front and went with them to help carry their bags. Ty hadn't unpacked anything the night before (not that he brought much), so gathering his stuff up was quite easy. Out in the hall he was amazed to see that Celeste was ready with her bag in hand. "Wow... that was quick!" He hadn't had much experience with women, but the little he did know was that it usually took them longer to get ready, so for Celeste to beat him out to the hall kind of took him by surprise.

Murshid hurried them downstairs and out to the car telling them their checkout with the front desk was all taken care of and making an odd joke at the expense of the seriousness of the situation. Although he kept assuring them they were in no danger, it almost sounded like he didn't believe his own words, as he rushed them out to the car. Carelessly tossing their bags into the trunk like dirty laundry again, he slammed their doors shut behind them and in no time was behind the wheel racing back onto the road as though he was going to be late for happy hour somewhere.

As Murshid pulled out into traffic, they narrowly missed a collision with a black Cadillac Escalade with dark tinted windows speeding into the courtyard of the very hotel they had just left. Ty noticed Murshid checking his rearview mirror as he sped away, then shook his head, wondering how anyone ever survived traffic in this country, and hastily fastened his seatbelt.

CHAPTER 36

NEVER IN A million years did Ty think he'd get to see the Baalbek ruins in person, but here he was, staring in awe at the largest stacked carved stones in the world. Although their trip to Lebanon had been unexpected, it turned out to be a nice surprise and very relaxing.

After finally getting a chance to look at the map that Murshid had given him back in Cairo, it hadn't taken long for Ty to figure out where he wanted to go next. It just so happened that the most intriguing ancient ruins on the planet were now only about 800 kilometers away in Baalbek, Lebanon. They were allowed to leave the country, Murshid said, as long as they had their paperwork in order. To Ty's elation, and thanks to Dr. Eisenberg's insistence early in class, this had been taken care of a couple of months ago.

They had driven west from Cairo, away from the Delta of the Nile and out through the barren desert, eventually coming to the coast of the Mediterranean Sea. They ended up at the ritzy resort area of Marina El Alamein where a private yacht was waiting for them with all the comforts of home. They were told that the National Archaeology Association had members throughout the world who were more than willing to help students with projects such as theirs, and fortunately for them a willing member was here with a boat and the time to take them to Lebanon.

Ty caught up on much needed sleep on their journey to Baalbek and was feeling energized again. Now he was ready for what lay ahead. The new scenery left him speechless. Some of the ruins were of Heliopolis, which was built by Alexander the Great in fourth century BC in honor of Zeus. The most recent ruins (which included the Temple of Jupiter) were credited to the Romans, but according to local folklore, the original construction was built by none other than Adam and Eve's son, Cain. Could there be even a remote possibility of truth to this legend? Might Ty actually be gazing upon something that had been constructed shortly after the dawn of mankind?

Ty remembered reading a story of how Baalbek got its name, and according to the local legends, it was named after the Canaanites deity, known as Baal. Ancient wisdom, passed down by the local people, also had it that the largest of the stones were erected by a race of giants after a Great Flood. Ty thought that, while interesting, it didn't make any sense. *After* the Great Flood? How could this be true if the Creator had caused the Great Flood to rid the earth of the troublesome half-breeds? It was becoming obvious things had been covered up, but why?

It was apparent that the stone wall captivating the small crowd, including Ty, had been constructed in various stages based on the different stonework in the individual tiers. At the very bottom were three rows of very weathered smaller blocks that appeared to be roughly five feet square. On top of these was a row of very weathered larger blocks that were around ten feet high and close to thirty feet long, all with a beveled edge. Stacked atop the beveled stones was a row of three even larger blocks known as the trilithon that were probably fifteen feet tall and sixty feet long and featured substantial weathering. At the very top were several rows of much smaller blocks that appeared to be hardly weathered at all.

If the latest-known construction was completed by the Romans between 64 BC and 312 AD, then judging by the difference in weathering of the enormous foundation blocks they sat upon, it was apparent that a very long time had passed between building phases. The big question was, *how much time?* he wondered. What was civilization like all those years ago? And true to everything he'd read, the older construction seemed more advanced than the newer. Time and time again, this was the same story. Unless the wall was built from the top down, which it obviously wasn't, then what possible reason would there be for the older workmanship to be that much better? And what could possibly have happened to impede the amazing megalithic construction and bring the work to a halt, only to be completed at a much later date?

Standing there, witness to the actual evidence and literally able to touch what might be the oldest construction on the planet was nothing less than surreal. Ty could feel himself drifting into the past, caught up in speculation at what the world had looked like when construction in Baalbek was just beginning. Was it really a race of giants who built this place? Or maybe it was the Watchers who were able to manipulate nature and stack the stones by somehow defying gravity. Or, he thought almost reluctantly, maybe it was nothing more than the use of pulleys, levers, and lots of manpower.

There was one more building block he had to see before they moved on, and that was the largest known carved stone in the world, the Stone of the Pregnant Woman. It was only a quarter of a mile from the Temple of Jupiter ruins, so it was a quick walk and the weather couldn't have been better: seventy degrees and not a cloud in the sky.

Murshid wasn't as informative about these ruins as he'd been with the pyramids. Then again, there really wasn't anything certain about the civilization behind this stonework either. A lot was known about the work the Greeks and the Romans did, but whoever was behind this remained a mystery.

He was still amazed at how little any of this seemed to impress Celeste. Although she seemed more than willing to continue on with whatever he wanted to see next, she just didn't seem to be very interested.

It had only been minutes, but it was apparent they were getting closer to the megalith as they approached a group of more tourists. Then there it was, the largest known carved stone block on the planet. He stood there in awe, staring in disbelief; it was simply so unbelievable that anyone past or present could've handled something so enormous.

The Stone of the Pregnant Woman (or the *Hajar el Hibla* as the locals called it), was close to seventy by fourteen feet and sixteen feet tall. Almost twice the size of a Greyhound Bus! The stone seemed to protrude from the ground at an angle, with the bottom twenty-percent covered.

Whatever happened to make the builders put all the effort into carving this huge stone, only to leave it lying on the ground was obviously something catastrophic.

Was it possible he was looking at the work of the *Nephilim* or, as the Bible so eloquently called them, "the men of renown"? Or perhaps that of the Watchers themselves? A strange feeling came over him. Was this the place where the Watchers had appeared on the planet?

The tallest mountain in the background came to Ty's attention as he remembered what he'd read in the Book of Enoch. Could that be the mountain where the Watchers descended from the heavens eons ago? Ty still remembered that the name of the mountain, Mount Armon, was now called Mount Hermon.

Ty pointed at the mountain and asked Murshid if that was Mount Hermon, but as soon as he asked, he realized that Murshid probably wouldn't know. He didn't, but without batting an eye Murshid turned to one of the locals and speaking in Arabic he asked him. The local shook his head then said something back to Murshid and pointed to the south.

"He said mountain called Hermon fifty kilometers that way. Why you ask?"

Ty didn't want to bring up the Watchers, but if the Book of Enoch was true, then he had to see the mountain.

He played coy. "I can't remember what it was, but I read something a while back that made that particular mountain sound interesting. Can we go to it? That is," he added, belatedly remembering his companion, "if you don't mind, Celeste."

She nodded, seemingly willing enough, but it seemed to Ty there was still no discernable spark of genuine interest in her face, or manner, when she replied. "I'm game. I say we see as much as we can while we're here."

Ty looked from Celeste to Murshid to see if he was agreeable.

"We take taxi back to boat, get bags, and go." Murshid said as he turned and started back in the direction from which they came.

In a matter of minutes they were in a taxi, a rather disreputable vehicle which, Ty mused, looked like the pick of the litter from one of the nearby junkyards as they rattled dustily down the road.

After several minutes of listening to the driver and Murshid in what sounded like a heated debate in Arabic, Ty asked Murshid if there was a problem.

"Well, I have bad news and not as bad news regarding mountain, but nothing that can't be... how you say... *worked out?*"

Ty matched their guide's light tone. "So, what you're saying is, bad news followed by more bad news? Well... what's the bad news then?"

Murshid looked into Ty's eyes. "Bad thing is, top of mountain across border in Syria. Means men with guns. Other bad thing… United Nations outpost on very top. Means more men with guns."

Ty sat back in his seat, wondering about the situation that was unfolding, watching the road impassively as the car moved forward, drawing closer to Mount Hermon.

CHAPTER 37

E VEN THOUGH MURSHID considered the circumstances regarding the top of Mount Hermon a "minor" obstacle—because
of the poor relations between bordering countries—he still wanted to stop for the day to make a plan, and embark on their
mission early in the morning. They decided to stay in the small
town of Chtaura, about halfway between Baalbek and the apex of
Mount Hermon.

Celeste had decided to go wander through the village after
they were checked into the small inn just on the edge of town but
insisted the others didn't need to join her. Parting ways at the
door, Murshid took Ty to a small coffee house across the street
and left him with Abdullah, their taxi driver, while he made plans
for the following day. It was a slow time of day for the local businesses, and Chtaura wasn't in an area popular with tourists, so
Abdullah and Ty had the place all to themselves.

After chatting with Abdullah over a couple of cups of coffee,
he now knew that not only was it common knowledge that the

current regime in Syria wasn't friendly toward Americans, but also that there'd been issues regarding the border ever since the Syrians pulled out of their twenty-nine year occupation of Lebanon. Ty was uncomfortably aware that both he and Celeste, having blonde hair and blue eyes, were going to stick out like a sore thumb.

For the most part, the border wasn't patrolled very well, which made it almost like a thoroughfare for arms' smugglers who were proponents of terrorism. Though border control might be lax, that wasn't necessarily a good thing, as running into any smugglers would probably not bode well for anyone who was an American or even an American sympathizer. At the top of the mountain would be a different story, though, with the UN outpost being heavily guarded.

That's when the thought hit him. What were the odds of there being a UN outpost on the very spot where the fallen angels had descended? Was it just another coincidence? Of all the mountain peaks in the world, there just so happens to be a UN outpost on the exact spot where the Watchers arrived? With all the conflict in the area, it would make sense for the outpost to be put there, but in the exact same spot? As intriguing as Mount Hermon might've been, it had just become even more so.

Abdullah noticed the distracted look on Ty's face. "What wrong, boy? You look as if you saw… how you say… *spirits?*"

Ty looked at Abdullah and asked, "What do you know of Mount Hermon's history? I don't mean anything recent with Israel or Syria, but old, real old history. Are there any ancient legends about this place?"

Abdullah snickered a little. "Ah! You have heard stories of the fallen ones… no?"

Ty nodded eagerly, then asked, "What can you tell me about them? I mean… were they real?"

Abdullah leaned back in his chair, considering. "Stories go way back… back to before flood… as you must know, but are they true?" He gave a slight shrug. "Who knows? I do not think so, many used to believe, that much for sure."

"What do you mean… used to believe?"

"There are temples all over mountain, old temples here long before Romans came. Romans built on top of ancient ruins. All temples face mountain top," Abdullah said informatively, then continued. "Something found in ruins of temple at very top long time ago…"

Ty's curiosity piqued, he leaned forward in his seat. "What… what did they find?"

"Ancient stone with inscription says some kind of oath, but that is all I know."

Ty felt a thrilling shock run through him, but thought he concealed it rather well. Of course he found it interesting. It was on the top of this very mountain that according to the Book of Enoch the fallen angels (or Watchers) made an oath to each other regarding the great sin they were about to commit with the daughters of men. Was it possible the fantastic story in the Book of Enoch was true?

The thought of the UN outpost resurfaced in his mind. Might there be something else up there, something that was being concealed for some reason? He queried Abdallah. "Do you know where these temples are?"

"No. But, I know someone who know much more of mountain. You like to meet him?"

Trying for nonchalance, Ty responded casually. "Sure, as long as it's no trouble, that is."

Abdullah got immediately to his feet. "No trouble at all. Stay here for moment." Without further comment, he turned and went outside.

As he sat there alone, Ty looked around and realized three other people had come in while they'd been talking. Two of them were an elderly couple and the other was a man who looked to be in his early thirties, eyeing Ty in a rather unfriendly fashion, as though he shouldn't be there. Now he realized just how far away he was from home and how out of place he was. Until now, the adrenaline had masked this, but sitting here by himself made him feel very alone. Sure, he had Murshid and Celeste, but he obviously didn't really know much about either one of them. Not only that, but Celeste just seemed so distant during this entire trip... not what he'd been hoping for at all.

Ty remembered he really should get in contact with his dad. Looking around the room, there wasn't a payphone to be seen. Had things not happened as fast as they did and he'd known in advance that he'd be traveling across the world, he unquestionably would've let his parents know where he was going. Now he was wondering if they were starting to worry about him. Though it'd only been three days since he'd been gone, it seemed like much longer. The excitement of being on an adventure with Celeste had been a dream come true. There really wasn't anything else he could've done, except to maybe not go, but that wasn't an option. After chatting with Abdullah for the last hour, he felt comfortable enough to ask the taxi driver if he could use his phone... providing he had a phone as Ty hadn't seen him use one yet.

While he sat there waiting for Abdullah to return, he started to think more about the ancient temples scattered across the mountain, all facing directly at what was now a UN outpost. What else was on the top of Mount Hermon? Could it be the world leaders were hiding something? It wouldn't be the first time, but why? What sort of knowledge might the powers-that-be want to conceal from the rest of humanity that would require to be heavily guarded day and night? Sure, it could still all be a coincidence, but over the last several weeks the word coincidence had taken on a whole new meaning.

Ty sat alone in the dim little room, a world away from everything he knew—everything that meant familiarity, security, and safety—envisioning this strange and ancient land at the dawn of human history. What if it were all true? He could feel the age of this place, almost mystic in its venerability. Here, so far from his comfortable, normal modern life, it seemed almost possible—the idea of God-like beings walking the earth… could they have done so? Could the strange marriage between the Watchers and the daughters of men really have taken place?

A shaft of light fell across his face, illuminating the room as the door swung open. Ty glanced up, his thoughts interrupted, only to see the light snuffed out as two men entered. It was Abdullah with an elderly man of Arab descent who was dressed wearing the traditional long, white tunic. They came over to the table where Ty was sitting, and Abdullah said something to the elderly man in Arabic who then looked at Ty and nodded his head. Abdullah told Ty that the man, who spoke no English, was Rashid, and that he'd lived in the village his entire life. Rashid knew more about the area than anyone else and was willing to answer any questions. Ty stood up and shook Rashid's hand, smiling. The old man smiled back, and as Ty looked into his eyes he felt, once again, almost as if he were looking back in time. Each wrinkle on the old man's face seemed as though it had its own story to tell.

Ty didn't really know where to start. He was full of questions. Not knowing how to begin, he opened his mouth, and just like that it seemed as though his questions came bubbling forth of their own accord, and he blurted out everything that was on his mind: What happened on top of Mount Hermon that's written about in the Book of Enoch? What was the writing found at the top? Why is there a UN outpost up there? As soon as he was finished, Abdullah started relaying his questions to Rashid in Arabic.

The joyous look that had been on Rashid's face faded as a more serious one crept into his eyes. When Abdullah eventually finished the translation, Rashid sat silent for a moment as he stared intently into Ty's eyes, as though he was trying to read him, trying to discern whether or not his questions were genuine. After a few charged moments of silence had passed, Rashid proceeded to talk. Although Ty didn't know what Rashid was saying, it was obvious that he was very passionate about the subject. His excitement built as Rashid spoke, and he leaned forward in anticipation of what he was going to hear.

After a few minutes, the old man was finally finished and Abdullah begin to relay his lengthy message. Apparently Abdullah had been right about the temples scattered across the mountain. Supposedly, they all had been built by a civilization long before a Great Flood, then rebuilt by the Romans at a much later date. They had all been built to face to the summit of the mountain. Abdullah had also been right about the stone found at the temple gracing the summit, which bore the inscription, *According to the command of the greatest and Holy God, those who take an oath proceed from here.*" Again chills ran up Ty's spine when he heard the translation of the inscription.

When he'd first read about the fallen angels and the oath they'd taken, it all seemed so implausible that he hadn't given much credence to the idea that any of the story could be true. Maybe a small grain of truth, had been his logical conclusion, buried deep in the legend somewhere at best. But now... now it seemed the fantastical tales were starting to become a reality, and the mountain where it all began was staring him in the face.

Then he realized Rashid hadn't said anything about the UN outpost. "What about the UN building at the summit? Are they hiding or maybe protecting something up there?"

After Abdullah's quick translation, Rashid briefly glanced at the other patrons then reached into his pocket and took out a folded piece of paper, pressing it into Ty's hand with a surprisingly strong and wiry grip. He regarded Ty gravely, then dropped his hands, turning to Abdullah with a brief response. Abdullah looked confused and perhaps a bit taken aback, but relayed his message. "Said some things best left alone. There is reason it called forbidden place."

The forbidden place? What, exactly, did he mean by that? Ty didn't know how to respond; it only made him want to know even more. Rashid said something else to Abdullah, looked at Ty and nodded, then started to get up as if he was ready to leave.

"Wait… please. Is there anything else you know that you can tell me?"

Abdullah responded directly to Ty. "Has to go now. I be back soon."

Abdullah and Rashid walked outside, leaving Ty alone to ponder what Rashid had said. *Best if left alone?* Maybe if he didn't have the curiosity of a cat he could leave it alone, but the old man's warning had only served to fuel his obsession that much more.

Ty unfolded the piece of paper Rashid had given him. It appeared to be a map of the mountain with several points plotted on it, each with some writing next to it. There was also a point at the very summit. As he sat there alone, he pondered… what was he uncovering?

CHAPTER 38

T Y AND CELESTE had just finished an early breakfast and were heading down the road with Abdallah and Murshid for their first mountain temple exploration. Ty felt well rested after a night's stay in the quiet town. Although the rooms were small, they were very comfortable, but what pleased him most was that he was finally able to access a phone to call his dad. He had asked at the front desk earlier in the morning if they had a payphone, to no avail, but as Ty was retreating to his room, a nice Arab gentleman had overheard the conversation and offered him the use of his phone. Ty gladly accepted and though he was only able to get his dad's voicemail, he left a lengthy message as to where he was, who he was with, where they were going, and that everything was fine.

Ty had time the previous night to look at the map of Mount Hermon the old man had given him. After Abdullah had translated the writing on it for him, they'd pinpointed the known temples that checkered the mountain's landscape. He'd used an old computer in a back room of the hotel that was reserved for guests, and even though the internet access was very limited, he was able to find some information on the ancient temples along with some photos.

Interestingly though, there was little information about the temple ruins at the summit. What little there was seemed to dry up after 1953. As much as Ty tried to research, there was absolutely no further information, which seemed extremely peculiar. If something was being hidden up there, whoever was responsible for it had gone to great lengths to keep it from being exposed. Even Google maps had an area of the mountain with a different photo superimposed over part of it. Another coincidence?

He was also amazed to find out how much Mount Hermon was mentioned in the Bible. The southern end of the mountain was the northern border of the Promised Land for the Israelites; Noah's son, Ham, had settled there after the Great Flood, and even Jesus himself had spent time there. Something even more intriguing, though, was that Og (one of the giants) had lived in this same area. Joshua (who succeeded Moses as the leader of the Israelites) himself referred to the area as "the land of the giants." So according to the Bible and the Book of Enoch, this was the area crawling with the half-breeds of God-like beings and humans that had set off the chain of events culminating in a worldwide flood to rid the earth of these abominations.

Further research had uncovered a story about the gates of Hades, which were supposedly at the foot of Mount Hermon where two caves were located. Ty remembered that according to the Book of Enoch, the Creator banished the leader of the fallen angels under a mountain for his sins. Was it possible this was the mountain? If it was the first place they set foot on the planet, then it might be fitting to condemn the conspirator of the rebellious ones to an earthly grave under that very spot. Maybe that's why it was known as the forbidden place.

After a little over an hour on the dusty road, they were closing in on the small village of Ain Hircha, located at the 3,900-foot level of the 9,200-foot mountain. This was as far as they could drive. They were also getting closer to the snow level, but thanks to Murshid, they had the proper local apparel to stay warm for the forty-minute hike. The attire would also help them to "not look so American," as Abdullah had pointed out.

Even though he'd seen several archaeological wonders in the last couple of days, Ty was finding the excitement that came with the anticipation of each of the upcoming sites only became stronger.

The road to Ain Hircha was anything but well-traveled, which was probably a good thing considering how narrow and winding it was, but it only seemed to add to the experience for Ty. As they crested the top of a little knoll on the barren mountainside, the road dropped into a beautiful scenic small covered with a beautiful tree he'd never seen before. Then he realized… these must be the famous cedars of Lebanon! They were fairly tall and bushy with thick trunks that gave them a surreal appearance as if they knew the secrets Ty was searching for. Amongst this Biblical forest were a few small houses scattered around. The village wasn't much bigger than the campus area back in Alexandria.

They slowly drove through the quaint village and the snow-covered mountain looming over them was so close now it appeared as though Ty could reach up and touch it. They found a parking spot in the road a few miles out of town. It was obvious that Murshid and Abdullah knew where they needed to park, because there wasn't anything posted that might indicate a trailhead. Once they were all out of the car, it wasn't until Abdullah said something in Arabic and pointed in a direction that Ty could see the ghost of a trail that could be seen ever-so-faintly angling up the hillside.

As they were donning their warm clothing, for a split second Ty thought he might've seen a look of disgust on Celeste's face. This would've been the first time she expressed anything other than willingness to participate in the adventure. However, when she saw him looking at her, her expression quickly changed to one that seemed of excitement and she commented on how she was enjoying herself and wondered what they might find at the end of the mountain path. Ty sure couldn't figure her out, even after all the time he'd spent around her the last few days. He'd tried more than once to let her pick a place to visit, but she'd always refused. If she didn't want to go on any of their excursions, she surely could've spoken up, but it was too late now.

Then Ty realized something. It had been apparent that Celeste wasn't that interested in the sites they had been visiting, but she hadn't even wanted to partake in any real meaningful conversation at all. Ty knew he most likely wasn't the most interesting person in the world, but why didn't Celeste want to get to know him at least a little better? Back at school, she had always appeared to be interested in him, but now they had a perfect opportunity to become more acquainted, she only seemed open to a little small talk at most. Ty wondered what it was that he could have done to squelch what little spark there had been. Whatever was going on with her, he wasn't going to let the idea of her not wanting to climb the mountain get in the way of his desire to see what secrets it might hold.

At least the weather was relatively nice. The warmth of the sun felt good on his face, but he could see they were going to get into some snow eventually as they ascended the mountain. As the peak of Mount Hermon was seemingly watching over them during their hike, Ty thought he could make out a small building on the rocky mountainside, still off in the distance, just a few hundred feet above the snowline. The higher they went, the more obvious it became the small structure was most likely the ancient temple they were looking for, as he could just make out that it was constructed of stone blocks.

Ty was staring at the temple when he saw a rather tall figure wearing local Arabic garb emerge from the back, stopping for a moment to look at their group, then proceed to walk away in the opposite direction. There was something different about the way he moved as he walked that seemed somewhat peculiar... very... odd.

Abdullah spoke up, "Probably he walk down from Ain Aata, other village farther up mountain."

They were close enough to the structure now to see that the stones were well weathered... almost matching those at Baalbek, just much smaller. It was about the size of a three-car garage, only with much taller walls and oriented facing the summit of Mount Hermon. It appeared to be in good condition, but it most likely had been restored several times. The base had obviously been there long before the rest of the construction; there was a noticeable difference in the weathering of the stones. The temple looked as if it had a gable roof at one time, but whatever materials had been used for that were long gone. The walls were intact and as they walked around to the front they noticed the doorway was also intact, even though the stone beam over the doorway was broken in half.

They were making fresh tracks in the snow, so they knew no one had been to the temple from the same direction they'd come. The only other tracks in snow were those from the tall stranger who'd just left, leaving on a path up the hillside.

Although this temple was considered to be a "small" one, standing in the doorway made Ty feel like a child. Why did they need such high doorways?

As Ty speculated about the temple and its origins, he gradually became aware of an exchange between Murshid and Abdullah. It was their tone that got Ty's attention and broke his train of thought. They were standing in front of him, blocking his view of something that they seemed to be discussing in their native tongue. From where he stood, all he could see was the remnants of what looked like four Corinthian columns built into the side of the stone walls and a short divider wall toward the other end of the structure.

Celeste was standing next to Ty and followed him as he went over to see what their guides were discussing so intently.

"What is it?" he asked, still not noticing anything special.

Abdullah pointed to a stone bowl just past the divider wall. "Libation."

Ty looked from the bowl to Abdullah in incomprehension. "Li... what?"

"Look." Abdullah pointed to the stone bowl. "Wine in bowl... is offering to the gods. Tall man who left here gave offering of wine to the gods."

From the single set of tracks in the snow, it was obvious that no one else had been there recently. Considering the bowl thoughtfully, Ty realized that whoever had left the offering would quite possibly be a wealth of knowledge regarding the secrets this mountain held. If he could only talk to him, there were so many questions he could probably answer.

He stepped outside and looked up the hill. The man was still in sight about a hundred yards away, not appearing to be in a hurry. Turning back to Murshid and Abdullah Ty asked, "If I can get that man to come back to talk to us, will you translate so I can ask him a few questions?"

"Sure, better hurry before he too far away. Is all uphill you know."

Ty cupped his hands around his mouth and yelled, "Hello... hello!" It was enough to get the man's attention. Ty waved and hollered the greeting once more as he started up the path to meet him, but instead of waving back and waiting for Ty, the stranger just turned and continued walking away. Turning back to Murshid and Abdullah, Ty told them he'd run up to see if he could get the man to stop and asked if they'd follow him. They nodded and motioned him to get going. Ty started out in a slow jog, but when his target glanced back and saw him coming, he started to jog as well.

Although they were now above the snow line, the faint trail was at an angle that had allowed the warmth of the sun to melt the snow and leave the ground firm. Firm enough that Ty wouldn't have to worry about his footing. Because of what they'd hiked already, he was warmed up enough to hit the trail at full steam if need be.

Taking off the cumbersome long-flowing outer garment, he left it on the ground and put it in high gear just as he had many times before, out of the starting blocks. Although instead of racing toward a yellow tape stretched across the track a hundred yards away, his finish line now was the tall stranger ahead, wearing something similar to what Ty had just taken off. Always the fastest kid on the block, Ty was closing in fast, just as he'd done with most of his opponents since childhood.

The gap between the two men was narrowing dramatically until the man turned around and saw what was happening. Then, like a prized race horse held in check, waiting for the right time to make his move, the stranger accelerated into an effortless graceful lope that widened the gap between the two just as fast as it had closed only a moment ago. With the judgment born with years of race experience, Ty realized there was no way he was going to catch him and he reluctantly slowed and came to a stop. *What the hell?* Ty thought in disbelief of what had just transpired. Maybe it had been the thinner air he wasn't used to, but having someone run away from him like that was an experience he'd never had before... ever!

As he stood there and watched the man disappear over the ridge, he could hear Murshid and Abdullah laughing as they were walking up to meet him.

"Guess he has nothing to say." Abdullah was roaring with a deep laugh. "Maybe next time you... how you say... *eat your Wheaties?*"

"Ha ha, very funny." Ty was trying to catch his breath still in a state of bewildered shock.

Murshid and Abdullah turned around to head back to the temple, loudly making fun of Ty and roaring with laughter. Ty was the last one to get there. Celeste, however, was still gazing up the hillside with an air of puzzlement.

"I thought I heard you were fast... fast enough to probably have gone to the Olympics? But, it... it was like you were standing still," she said with a glazed look on her face, somewhat under her breath as if distracted by what she just saw.

"Oh, don't tell me you're going to rub it in too?" Ty was still breathing a little harder than normal. Glancing at Celeste he saw no sign of teasing. She completely ignored his little joke. She seemed to be in deep thought, and the look on her face... was as though she had just seen a ghost. He looked away, back in the direction he had just come, and felt a chill creep over his cooling skin. She was right, whoever the guy was, he just outran a potential Olympian with ease... it just didn't add up, there was no way the air was that thin.

As he considered what had just transpired, staring up at the horizon, he heard a woman's voice and turned to see Celeste had walked away, back closer to the temple and was just taking her phone away from her ear. The voice he'd heard was obviously hers but what was odd (besides the fact that her phone was now miraculously working) was that he could've sworn she was speaking in German.

THE LEADER OF the small squadron of aircraft in the sunbaked, abandoned hanger in northwest Iraq nodded to his crew as he hung up his phone. The call was finally in and it was time to move.

CHAPTER 39

GRANT, ALONG WITH his partner, Dan Clancy, had arrived in Cairo less than twenty-four hours ago and were now back in the air en route to Beirut. The good news was that when they had landed in Cairo, Grant finally had a message from Ty letting him know where he was and that he was okay... the bad news was that he was now three countries away in a remote region in Lebanon.

What made the bad news even worse was that there were reports just now surfacing that the small village of Ain Aata—which was close to where Ty was last known to have been—was the target of some sort of air assault. Grant couldn't help but think whatever had happened in Ain Aata, it was somehow connected to his son.

After having several hours to ponder the wild story Tom had told him about what ODESSA's plan with a *Nephilim* was thought to be, and given the chain of events that had been unfolding before his very eyes, he hoped it was a big mistake, but deep down he knew it was all probably linked together. The only thing to be done now was to find Ty and hopefully start detaining the players who were using him to help make this nightmare a reality. Grant knew he needed to try to put a stop to their plan somehow. After all, when they got what they needed from his son, what would they do with him then? Hopefully, he wasn't already too late.

After their plane landed and they were rushing through the crowd of outbound travelers, a very attractive woman wearing a long Arab dress and an open-faced headscarf brushed passed Grant as she hurried to catch her flight. Grant noticed something a little out of place with the woman, turning and watching as she passed. The woman disappearing into the crowd was wearing hiking boots.

Once they'd cleared customs, a representative from the U.S. Embassy was there to meet them with more information about the assault on Ain Aata, and the news wasn't good: there were no survivors. The entire village had been wiped out. There still wasn't a motive known for the attack, but what they did know was that a small squadron of aircraft had somehow flown under the radar into Lebanon from over the Syrian border just north of Damascus. Then continuing toward Baalbek, they had zigzagged along the northwestern edge of the Mount Hermon range before coming in for a low pass over Ain Aata and dispersing a nerve agent over the entire village, killing everyone. There were reports that a large dual-rotor helicopter had come in trail, landing momentarily, then taking off in the opposite direction. The four C-123s that had dispersed the nerve agent had all been shot down by Lebanese forces just before crossing the border back into Syria killing all on board. The helicopter had also been shot down only a few minutes after taking back to the air, and so far no survivors had been found.

Different sects of the Muslim faith had long committed acts of terror against one another. Something of this magnitude, though, against the small village of Ain Aata, where the inhabitants were known for keeping to themselves... it didn't seem to align with religious differences as the cause of the atrocity. For now, whoever was responsible and their motive for the attack was unknown.

Grant was putting together a plan to find his son, trying to suppress the fear writhing in the shadowed corners of his mind, when his phone rang and his luck suddenly broke. It was Ty.

CELESTE HAD BEEN speaking German on her short phone call back up at the temple ruins, Ty was almost sure of it. This, coupled with the fact his abductor the other night seemed to have a thick German accent also seemed to add up to something that wasn't right. And even the thought that Murshid might have slipped out a tinge of a German accent the other day was now a concern. If Murshid and Celeste knew each other, neither had given any hints to it, but something smelled bad. If they were all connected, what did it mean? Ty couldn't think of what he'd been involved with that might relate to anything German at all.

Though Celeste denied she had been speaking in German, she did acknowledge that a call finally got through from her mother. Celeste said that her father had had a terrible accident and was in critical condition, the reason they'd driven two hours to get to the Beirut International Airport so she could catch a flight back to the States. The fact that her phone miraculously was now getting reception didn't sit well with Ty either, but calling her a liar wasn't going to help the situation at all. She did seem obviously distraught though, and didn't talk much on the way (which he was used to by now anyway). She said her mother had set her up for a 2:00 p.m. departure. Now with Celeste gone, Ty needed to decide what he was going to do next: either stay for the remainder of the trip or look into going home early as well. With Ty's circle of trust shrinking fast, going home now seemed like the best thing to do.

Abdullah and Ty had stayed with the car while Murshid took Celeste into the terminal, but Ty had decided before they left, he should try to call his dad from a pay phone inside, in the hopes of actually talking to him this time. To his surprise, his father answered. Even more surprising than the fact that there were still pay phones to be found somewhere, was where his father was... he was outside the very terminal Ty was calling from! His father said only one thing. "Stay where you are and I'll be right there." It was the exact same phrase he'd used when Ty had been involved in a minor incident years earlier, and he knew enough to do exactly what his father told him.

As Ty hung up the phone his mind was racing with questions with the first and foremost being... why was his dad *here?* Something was obviously wrong, but what could it be? Then he wondered. Had something happened to his mother? He was pacing back and forth in front of the phones with these thoughts running through his head when his father and two agency looking types came through the automatic doors.

Ty immediately ran over to his father, thinking that the worst may've happened. "What's wrong, Dad? Is Mom all right?"

His dad, looking relieved, enfolded Ty in a fierce embrace. "Your mother? Of course she's fine. It's you I was worried about, son. Are you okay?"

"I'm fine and happy to see you, but what the hell are you doing here? I mean... what the hell is going on?"

"Where's the girl? Is anybody else with you?" his father said quietly under his breath so only his son could hear.

Ty could sense the seriousness of his dad's tone. "Celeste? She just caught a flight back to the States, and our guides are waiting for me out in the car. Why? What's going on?"

"What flight did she get on, and where's the car?" His father was still speaking quietly.

"I'm not sure what the flight number was, but she was going back to D. C., and the car is parked out front. What's going on, Dad?"

Grant stepped back and whispered something to his partner who nodded then turned and left, then fixed Ty with a level gaze. "Go out like you're getting back into the car. But, son, whatever you do, do not get in. Understand?"

The intensity in his dad's eyes forestalled the questions that Ty had been about to ask. Biting them back, he nodded and walked out the automatic doors with one of his dad's men right behind him. When he looked to where his ride had been waiting… the car was gone. He looked up and down the curb, but they were nowhere to be seen. "What the hell?" he said out loud in bewilderment. Then, squaring his shoulders, he turned and re-entered the terminal.

"Dad, *what's going on?*"

Grant put his finger up gesturing for Ty to wait a second as Dan returned and was whispering something to him. It was obvious that whatever Dan told his father was making the wheels turn in his head. Then Grant turned to the man that Ty didn't recognize.

"We need a private place to talk. Is your car in the parking lot?"

The man nodded and everyone followed him out the door, Grant staying close to Ty. A couple of minutes later they were across the road in the covered parking lot sitting in a black Cadillac Escalade with dark tinted windows. Once the doors were closed, his father began to speak.

"First things first, Ty. Not only did we check for all the flights going to D.C. for your lady friend, which there were none by the way, we checked all flights out of Beirut in the last two hours and no one by the name of Celeste Peterson was on any of them, so I have to ask you. Are you sure she got on a flight at all?"

Ty didn't know what to make of the entire situation, but he trusted his dad wholeheartedly. Until he knew what was happening he had no choice but to cooperate and answer the questions his dad had before he started asking questions of his own.

"Well, I do know she went inside the terminal for sure, but I stayed out in the car, so I really don't know if she actually got on a flight or not." He couldn't help himself. "Do you think something happened to her? Why wouldn't she have gotten on her flight?"

"Don't worry, son. I'm sure she's fine, but I don't think she is who you think she is."

"What do you mean? Who is she?"

"I'll get to that in a minute, but for now just try to think. Is there anything you can remember about where she might've gone instead of D.C.?"

Now he was in a fog about the whole situation, but responded obediently, nonetheless. "I think I saw her write down a flight number when she was on the phone with her mother. But I never paid any attention to what it was. Murshid—our guide—went in with her. And, I don't know if this is relevant or not, but I think she might've been speaking German while she was on the phone." He paused for a moment thinking back, then said, "And, Dad, I'm pretty sure I've heard a couple other German accents, maybe even from our guide, Murshid."

Ty noticed his father exchange a glance with the other two men, then looked at him and said, "Keep thinking if there's anything that might help us find her, and in the meantime, we'll get some pictures for you to look at." His father already had his laptop opened. With the help of some CIA software he was able to bypass a few security systems and *voilà*... passports of everyone who'd traveled out of the Beirut International Airport in the last two hours were accessible. With a few more strokes of the keyboard, the system narrowed it down to just the female travelers. Grant handed his computer to Ty.

"All right, son, find her. But assume she'll probably be disguised."

Ty nodded and started scrolling through the photos. There must've been at least 500, but if she had flown out of Beirut as she said, then hers would be one of them.

AS TY WAS looking for a photo of Celeste (or whoever she really was), Grant was on the phone trying to get more details about the assault on Ain Aata. Though the facts were still rather murky, one report stated a vehicle was seen coming off the mountain on the road from Ain Aata shortly after the attack was first reported. Was it possible there had been survivors of the horrific attack? And if so... who were they and where did they go? With all the aircraft shot down after the assault, then it would appear the aggressor's mission had failed, but from what Tom Bruiner had told Grant... he was afraid things were far from over.

Although Grant didn't know if it was the right decision, he chose not to tell his son that Tom had mentioned Ty was thought to be special by whoever had been using him in this elaborate scheme. Maybe later he would, but for now... he chose to wait.

As for his son, it'd only taken him one time through the passport photos to find the one of the once girl-of-his-dreams. And her destination? Not Washington, D.C. or even anywhere in North America. The innocent girl from Ty's class had purchased a one-way ticket on Air France flight 3452 to Buenos Aires, Argentina. Even though the woman in the picture had the name of Elke Shultz and jet black hair, there was no doubt it was her. And, everyone in the CIA knew the significance of the name Shultz. It was the name of Heinrich Himmler's forgotten mistress.

CHAPTER 40

A LTHOUGH GRANT DIDN'T want to believe his son was caught up in some kind of muddled Nazi ruse, there was no looking the other way now. With the woman they were now pursuing having the same last name as a mistress of a deplorable infamous Nazi and the story that Tom had told him, there seemed no escaping the nightmare.

Grant knew that Heinrich Himmler, one of those directly responsible for the Holocaust, had weaseled his way to the head of the Nazi SS in 1929 and remained in power until its demise in 1945. During his reign of terror under Adolf Hitler, Himmler founded the scientific institute *"Ahnenerbe"* or "Inheritance of the Forefathers" whose mission was to prove the superiority of the Aryan race and, in doing so, prove they were descendants of the people from the lost continent of Atlantis. Not only was Himmler looking for the lost continent, but also biblical artifacts such as the Holy Grail, thinking that if found, he could somehow gain superhuman powers. (Coincidentally, *Ahnenerbe* was the same organization that

constantly clashed with Harrison Ford's character in the famous
Indiana Jones movies.) When Germany fell to the Allied forces at
the end of World War II, Himmler took the cowardly way out, and
committed suicide before he could face justice for his crimes
against humanity.

It was well known, especially to someone with Grant's intel,
that Himmler kept a mistress other than Hedwig Potthast. Her
name was Zelma Shultz, and she also gave him an illegitimate
child. There had been rumors that this little bastard had disappeared shortly after birth. It wasn't until years after the war had
ended that whispers started to surface about the lost Himmler
child. Now the child would be well into his seventies, and according to Tom, it seemed as though perhaps this lost Himmler
shared one of his father's goals... breeding the perfect soldier. The
thought made Grant cringe.

This, coupled with the fact that many (including Stalin and
Dwight Eisenhower) believed Hitler's death to be staged and that
he and Eva Braun may have escaped to Argentina gave rise to
some concern that the last of the Third Reich had yet to be seen.
Grant knew there was some creditable evidence to support this
theory, such as the fact that both Hitler and Braun had false teeth
made only days before the fall of Berlin. Reports stated that both
of the corpses identified as Hitler and Braun were found to be
wearing those exact false teeth and interestingly enough, they
didn't quite fit. More than one German U-boat had surfaced off
the coast of Argentina several days after Berlin's fall along with
many different alleged sightings of Hitler in La Falda, Argentina,
where he may have had a safe haven supplied by the proprietors of
the Eden Hotel, Walter and Ida Eichhorn.

There was some dispute surrounding the truth of any of these
reports, but with the girl's possible pedigree—who his son had been
traveling with for the last few days—made her disappearance give

the story Tom told Grant even more credence. Grant still had to consider that Tom's testimony about ODESSA might just be a smoke screen to steer the CIA away from infiltrating his organization, but that was a chance he had to take. One thing Grant knew for sure was that with the disappearance of Ty's teacher Dr. Eisenberg, along with Murshid and Abdullah, there was only one other player involved in this crazy scheme whose whereabouts was known. That was Celeste or Elke or whoever the hell she was, and as soon as her flight landed in Buenos Aires… that trail would most likely dry up until it was too late. Grant took a deep breath, staring off into space mulling over all that was transpiring.

The CIA had operatives all over the world, and South America was no exception. The only problem was if Elke Shultz changed her appearance enough to fool the agent who would be waiting for her arrival into Buenos Aires, then the chance to derail the diabolical plot that was unfolding would be lost. There was, of course, a possibility the plan had already been foiled by the Lebanese Air Force when they shot down the aircraft responsible for the catastrophe at Ain Aata, but it was too risky to leave it to chance. Grant knew the best opportunity they had to identify the woman upon her deplaning in Buenos Aires and hopefully following her to the bigger fish, was to have the one who knew her face the best in wait when she arrived: Ty… but they were still in Beirut.

At least with the CIA now involved, Grant would be able to pull a few strings and have Air France flight 3452 divert to an alternate airport along the way. This would give them time to get there first and lay in wait, so magically after a quick phone call… flight 3452 encountered a mechanical problem that forced them to make an intermediate landing in Lagos, Nigeria. Within an hour-and-a-half, Grant, Dan, and Ty were lifting off the tarmac at Beirut International. Destination: Buenos Aires, Argentina.

———✕✕✕———

AS THE BOEING 747 was taking to the air, Ty had one last view of Mount Hermon and couldn't help but wonder. *What was at the summit and why was it being hidden?* The UN was stationed there for a reason. Deep down inside he knew one day he'd find out, but that was going to have to wait for another time. Now they were on their way to try to stop a madman's dream from becoming a reality.

With the long airplane ride ahead of them, Ty's dad finally had some time to fill Ty in on what he knew of the situation so far. "Well, son," his father started to speak, "I don't really know where to begin, so here goes. The long thought dismantled organization of ODESSA, who were the organizers of the ratlines to help Nazis escape Germany after WWII, apparently is anything but that. If your buddy Tom's suspicions of the situation he warned me about are true, then the Nazis' dream of creating the perfect soldier has become the obsession of one of the illegitimate offspring of none other than Heinrich Himmler."

Ty had to interrupt. "So you talked to Tom? Is he involved in all of this after all?"

"We had a little talk with Tom." Grant said with a look of sincerity, "and though he's involved all right, he's not part of the group we're chasing down now. He's your friend, and you don't have to worry about him. I'll tell you a little more about him in a moment." Grant looked out the window as the desert passed below, then back to Ty and continued. "It's not the fact that they have a plan of creating the perfect soldier that's so unbelievable, but how they intend to make it happen." Grant paused again as if he was still trying to convince himself of what he was saying was true.

"What, Dad?" Ty jumped in. "And what does Celeste have to do with it?"

Grant took a deep breath, then continued. "Through the blood of the *Nephilim*, the giants from the Bible. I know it sounds absurd, but there's enough evidence to support this... this "Jurassic Park" concept and that indeed there is someone who harbors this insane notion. As to why you'd been "recruited" to somehow lead them to a *Nephilim* descendant? I have absolutely no idea."

Ty couldn't believe what he was hearing, but thinking back on it now as his father was talking, there was no doubt he'd been recruited. The school's computer system being down during registration, the perfect girl "luring" him into an archaeology class, and then being lucky enough to go to the Middle East with her. The fact that his cell phone quit working right after she asked to use it, made it obvious now, that whoever was behind this scheme didn't want him to have access to any communication with, most likely, his father. What had just transpired up on the side of Mount Hermon and getting his doors blown off by a tall, lanky native. Then the call Celeste had made was no doubt to let her subordinates know someone with "giant" blood in their veins had been found, which must have triggered the gas attack on the unsuspecting village. As crazy as the thought sounded, Ty knew he was fast, and it would be very unusual for any of the top sprinters in the U.S. to edge him out of a race let alone some random Lebanese villager who took him out with ease.

Grant seemed to become more convinced as he spoke. "It appears there are many people on the planet who believe in the existence of the *Nephilim*, but leave it to the Nazis to actually try and somehow harness their genetics to produce a super warrior." He paused, then laughed a little before he said, "I'm just surprised we didn't think of it first."

His father told him it was likely that whatever their diabolical plan was, it most likely wouldn't succeed. Ty could tell from his dad's tone though... he was worried. He was obviously determined to make sure their plan failed, especially after Ty had been used as a human pawn in the elaborate scheme.

"So what about Tom?" Ty asked. "How is he involved?"

"Does S.O.J. International, mean anything to you, Ty?"

Ty thought for moment, but nothing came to him. "No. I've never heard Tom or anyone else mention S.O.J." Then he remembered something. "Wait a minute. I may have seen those initials a couple of months ago. Remember that weird guy I went to see out across the Chesapeake Bay I told you about?"

"Yeah, I remember. What about him?"

"In his collection of giant memorabilia, he also had an old dagger with the same lettering on it. He acted a little odd when I saw it too. What does it mean, Dad?"

Grant looked at Ty then out the window as if in deep thought. "I don't know, son. I don't know."

Ty could tell from the look on his father's face after he spoke that he was keeping something from him, but for now, he decided to let it be.

THE FLIGHT SEEMED to go by rather quickly, and no one involved knew if this was a good thing or not, but they did know one way or another, this thing had to be put to bed… permanently. As soon as possible after landing and clearing customs, Grant was putting the plan they had devised into motion. Everything would be in place by the time Celeste's—Elke's—flight arrived within the hour. Besides Grant and his partner Dan, there was also another agent, Selena Lopez, who'd driven down from Paraguay to help (ironically another place where Hitler may have spent some time in his twilight years).

The plan was to disguise Ty so he was unrecognizable to Elke and position him at the gate where the deplaning passengers exited.

Dan would accidentally bump into her while Grant would plant a small transmitter hidden in a pen on her. If the plan worked, she could be tracked anywhere, and with any luck, they would find the madman that was behind this insane plot.

It was a bit of a scramble, but they were able to get everyone in place just in time. Everything started off without a hitch. Ty was totally unrecognizable in sunglasses and a hoodie that fit him at least two sizes larger than the rest of his clothes, pretending to be absorbed in reading a local paper. Selena was waiting in her car at a pull out before the first intersection on the only road leaving the airport, ready to tail Elke.

Once the Air France flight 3452 arrived, passengers began trickling out. After about a third of the people were off, along came a young woman with jet black hair and dark glasses wearing clothing similar to what the local wealthy women of Argentina wore. As different a look as she had now—compared to the beautiful blonde who Grant's son had been so infatuated with for the past several months—Celeste's change in appearance obviously wasn't enough to hide her mannerisms from Ty. Even Grant himself recognized the hand-bag from the woman he'd seen wearing hiking boots several hours earlier that caught his eye in the Beirut International terminal.

Ty turned the page of the newspaper indicating he had spotted her, but at that exact moment Dan was jostled by a passenger who was obviously in a hurry because of the late arrival, causing him to miss Ty's signal completely. Grant, however, saw his son's signal and proceeded as planned by forcing his way through the outflow of passengers until he was right behind her. Once in position, he had to wait for a good opportunity to plant the pen, but as they neared customs he was running out of chances. He'd have to make his move quickly or risk losing her. With time running out, the only thing he could do was slip the pen in an open pocket on the outside of her purse and hope that customs didn't accidentally find it somehow.

Since the flight from Beirut had been late arriving, there were more people than normal in the terminal for this time of day, so the custom agents were a little more hurried than usual: they let Elke pass through without any additional searching. Now, as long as she didn't somehow find it herself, they'd be able to track her wherever she went.

Grant followed her from a distance through customs. It was only a couple of minutes and she was out the door where a black Mercedes Benz with dark tinted windows was silently waiting. Now all he could do was wait until he got word from Selena.

It wasn't long after they got their car when she called. She told him she was getting a strong signal and gave him directions on how to follow. It was a good thing Grant and the crew got a little sleep on the long flight because it turned out to be a long drive. From the map Grant had, he could tell they were going to a very remote area at the base of the Andes close to the Argentina-Bolivia border.

They came around one last corner to see Selena's car parked on the side of the road. It was obvious where the Mercedes Benz had finally stopped… at the end of the road at the base of the mountains at what looked like a fifteenth century European castle. It appeared to be nothing less than an impenetrable stronghold.

IT HAD BEEN a long time since Elke had seen her grandfather. Though his ways seemed far too radical for her, he was family. Raised with a strong sense of familial duty, she was happy to do what he asked of her.

Elke knew that the atrocities which her great grandfather had been accused of during World War II caused her mother to take her grandmother's last name of Shultz. Her grandfather, on the other hand, was proud of what his father (Heinrich Himmler) had accomplished and wasn't about to take any name other than Himmler. Even though his father had never known of his birth, Rudolf was proud to be Himmler's son and proud of his father's vision and bold actions. Like his father, Rudolf, also believed the Aryan race to be superior and was deserving of the highest pecking order.

Elke's grandfather was still lying in the hospital bed with tubes running into him, but he was awake and his face lit up when he saw his granddaughter. Elke returned the smile and with perfect German was the first to speak.

"You look tired, Grandfather. How do you feel?"

"Still groggy, but seeing you and just being awake tells me that everything must've gone well?"

Elke glanced at the man who, wearing a lab coat and scrubs, was examining a chart in the far corner of the room, but her grandfather seemed unconcerned by the man's presence.

"Yes, I did exactly as you asked. Now what do we do?" She said, still not knowing what her grandfather's plan was.

"Oh my dear. Now we'll reap the rewards. And you my precious... you shall be a queen!"

Elke had absolutely no idea what he was talking about. She walked around the other side of the bed to get a little closer. This also brought her closer to the machine that was monitoring the old man's heart. Then they heard it... *chirp... chirp... chirp.* The rhythmic chirping was coming over the heart monitoring machine, and the man dressed in doctor's garb rushed over, frantically checking the other readings and then the connections. Elke stepped back to get out of his way, then the chirping stopped.

With all eyes on Elke now, the doctor asked, *"Could you step back over here again, please?"*

She did as she was asked, there it was again… *chirp… chirp… chirp.*

"Is your cell phone on by chance, Fraulein?"

She took her phone out. *"No, I haven't used it since I got here."*

"May I hold your phone for a moment?" She nodded and gave it to him. *"Please go back to where you were again, Fraulein."*

Again she did as she was asked only to hear the chirping once more. Distressed, she jumped back and started digging frantically through her purse. Then she found it… a pen that she didn't recognize. The doctor took it from her and moved it closer to the monitor. The chirping grew louder. It was obviously some kind of transmitter. It was also apparent whoever put it there had access to some extremely high technology… that much they knew immediately.

CHAPTER 41

WITHIN AN HOUR Grant, Dan, and Ty had rendezvoused with Selena and were now in a position about two miles away from the fortress where Selena had seen Elke disappear. They could see the grounds easily, everything was unobstructed including the road leading up to the main gate.

"Well, Selena, what do you make of it?" Grant asked as they got out of the car, looking for her assessment of the situation.

"Even though there isn't a moat, which would've fit in quite well by the way, there might as well be. There's a concrete wall about twenty feet high surrounding the place and a gate which appears to be built out of iron bars. I've also seen several guards carrying machine guns."

"That figures," Grant said dryly. "Whoever owns this place is obviously partial to their privacy... that much is certain. But, somehow, we're still going to have to put a stop to what they're doing in there," Grant was glassing the place with binoculars. "I don't know how we're going to be able to do that with a surveillance-only authorization." He put down the binoculars and looked at everyone. "Unless we don't follow orders, that is."

Dan and Selena seemed skeptical about the story of the "giants" from the Bible, but had been amazed they'd never even heard the contents of Genesis 6:4 before as they said they both had been raised as Christians. As hesitant as they were, they didn't let their doubts get in the way of their professionalism. It was clear from what they'd seen so far that something way out of the ordinary was going on. The armed guards patrolling the grounds were proof of that.

Dan spoke first. "Well, I can't speak for Selena, but you can count me in." He'd worked with Grant several times over his twenty years with the CIA, and they had earned each other's trust more than once, so if Grant was in, so was Dan.

Selena took longer to deliberate. She'd only been with the Agency for five years and said she hadn't come across a time where breaking the rules had been an option. "So what happens if we storm in there and it's just an eccentric old man living there minding his own business?" She said, thinking out loud. "What then? I'll be damned if you two screw this up and I wind up applying my training as some frickin shopping mall guard."

Grant nodded understandably. "I know Selena, all of our asses are on the line if we go through with this thing. I've made two calls to the boss all ready, and there just isn't enough proof yet to convince him there's a need to act. Hell, I even told him what I really think is about to happen and judging by the long pause after... well, let's just say I'll probably be taking some inkblot tests when I get back. Really though, I don't think we have the luxury of waiting until there's more evidence anyway." He paused for a moment, looking at everyone else, then back to her. "There's no guarantees. I'll understand if anyone wants to back out. But... if we are right about what is going on in there... God help us all if we do nothing."

She paced back and forth, staring at the ground then at the fortress several times and maybe swayed a little by peer pressure, she finally looked at Grant and said, "Okay. I'll do it. But if this turns out bad, you pay my rent until it's fixed."

Grant smiled at her thankfully, then began to address everyone. "Okay then. Well, the way I see it, if the madman in charge is going to try to produce a super solider somehow with *Nephilim* DNA, then there's no way we can know for sure just how much time he needs to make it a reality." Grant still had a hard time actually believing what he was saying, but knew he had to continue. "If a clone of some kind is their plan, then it would take some time for cell growth before they'd have anything for us to worry about, however, and believe me, I know just how crazy this sounds, but if they have some way of intermixing the DNA with a grown human... well, let's just say that the threat would be much more imminent. With any luck, that's not even possible, so we should have some time to come up with a plan that would shut this thing down long before the birth of any kind of super Nazi would be physically possible." He paused looking back toward the castle, then said, "May God be with us. Now let's get busy and make a plan."

Inside the complex, they could see two other smaller buildings from their vantage point. As for what their purpose was, Grant couldn't tell... maybe storage buildings. Six large generators could also be seen, most likely used to power the place. It didn't quite make sense why there were so many, though, as only one could be seen spewing exhaust.

They'd only been watching the place for a few hours with no traffic in or out when a black moving truck arrived at the front gate. The truck was let in immediately and then pulled around the side of the imposing manor building, backing up to a side entrance. Although they couldn't see everything that was transpiring, there were at least six men with machine guns standing around the truck. It was obvious something was being unloaded, but with their vision obstructed by the truck it was impossible to see what it was. After a few minutes of activity, all but two of the men with guns were out of sight, then the truck pulled away from the side of the manor and parked next to the three other vehicles lined up in a row next to the main drive.

Then it hit Grant. "There had been a vehicle seen leaving Ain Aata shortly after the attack. I have a sick feeling that they had found who or *what* they were looking for."

"You don't mean... a giant?" Selena sounded skeptical.

"Could be. And if they did, then it's likely that what we've just witnessed was the arrival of someone whose blood is carrying *Nephilim* DNA." Ty said, though his concern was noticeably laced with excitement.

"Do you think it's possible that they're still alive? I thought there had been no survivors in Ain Aata." Dan said with seemingly genuine concern.

"Who knows." Grant narrowed his eyes in thought. "Maybe they administered an antidote in time to reverse the effects of the nerve agent. Whatever the case, it looks as though there's a good chance that operation "Super Nazi" is a go. Now the question is, how much time do we have to see to it that the outcome of this insane plan is a failure?" The tone in Grant's voice was all business now.

It was doubtful they could get a better vantage point without the risk of being seen, so they stayed where they were to keep an eye on the place and try to come up with an idea. Getting the local authorities involved wasn't an option as they had no proof to back up any of their wild accusations. (There was also the chance the local authorities were being paid to look the other way.) Unless they saw something more damning soon, there wasn't enough evidence for Grant to get any more involvement from U.S. Forces either, even though a surgical air strike would put this whole thing to rest once and for all. Whatever plan they devised was going to have to be simple as they didn't have much to work with... including time.

The first thing they needed to do was find a way to get in, and that didn't appear to be too easy a task from where they sat. By the time night fell they had all come up with various ideas, all of them were risky which most likely wasn't going to be avoided.

There'd been no additional traffic into or out of the entire area, but around noon the following day, the other five generators started running; two days later all six generators were still operating nonstop. Judging by their size, whatever was going on inside was taking an enormous amount of power. If they didn't come up with a good plan soon, Grant was getting the awful feeling that it'd be too late.

It was Ty who finally noticed something and made a suggestion.

"I think I have an idea, Dad."

Grant lowered the binoculars. "What is it, son?"

"Do you guys notice the similarities between this fortress and the ancient city of Troy?"

Grant frowned, looking thoughtful, then slowly nodded. "A Trojan horse. What better way to get inside a fortress crawling with armed guards than having them open the gate for us willingly? Good idea, Ty."

AFTER ONLY A couple of hours and a little head scratching, they all agreed on what to do. The simplicity of the plan almost made it seem too easy. Selena, who was quite an attractive woman, would conveniently break down in her expensive sports car just outside the gate. She'd then call Ty, posing as her brother, who'd come to give her a ride back to town on his motorcycle. While she was waiting for her ride, she would attempt—aided by her abundant natural charms—to convince whoever was out front to help her push her car and let her leave it inside the gate while she got help. If animal magnetism could prevail yet once again, as long as they weren't suspicions enough to look inside the trunk, where Grant and Dan would be hidden, they'd be in.

With just two men against the unknown number inside, trying to slaughter them all in their sleep as the Trojans did would be a suicide mission. However, there was a simple solution that, if it worked, would shut down whatever was going on inside and still give Grant and Dan time to get out unharmed: sabotage the generators. Shut their power off and whatever they were doing inside would come to a halt, plain and simple. If done right, Grant and Dan would be able to get back into the trunk and wait until morning for Selena to return. As long as the sabotage wasn't apparent right away, nobody would even think to check the car until it was long gone and they were safe.

Oran, Argentina was the closest town of any kind, and though it wasn't very industrialized, they were able to obtain everything they needed to get their plan underway. They rented a motorcycle from a local shop along with a helmet to shield Ty's face when he played his part in the operation. Selena was absolutely sure she'd been out of sight when she was following Celeste from the airport, so her red BMW sedan was a perfect car for the job. The fact that it was German-made probably wouldn't hurt either. She was also able to obtain an outfit appropriate to the task at hand, exchanging her professional attire for tight fitting, skimpy apparel, though she didn't look happy about it. Judging from the response from her male co-workers though, it was perfect.

It wasn't until they'd cleared out the trunk to make room for

Grant and Dan that they discovered a small, but extremely significant problem. Dan was too big.

"I'm sorry, but I just can't make myself fit." Dan was obviously distraught, but no matter how hard they tried, it wasn't going to work. At six-foot-six and 280 pounds, it was physically impossible. For a few bleak minutes, it looked as though they'd have to come up with another plan.

Then, Ty spoke up. "It looks like we're left with only one alternative... me."

Grant didn't hesitate. "No! There's no way I can allow that. We're going too far out on a limb as it is, son, and not only that, but your mother would kill me."

"But, Dad, what other choice do we have? We might not have time to come up with another plan." Ty pleaded his case for several more minutes...at six feet and 180 pounds he was able to fit alongside his dad with room to spare. It was, he argued, the only viable option.

As reluctant as Grant was to have his son involved even as Selena's brother, having him go into the lion's den was out of the question. Going in alone, however, was also not plausible and time was running out. So, as much as the decision troubled him, Grant finally reluctantly agreed. Ty, on the other hand, had absolutely no problem with the idea at all. In fact, he seemed thrilled to be on a mission with his dad. The wrath of Marion, should they ever have the courage to tell her, would have to be a matter for another day.

THEY WAITED UNTIL two hours before sunset to embark on operation "Power Outage" so Grant and Ty wouldn't have to be cramped up together in the trunk any longer than necessary. This would also give anyone on the inside less time to think of searching the BMW. At 7:45 p.m. they left Oran, making the twenty-minute drive up the windy road to the fortress with Dan in trail on the motorcycle. Dan followed as long as he could, getting as close to the stronghold as possible without being seen.

Everything was going as planned so far, and just when Selena reached the gate, she quickly shut the car off and put the good key in her bra. She then inserted the one they'd dismantled the security chip in and put it in the ignition. There was no way the car was going to be able to start.

Acting frustrated, she made enough commotion to draw attention from one of the men inside the compound to come to the gate. Although he wasn't carrying a gun, she knew he must've set it down just out of sight; the past couple of days all the men had been heavily armed.

He was young, probably in his early twenties, and seemed more than interested in their new guest. Right away she could see that he'd been away from the opposite sex for a long time as he couldn't take his eyes off her scantily dressed curvy figure. It seemed he only knew a little Spanish, but he obviously understood what she was asking; he opened the gate and walked through to see if he could get her car started. An attempt which, of course, she knew to be futile.

While she made the call to Dan, the man made a call of his own, and in a matter of seconds another man—who appeared to be slightly older—showed up... again no gun in sight. He appeared upset with the younger one, and after a lengthy conversation in German, he calmed down enough to look at Selena and address her in rough but intelligible Spanish. *"How long you want to keep car here?"*

She could see he wasn't as interested as the younger man, so she worked a little harder. Bending over to adjust the strap on one of her sandals, displaying the low neckline of her tight fitting top, she said coyly, *"Tomorrow. I'm sure we can be back tomorrow."*

It was clear he'd been looking her over as she spoke even though he was trying not to.

"And your brother? When will he be here and give you ride?"

She looked at her watch. *"In about fifteen minutes."*

He looked her over one last time. *"Okay… you can keep car here, but only one night."*

"Thank you very much. Maybe I'll see you in town sometime?"

He faintly smirked, but ignored her suggestion. *"Get in… you steer and we push."*

She didn't hesitate to oblige, but couldn't help but think if they decided to ask to see in the trunk, the politeness would come to a screeching halt, and things would get messy real fast.

CHAPTER 42

WAITING IN THE trunk for five hours had seemed like an eternity, but with each hour that passed, the chances of being discovered greatly diminished. Ty couldn't help but notice the irony of the guard being taken in by the beauty of the opposite sex. It was the same as what had happened to him several months before with Celeste and the same as the fallen angels had with the human women eons before that, starting this whole crazy ride. Hopefully the end results would be just as effective.

"I haven't heard anything out there for a while, so I'm going to take a look," his dad whispered, then popped the trunk and slowly opened it—just a hair—to see what they could.

Ty nodded and stayed quiet but intently looked out the tiny opening with his dad.

A light breeze whiffed across the grounds as they peered from the cramped quarters of the trunk. Luckily, the car was parked in the right direction so they could see all around them, including the main building, the two smaller structures, and what they came for, the generators. Still no security cameras either, at least none in sight.

After observing for ten minutes, they noticed the night watchman casually walk in front of the main building then disappeared into the shadows around the back. It was apparent he must be patrolling the entire circumference of the building. Ty saw his dad look at his watch, then they waited. Fifteen minutes passed before the same man emerged from the shadows on the other side of the building. The same time as they had noticed from their surveillance the past few days. Again Grant checked his watch and waited… fourteen minutes passed, and once again the watchman came forth out of the shadows from the other side.

Once more his dad clocked the time then whispered, "Okay, Ty, get ready. When he returns in the next fifteen minutes, we'll wait for him to walk around the front, and then when he gets behind the building again, it's time to take care of business."

Ty acknowledged his dad with another nod.

Fifteen minutes went by and nothing… sixteen minutes and still nothing, then at seventeen minutes, there he was. This was it—as soon as the guard vanished behind the generators, they'd make their move.

The time it took for the guard to walk the front grounds again seemed like an eternity, but as soon as he was out of site, Grant quietly opened the trunk and they crawled out. What little wind there had been, had all but dissipated, and the only thing that broke the silence of the night was the rumble of the generators in the distance. Keeping low and trying to stay in the shadows as much as possible, they crept through the low cut grass to the generator enclosure. As they got closer to their objective, the noise from the six diesel engines powering the generators grew louder, masking the rattle from the chain-link fence as they began their climb over.

Both Ty and Grant were dressed in black and were almost invisible once they were inside the enclosure that surrounded the roaring power plant. Grant kept watch while Ty went to do his part, which was to take out the generators.

Their plan was simple, and it was something Ty's father remembered that happened to his brother-in-law's sawmill in Montana years ago that gave him the idea. Apparently, Grant's brother-in-law's disgruntled neighbor didn't like the noise from the mill, so he put sand into the engine to try and ruin it. Grant just had to refine the plan somewhat, to give them time to return to the car before anyone knew anything was wrong. If everything went as intended, Selena's car, along with Ty and his dad, would get safely towed out of the complex in the morning before the effects of the sand started to do the irreversible internal damage to the engines.

To pull this off, they'd filled six plastic bags with sand. Ty would pull the covers of the air cleaners off the engines and poke a hole in the internal air filter and the bag of sand, then place the bag into the air cleaner canisters and reinstall the covers. They figured this would only take a few minutes and give them just enough time to get back to the car before the guard came back. Sometime later the following day, the engines would've ingested all the sand and scoured up the piston walls enough to lower the compression of the engines. They'd lose the power required to spin the generators, thus bringing their adversaries' scheme to a halt. It was such a simple, yet effective plan, and though they couldn't be sure exactly when the engines would fail, they knew they most certainly would.

Everything was going exactly as they had hoped. Ty's heart raced as he started to open up the first air cleaner. He had no more than started to unscrew the retaining cap when... lights came on from all around, momentarily blinding them. Everywhere he looked a flashlight was pointed at them... a flashlight and the gun barrel it was mounted on. Adrenaline flooded Ty's body ushering in an emotion that had been avoiding him up until now... fear. They'd been busted. *How the hell could they've found us?* He thought. *It seemed for all the world like they had been waiting for us... almost like they knew we were coming.*

Ty's dad dropped his gun and slowly raised his hands and Ty followed suit. Ty knew they were at the mercy of the gunmen. Both he and his dad had their hands tied behind their back, then were escorted from the enclosure with the barrel of a gun jabbed into their spine. It was almost like he was in a dream. Seeing his dad not in control of the situation at hand was something that he'd never experienced before. The distress he felt intensified.

They were led at gunpoint to the manor through the front entrance. It was cold inside, a damp cold that cut right through Ty's anxiety and settled deep into his bones. The place had the faint musty smell of an old basement. Then the shock of the sight in front of him hit like a sledgehammer. It was like he'd stepped back in time. Back to... Nazi Germany! Everywhere Ty looked was covered with Nazi memorabilia, from the famous red banners with swastikas draping down from the high ceilings, to the Nazi uniforms on display. And even portraits and photos on display of the furious Fuhrer himself... Adolf Hitler. Ty was chilled by what he saw as he and his father took in the eerie sight. It seemed clear that whoever lived here was intent on bringing back the power of the Third Reich.

It was only a matter of minutes before Ty saw an elderly man being pushed in a wheelchair emerge from a hallway from their left. Though he wasn't anyone who he or his dad recognized, it was obvious by the demeanor of everyone else in the room that he was in charge; the stiffening up and raising of their right hands like good little Nazi soldiers made that quite clear.

Then the old man spoke in perfect English, but with a thick German accent. "Forgive my immobility, but it's the result of being asleep for the past six months. Atrophy of the muscles is unavoidable," he said, then looked at Grant. "I assume this must be yours?" He held up the pen containing the transmitter that Grant had slipped into Celeste's purse. Ty and his dad were silent and Ty thought to himself, *how in the hell did they find that?*

"You don't have to answer. Allow me to introduce myself. I am Dr. Rudolf Himmler... son of Heinrich Luitpold Himmler." Neither Ty nor his dad betrayed any surprise at his revelation. It was just as they had feared, although hoped against.

If Himmler was waiting for a reaction to his identity, he was disappointed when Grant finally spoke. "It's me you want. Let my son go, and I'll tell you anything you want."

Himmler spoke to him calmly. "Oh, don't worry, Mr. Larson, you don't have anything I want. Nor do I have any intention of hurting your son. Rather, I would like to thank him."

"Thank me? For what? What did I do for you?" Ty asked, as he winced with disbelief.

"You led us right to one of them. One of the men of old, men of renown. I'm sure by now you must know who they are... the *Nephilim*! You see, had it not been for you, my boy, none of this would've been possible."

"What do you mean... 'had it not been for me'? I had no idea what the hell you were trying to do." The fear in his body was being pushed aside with anger taking its place.

"Exactly! You had no idea whatsoever. That, my son, was how it was all possible! We've been trying to capture one of these things for years. We'd get a tip where one might be, but every time we'd show up to lay a trap, it would be gone. It was almost like they knew we were coming. In fact, that's exactly what was happening," Himmler took a moment to let his words sink in before he continued. "You see, my boy, among their other *unearthly* abilities, the *Nephilim* could read our thoughts. That's why they always disappeared when we would show up... they *did* know we were coming! And you, my boy, you had no idea you were looking for them... nobody knew except me... and I was deep asleep as everything unfolded, that is, except for devising the plan itself, I'm proud to say. It was a thing of grandeur, utterly magnificent!" Himmler said proudly as though he expected an applause.

What the Nazi was saying made no sense to Ty. The madman could see the look of confusion on both Ty and his father's face, so he continued. "You both look confused. Then let me pose the question to you. If the only one who knew of the plan to catch one of these elusive beings was in a deep sleep... then how would they ever know someone was coming for them? I and I alone, was the only one who knew what was happening!" Then Himmler laughed ever so slightly and said, "Thankfully, I must have been dreaming of something else while asleep."

Ty's skepticism was still in control of his thoughts when he blurted out. "But what about Celeste—Elke—or whoever the hell she is? What about Dr. Eisenberg and everyone else? For God's sake, what about the pilots you used to kill that entire village?"

"Precisely, my son! Do you think a whole squadron would intentionally gas an entire village knowing they would probably be shot down themselves for their actions? No one on board those airplanes knew they were carrying poisonous gas." Himmler laughed again, only this time the tone revealed the evil that consumed his soul. "Idiots! They thought they were cloud seeding... trying to make rain in the desert! A small sacrifice for the greater good." He paused for a moment as though he had just won the Nobel Prize for his accomplishment, then continued, "As for Elke, my beloved granddaughter, all she knew was to... shall we say entice you into Eisenberg's class. That and to put you on the path of the great Edgar Cayce... just a little push to get you started in the right direction. The only other thing she was to do was to keep you away from a phone and report if she saw something... something unusual, shall we say? While in *your* company." Again, he paused and laughed with arrogance seething from his core. "Until now, she had no idea what a *Nephilim* was. All *anyone* knew was just enough to make another event happen, which led to another and another, until... until I got my goddamn Giant! And for that, I thank you, my son. I sincerely couldn't have done it without you."

Suddenly, the pieces were all starting to fit together. Ty had been tricked into taking the trip to the Middle East. Lured into a trap by a beautiful woman months ago, then used as a pawn in a psychopath's diabolical scheme. Something still didn't make sense though, so Ty had to question the madman. "But why me? How the hell did you ever pick me? What made you ever think I'd lead you to one?"

Himmler's look was questioning, yet unyielding. "Oh young one, you still have no idea of who you are... do you?"

What did he mean by that? 'I still have no idea of who I am?' It was as though there was something he should remember... something that was on the tip of his tongue, but just out of reach.

Interrupting his thoughts, Himmler continued. "It doesn't matter now, boy. Let's just say that not only do you have the naivety that comes with innocence, but more importantly you have the pedigree... seeking the truth is in your blood... *literally*! And with some expected help from the CIA..." he glanced briefly at Grant, "Oh, it was a *slight* gamble all right, but one I was willing to take. I was confident you'd track one down for me! And just as I thought—"

Grant cut him off with his face turning red as his emotions were starting to flair. "The CIA did nothing to aid you... you psychopath!"

"No? Who was it that kept the Giant hunters out of the way?" Himmler questioned him, keeping his cool.

"Giant hunters... just who are you referring to?" Grant was visibly upset, but also seemed confused.

"Your son's good friend... Tom, I believe? He obviously didn't tell you who he works for." Again, Himmler laughed with arrogance. "Let me fill you in. The organization that Mr. Bruiner is with has existed since the waters of the Great Flood subsided. They have also been seeking out the leftover *Nephilim*... only their goal has been to extinguish the great blood line forever! Fools!" Himmler showed a bit of a temper. "Trying to wipe out... the *second* most perfect beings who have ever walked the face of the earth?"

Ty looked at his father thinking, *the second most perfect beings... what did he mean by that?* He was just about to question their host, when Himmler continued. "For some reason, and I still don't know how, Mr. Bruiner and all of those with S.O.J., or whatever the hell they call themselves, were able to get to the *Nephilim* without their knowledge and kill them! Sooner or later, they would've wiped them out completely! So again, I thank you and the CIA for all your help. Thankfully, even though S.O.J. is so extensive, they're also so secretive that it usually takes some time before the right hand knows what the left is doing. I was aware that one of them found something out about my plan so I had to stay one step ahead... and I was able to do just that." Himmler was oozing with arrogance as he spoke.

Ty felt sick to his stomach. How could he have been so dumb? There'd been signs all along the way, and he ignored them all... all because of a pretty girl. The look on his face must've been easy to read.

"Don't feel so bad, my boy, for it was lust all of those eons ago that made this all possible. The lust of beings much greater than you or I."

Ty knew what he was referring to: the fallen angels mentioned in the Bible, however, somehow that didn't make him feel any better. This Himmler was simply crazy, the same as the last. To be the reason why he was able to make this nightmare come true was almost too much for Ty to bear.

Ty knew that Himmler could see the look of disgust and horror on his face, and being the sociopath that he was, Himmler just had to gloat some more.

"Come! Let me show you what you came to see."

Himmler gestured impatiently, and the orderly wheeled his chair around. They were nudged from behind by the barrels of the gunmen to encourage them to follow their host. With the rogue Nazi in the lead and the gunmen in trail, Ty and Grant reluctantly followed to a hallway at the far side of the main room, which led them down a long ramp to an underground level and then through a maze of narrow tunnels, until they eventually came to a solid wall lined with some kind of ceramic casing. Himmler was wheeled to the side and pointed to a small portal in the wall, covered with a hard, clear material, which allowed the contents of the room inside to be viewed from where they stood. Himmler motioned to Grant. "You might want to look first, Mr. Larson."

GRANT, SOMEWHAT RELUCTANTLY, stepped forward and bent over to peer through the hole. In the center of the room was a bell-shaped machine that appeared to be made of some sort of metal. At the base of the machine were heavy electrical cords feeding into it around its entire circumference. Grant could almost feel it pulsating with energy just by looking at it through the tiny peephole.

"No comments, Mr. Larson? Do you not know what you are looking at? Do you not recognize *Die Glocke?* The Bell!" Himmler's voice was filled with excitement.

Despite his years with the Agency, Grant still found himself skeptical. Could it be? Was this the infamous Nazi Bell? This had probably been the most secret of the Nazi programs of all. It wasn't until 1997 that stories began to surface regarding the bell project. How could something have been kept a secret for so long after the fall of the Third Reich?

The bell experiments had supposedly been conducted toward the end of the war, deep underground in occupied Poland. Hitler had been obsessed with finding a super weapon that would defeat the allied forces closing in on Germany. Though the bell project was shrouded in secrecy, there had been purported leaks said to explain its propose, with whispers of everything from a time machine to an anti-gravity device, though most thought the latter the most probable.

According to the reports, the device stood about fifteen feet tall by nine feet wide and was made from some kind of hard metal and shaped like a bell, hence the nickname. Inside were two counter rotating cylinders filled with mercury, that when energized, would create an electromagnetic field that would produce a torsion field and be able to cancel out gravity. It was Albert Einstein's Unified Field Theory that gave the bell experiments merit for manipulating time-space, which in turn also gave the time machine stories some plausibility as well. But, most likely the purpose had been to create a propulsion system far superior to anything else in existence at the time. It was said to have required enormous amounts of electricity, which would explain the need for all of the generators outside. Judging from the appearance, the description also fit.

SS General Hans Kammler had been in charge of the secret weapon projects. When Nazi Germany finally fell to the Allied forces, Kammler and the Bell were nowhere to be found. However, before his disappearance, Kammler oversaw Hitler's order to execute all sixty-two scientists who had been working on the project, along with all of the concentration camp workers who had been used for slave labor. For years afterward, stories had floated around about both Kammler and the Bell's whereabouts, including speculation about both the United States and Argentina. The Germans had two large, six-engine transport aircraft, the use of one of which was requested by Kammler shortly before the fall of Berlin. Mysteriously, it has never been found either.

It seemed apparent that the Bell's whereabouts were no longer in doubt, but the question now was, what did Himmler's plan have to do with an anti-gravity machine? Although he refrained from calling him a madman out loud, Grant still had to ask, "I do recognize the Bell, but I'm afraid I don't understand the purpose. I mean… how on earth would that device aid you in obtaining your goal here?"

"Ah yes. What would I need with an anti-gravity machine?" Himmler's tone was condescending now. "Actually, Mr. Larson, you are correct. I have no use for such a machine. However, as informed as you are, you may not be aware that there is another trait of the bell. A lesser known trait, shall we say? You see, when the tests were being done with the Bell, there was something everyone thought was a bad side effect. Something that in reality, was a blessing. *My* blessing as it turns out."

"Oh?" Grant allowed a small measure of disgust to creep into his voice. "And what might one such as yourself consider a blessing?"

It appeared Himmler noticed Grant's tone, but still looked pleased by the question. "It seemed as though every time *Die Glocke* would operate, everything around it would die… all forms of life, plants included. Everyone thought it was some kind of radiation that was causing this, so lead was used as a shield, but to no avail. It wasn't until ceramic bricks were employed, that whatever the force was, it could be controlled," he casually explained.

"Eventually, someone took a closer look at the cells in the plants that had been affected, then we finally understood what was happening. The plants weren't just being killed off, rather, they were aging... aging at an incredibly fast rate... almost 1,000 times faster than normal!"

Whatever it was Himmler was developing from the *Nephilim* he'd captured would be full grown soon... real soon.

THE TONE IN Ty's voice was full of disgust, but also contained the tiniest bit of intrigue. "So that's what this elaborate set up is for? To clone a *Nephilim*... a giant? One of which you just murdered?"

"Clone a *Nephilim?*" Shaking his head, he said, "No, my boy." There was the condescending laugh again. "Come, let me show you!" Himmler was wheeled to another ramp that spiraled up and around the ceramic-encased room to a level directly above the bell. It was a room similar to that which housed the bell, also encased in ceramic, with a peephole identical to the one they had just looked through. Himmler motioned for Ty to look.

"That's the problem with you Americans... you always think too small. Why would I make a half-breed when I can create the *whole* thing?! The *purest* life form to not only ever walk the face of the earth, but exist in the entire universe! From the DNA of the *Nephilim* that you found for us, we were able to isolate and separate out, what I refer to as... the God gene, and recreate one of the Fallen Ones! A Watcher!"

Ty couldn't believe what he was hearing. Could it be possible? Could this madman have made a Fallen Angel... a Watcher? Perhaps even some form of God himself?

Half afraid of what he'd see, Ty bent down to look inside. In the middle of the room was a clear cylindrical case maybe six feet wide that went all the way up to the ceiling. Chills raced up Ty's spine when he saw what the case contained. Inside the giant test tube was a massive humanoid-like form, pulsating with an electric bluish sheen, looking as if it were made from pure energy.

He couldn't take his eyes off the thing.

Then... then he thought he saw movement. He checked the impulse to recoil, his fascinated gaze fixed on the creature in the test tube.

There it was again! It did move. It... it was alive!

THE END?

One more coincidence?

And it came to pass when the children of men began to multiply on the face of the earth and daughters were born unto them, that the angels of God saw them on a certain year of this jubilee, that they were beautiful to look upon; and they took themselves wives of all whom they chose, and they bare unto them sons and they were giants.

THE BOOK OF JUBILEES 5:1

PROOF

The Novel

Made in the USA
Las Vegas, NV
15 December 2021

38058676R00198